D1392834

NEIL HUMPHREYS

PREMIER LEECH

All the best

Neil Humphreys

mc **Marshall Cavendish**
Editions

2011

This is a work of fiction and the characters portrayed do not exist. Any similarity or apparent connection between the characters in the story and actual persons, whether alive or dead, is purely coincidental.

Published by Marshall Cavendish Editions
An imprint of Marshall Cavendish International
1 New Industrial Road, Singapore 536196

The publisher makes no representation or warranties with respect to the contents of this book, and specifically disclaims any implied warranties or merchantability or fitness for any particular purpose, and shall in no events be liable for any loss of profit or any other commercial damage, including but not limited to special, incidental, consequential, or other damages.

Other Marshall Cavendish
Marshall Cavendish Ltd. ... ... UK • Marshall Cavendish
Corporation ... White Plains Road, Tarrytown NY 10591-9001 ... SA • Marshall
Cavendish International ... oke: 12th ... akhumvit 21 Road,
Klongtoey ... Wattana, Bangkok ... Thailand • Marshall Cavendish (Malaysia)
Sdn Bhd, ... en Subang, Lot 46, Subang ... Tech Industrial Park ... atu Tiga, 40000
Shah Alam ... langor D ... Malaysia

Marshall Cavendish is a trademark of Times Publishing Limited

National Library Board Singapore Cataloguing in Publication Data
Humphreys, Neil.
Premier leet ... ... Marshall Cavendish Editions, c2011.
p. cm.
ISBN : 978-981-4328-42-5 (pbk.)
1. Soccer players – Fiction. 2. F.A. Premier League – Fiction.
I. Title.

PR6108
823.92 — dc22   OCN672105287

Printed by Craft Print International Ltd

for Fans

acknowledgements

Chris sat me down at his dinner table and said, "What about the English Premier League?" Interviewers at BBC radio said, "A novel about the EPL would be timely, you know." And then footballers started getting caught with their pants down. The exasperated reaction of the average, disillusioned fan provided the motivation to write this book. Being made in Dagenham did the rest.

In London, Martin offered support and some well-known journalists offered all kinds of things. That's why they'll remain nameless and I'll remain eternally grateful. Many of my heroes gave kind words of encouragement that ended up on the cover. In Singapore, Shawn, Mei Lin and Stephanie kept me an honest man and the boys in Bangkok did the business with the artwork. My beautiful wife and daughter also deserve praise for leaving me alone in my dark place.

This book would not have been possible without those in the industry who dropped their trousers, shafted every kid's dream and left the glory game haemorrhaging from within. This one's for you, guys.

one

THE sex had exceeded all his expectations. Scott had expected another actress. High-end slappers were always actresses. They were panting, wailing bullshitters. They made Scott paranoid with their histrionics. He couldn't focus on the job when he was always looking around for a camera. Nowadays, he always checked for a camera. It was too risky. No one wanted to "do another Lampard". That's what they called it in the dressing room. Tell any of the lads about a shag and the first thing they asked was, "Did you check for a camera, Scott, or did you do a Lampard?" Of course he checked for cameras—even those fucking camera phones that made his life a misery. Sometimes he even asked them straight out where it was. Scott had 60 cameras watching his every move and mistimed tackle every Saturday. He didn't need another one up his arse on a Saturday night.

In some ways, he had more time for the low-end slappers he shared with his teammates back in the youth team and the reserves. There was never any of that "What's David Beckham like?" and worrying about the plebs reading about it in the *News of the World*. No BAFTA-winning performances, no anti-climaxes, no floating around any clouds of uncertainty; if the sex was shit, you knew about it. There was something authentic about a fuck in a Ford Fiesta.

But Scott had come a long way. Low-end slappers never bothered trying anymore. They knew their place and he knew his. They played in different leagues now. It was always about the numbers. Like all English Premier League boys, he'd occasionally slip up on an away day to Southend, but everyone had a private weakness for a bit of rough now and then. Apart from the odd upset once every other season, Scott was purely Premier League now. He still popped in Faces over in Gants Hill with some of the West Ham and Tottenham boys, but that was him succumbing to nostalgia rather than temptation. They fumbled around on the dance floor, doing their best Arctic Monkeys, while he sat back behind the red rope, basking in his celebrity seniority. It was marked VVIP, squire, roped off, curtained off, might as well be fenced off, so you all knew the score. Fuck off.

Soho was Scott's playground now. Had to be. It was part of the game. He couldn't be seen drinking in his old Essex shitholes around the A13 any more than he could be seen shopping in Asda, unless he was signing the inside of a football computer game for some hooded plebs. Eighty grand a week bought exclusivity, but it came with rules. Don't fraternise. Keep them all at arm's length. There's nothing to see there anymore. Move along. Stay behind the rope, hide behind the champagne bottles and keep them in their pens where they fucking belong. Those old footballers in the eighties had it sweet. They played the game like past masters. They had dodgy 'taches, cheesy afros and tight shorts, but they had a blinding deal. They still had the plebs behind fences.

Scott could come out to play in Soho. Scott, Ross and Jimmy—proper mates, proper men, grew up together, went through the academy together, dealt with the media together and handled the plebs together. So they went to Soho together. They usually ended up at the Punk Club or the Soho Revue; no plebs and high-class slappers jumping out of their spray-on tans.

Too many Tottenham footballers for their liking, and one or two of the Spurs boys had been a bit naughty in recent seasons; got caught on camera by the paps getting too handy and that just pissed everybody off. The Premier League boys hardly had any private playgrounds left, so it was always irritating when someone got caught behind the bike sheds.

Scott knew what was coming. Ross had buggered off to the casino and Jimmy had some sponsorship deal to sort out with a suit pleb. Suit plebs were more annoying than regular plebs because they thought they were worthy of time and attention. They were fucking cash machines with less personality. But Jimmy was different of course. Jimmy loved being among the money men.

Scott was flying solo in Soho. That was only ever going to end with a phone call to a devoted, discreet cabbie, a nod to the manager, a "Can I use the back entrance, mate, and by the looks of this one, that might not be the only time tonight," a dash past the dozing snappers, nipping around them like Roger Moore in *Live and Let Die*, into the back of the cab, hand straight up the thigh. Welcome to the Premier League Club, darling. Congratulations, babe, you've passed the test. You're about to be rubber-stamped by a bone-hard celebrity. You've arrived. You've achieved. You've made something of your life. You've opened your legs to cross that red rope. You're a part of our world. Didn't the view from Mount Celebrity make the ride worthwhile? Did you enjoy yourself? Did you cum? Does it matter? The celebrity tour is over now, babe. Maybe I'll see you again. Maybe I won't. There are just too many tourists and not enough tour guides. But you've got your memories. No videos or flash photography, I'm afraid, that's no longer permitted. But you'll have a story to share with your other high-end slappers. You had a knockout game in the Premier League, you might even go on a cup run, but this particular journey ends here. I live in the Premier League. You will always be a tourist.

Jo was the exception. She had crossed the red rope and opened her legs so widely; she didn't need to go back.

She was Jo. Just Jo. No other name required.

Like Pele or Ronaldo, she was always going to be destined for football's elite. Women are blessed with either brains or beauty. Jo had neither. But she understood the future while intellectuals grappled with the present. In the past, fame was born; 21st-century fame could be made. Pamela Anderson had led teenaged ugly ducklings merrily down the stream towards adult self-esteem and salvation. Every mall and McDonald's in America had a Pamela Anderson doing her thing with her bleach bottle and her push-up bra, just wishing, waiting and hoping to be discovered or deflowered, whichever came first.

Jo saw it coming before it crossed the Atlantic. Talented singers, songwriters, dancers, actresses—creative people—were deluding themselves in the nineties. Talent is temporary, but fame is permanent. Talent is sucked in and spat out again with the pop culture tides. Jo had always laughed at the fickle fortunes of Gary Barlow and Robbie Williams. Did one suddenly become a shit songwriter and the other one turn into Gershwin? And then vice versa? The pair relied on talent alone to navigate their careers through the jungle of celebrity. If I'm a celebrity, Jo always thought, no one else is going to get me out of here. Pamela Anderson hasn't gone anywhere.

Jo saw the future in Pammy. If you're famous for being a talented songwriter, then you have a limited shelf life. Musical tastes change. But if you're famous just for being Jo and nothing else, then you're always going to be famous. Because you're always going to be Jo. Jo will never change.

And Jo had worked her way into the Premier League with breathtaking speed and determination. She had served her apprenticeship. She had carried out more than her fair share of

Ford Fiesta fucks and was extremely proud of her committed, dedicated work ethic. Always conscientious, she started locally to cut down on travelling time. A few broken-down West Ham and Leyton Orient players now earning their pension at Dagenham and Redbridge; a threesome with Southend's midfield when she was going through the obligatory "dirty phase" for the lad mags; an up-and-coming Cockney actor making a name in the hooligan movies and a household name in Britain's favourite soap opera. Out of respect for his children, she had refused to reveal his identity—until she was paid 50 grand by the *News of the World*. It would've been a hundred grand had there been photographs, but Jo got hammered that night and forgot to get out her camera phone, which really irritated her. She had always prided herself on her professionalism.

Now she was at the top of her game. The tabloids called her Britain's answer to Paris Hilton and, secretly, it was one of the proudest moments of her life. She was a visionary. She understood fame in the 21st century better than Clive James. Everyone else could go and get fucked.

Jo didn't need to rock the boat now. Her manager had just secured a second season of her reality TV show and she now had most of the nation's plebs on board. All she had to do was keep them and the paps sweet, and she was golden.

Jo had spotted Scott across the bar and was surprised to see him alone. Ross and Jimmy were always with him. They drove her to distraction. The three were joined at the hip. But she liked Scott. He wasn't particularly good-looking; slightly ferret-faced with too much hair gel in his fin, but he made her laugh. She raised her champagne flute to Scott and beckoned him over for a chat. A shag was out of the question, for obvious reasons, but at least she'd have a good night.

two

JO rolled over in bed and stared at Scott. What had she just done? Why had she even done it? Scott wasn't her type. In truth, she never really had a type; the career always came first. But now she had a type, a strategic type, and Scott didn't fit the mould at all. Ironically, their celebrity stars aligned now. When she played the numbers game, Scott ticked all the boxes. He was club captain, a regular on the back pages, some decent sponsorship deals and a near-certainty for England. That was always the goal; the England squad. Every player's dream was to make the England squad, and Jo was no different. That was Premier League and then some. No need for any fake bigging up after that. Max Clifford came to you once you made the England squad.

The irony certainly wasn't lost on Jo. For the first time in her career, she didn't actually need an England cap. It promised to do more harm than good. The TV show was not only a piece of piss, but the ratings were going through the roof. She was truly the queen of the council estates. She was once called the Boudica of Barking. That's what some ugly feminist journalist called her, and she loved it. The Boudica of Barking, the old hack had said. If Billy Bragg was the Bard of Barking, then Jo had to be the Boudica of Barking. Jo had no idea who Boudica, the Bard and Billy Bragg were, but her manager nodded positively over the journalist's shoulder. It was a compliment. It was a monster compliment: one was an old local singer and the other one did some plays, but she'd never seen him in anything. When Jo discovered who Boudica actually was, she made every effort to play up on the comparison. She went to a movie premiere dressed in a skimpy coat of armour and a Union Jack thong, behind a chariot being pulled by a couple of pit bulls wearing Union Jack vests. The paps loved it. She spent an hour on the red carpet. It was Leicester Square in November and she was freezing her tits off, but she didn't care. And the frozen nipples came out a treat in the tabloids.

From that moment, she was Boudica of Barking, but mostly in her mind. The media rarely picked up on it again. The broadsheets thought the title was a tacky joke and the lad mags weren't sure if their target audience knew who Boudica was. But Jo didn't care. She was the self-proclaimed queen of the council estates. From her humble beginnings giving hand jobs at the back of the Maths class for 50 pence a time to holding the nation's media in the palm of her hand at movie premieres, Jo had arrived. The girl with the harsh face, tied-back hair and grey tracksuit bottoms had gone, and she never wanted to see her again. Boudica of Barking attacked and devoured enemies, conquered armies and campaigned ceaselessly. She always marched forward. Jo never wanted to look over her shoulder, just in case she saw the minging girl in the dirty grey tracksuit bottoms scowling back at her.

But as Jo stared at the snoring Scott, she knew she had gone too far. She had conquered the paps and the plebs, but there was a very real danger of all that unravelling.

The plebs loved the tits and teeth on *Page Three* when it suited them. Behind closed doors, they behaved like Japanese businessmen with their depraved magnifying glasses. That was fine. That was acceptable. That was normal. They wanked over her pages while their wives did the shopping every Friday, regular as clockwork.

Publicly, though, they had to jump on their soapboxes like some fucking Victorian moralist; family values and all that bollocks. Never break up the family unit. Never. Jo shagged them, but never so hard that they got childish ideas about leaving their wives. Jo never crossed that line because she was aware that the tabloids could never cross that line with her. Footballers, actors, fresh-faced *Pop Idol* rejects; she slept with them and then smiled widely for anyone who paid for the next glamour shoot, the next interview, the next appearance fee. And the plebs applauded her all the way. Isn't she a remarkable businesswoman, they bleated. She certainly knows how to play the media. She's even writing books now. Isn't she a clever girl, they bleated. They always bleated. It was too easy.

The only trouble with the plebs, Jo always said, was that they were such fucking hypocrites. Boudica of Barking could load up the chariot and steamroller as many rising and washed-up celebrities as she could (only the A-listers were beyond her empire; even Boudica never conquered the gods) and the plebs all fell in line behind her dutifully. But there was one line the Victorian, hypocritical plebs could not totter across.

Jo was now married with a little girl.

She could already hear the plebs bleating in their text messages to the daytime TV brigade. You can't do that to children, can you? I mean, fair's fair, she's a talented businesswoman and all that, but it's not fair on the kids, is it?

Shame no one ever shared that advice with Jo's mother when Jo was a kid, but that didn't matter now. Jo preferred not to think about that.

The plebs had their morals. Rules were rules. Family values and all that. Boudica of Barking had strayed too far into enemy territory this time, and the plebs would surely desert her for the moral high ground. With the utmost reluctance, the tabloids would be forced to go after one of their most prized cash cows. As she gently caressed Scott's face while he slept, Jo felt like that girl with the harsh face in the dirty tracksuit bottoms again. She felt vulnerable. And she really hated that.

SCOTT heard the breathing. And then he smelled the breathing. That wasn't his wife. In truth, it often wasn't, but this was ... this was ... oh fuck.

Jo.

Jo.

Fucking Jo.

Of all the high-end slappers in London, he had to knob the only one who was off limits. The Boudica of Barking. The fucking back end of a Barking bus more like, that's what the other boys called her. Jo was everything Scott didn't look for after games. He was after the sporty, natural, athletic look. There was nothing natural about Jo. She was a walking, always talking Frankenstein's monster. The only things that remained from the Essex girl she had left behind were her eyes, and they were usually glassy and bloodshot. She'd had her knockers done—twice—because one of the singers in Girl Power said she still had Spaniel's ears after the first job, so she went crying back to the scalpel and had the pair ripped open again.

The lads always said her foundation was more solid than West Ham's back four. She was never seen without her makeup. Never. Her face was darker than Barack Obama's arse. The paps at Big Pictures reckoned they made more money out of her when they snapped her without her makeup on and looking like shit, than they did when they got her heading into a nightclub. They were two different women. Without the tan and the eyeliner, she looked worse than the hooded plebs who queued up for her autographs at Lakeside.

But Jo had made Scott laugh, really laugh, in a way that only two people from a shared background could. They were both from Barking. They both got the same jokes. That had really surprised Scott. He loved the crack in the dressing room. After the money, it was the only thing that really appealed to him about playing the game. Ross' pranks and piss-takes were the highlights of every training session. But he'd never laughed so long and so deeply before as he had last night. No matter how drunk they got, no matter how surreal their conversation got, there was always a flicker of recognition between Jo and Scott. Nicking the morning's magazines outside WHSmith at Barking Station after a night at The Spotted Dog, being dragged around the Barking market—all six stalls of it—by their mothers, drinking cider outside St Margaret's Church and pissing up the walls of Barking Abbey; they reminisced about it all. They had lived each other's lives at the same time without ever crossing paths. Even Scott had acknowledged that that was just mental.

Still, that was no excuse for shagging her.

Scott was disappointed that he'd let his guard down, but not angry. The sex really had exceeded all of his expectations. He didn't bother with the high-end slappers anymore, but when he had, he often felt like he was a conductor waving his baton around in the Royal Albert Hall. He expected Jo to be the new Wembley. But whatever she'd paid to have done down there—and she'd obviously paid someone, Scott hadn't felt like that since he'd been a teenager—it was worth every penny. Jo was no actress. She didn't have to be. She was a natural, in the bedroom at least. On that score, he could see what all the fuss was about. No one had ever done anything like that to him before.

Not even his wife.

That didn't bother him particularly at the moment. That wasn't even an issue. He'd been here many times before. He always used the same hotel. But he was in a tight spot, as it were. His Saturday night hotel room retainer was a perk of the job. He had earned it. Strikers kicked his Achilles' and elbowed him in the bollocks while the plebs in the stands told everyone watching *Match of the Day* what a useless bastard he was. He had nothing to apologise for. His away days were well deserved.

But Jo was off limits. He was a rising star now in the English Premier League. And Jo was Jo. He was risking more than just a caution here.

Scott felt her caressing his face. He was properly awake now. He had to open his eyes.

"You all right, babe?" Jo whispered.

God, she looked fucking awful first thing in the morning, Scott thought. What did they all see in her?

"That was a funny old night, weren't it?"

Jo smiled cheekily at Scott. She did have a seductive smile.

"Yeah, it was, er, a strange night," he nodded, smiling in spite of himself at the memory.

"It was a great night," Jo muttered.

"Can't argue with that."

Scott meant it, too.

They stared at each other. For the first time in 12 hours, they didn't know what to say. They didn't need to say anything. The dirty great white elephant in the corner of the room was doing all the talking. There was something so primitive, so raw about last night that it reached depths that were beyond their understanding. They both knew that neither of them could explain last night if they tried, except to say they would never experience sex like that again. Unless they did it again.

"I need to pee," Jo said, recognising that someone had to make a move before they both said something stupid.

"Yeah, yeah, of course, babe."

Scott watched her cross the hotel room. She was naked, obviously. When a body cost that much to put together, there was no logic in covering it up. And it was the perfect body, totally flawless.

He really was a lucky man.

Scott heard the tinkling in the bathroom and quietly picked up the phone. He slipped out of the bed and crouched down on the floor beside it.

"Hello, it's me, Scott," he whispered quickly. "I'm in the hotel again ... yeah, that one ... no, no, I haven't got time for that now, just fucking shut up will ya and listen. I've really fucked it up this time ... yeah, yeah, I know all that, but that was different ... I didn't shag my best mate's wife then, did I?"

three

SCOTT was shitting himself. He didn't want a kicking, not today. The trials for the academy were tonight and he was desperate not to play like a dickhead this time. He wasn't a complete spanner. He knew the coach had felt sorry for him. He knew he had been handed a second chance—his last chance—thanks to Ross and Jimmy. They'd been amazing, had the games of their lives. Scott had played football with them since they messed about together with tennis balls in the nursery, and even he had been shocked. Every pass, every dummy, every run, everything; it all came off—for them. Maybe that had put Scott off his game, but that was a feeble excuse. Scott was the most dedicated footballer in the school. Everyone knew that. Even Ross and Jimmy. But he'd played like a right twat at the trial.

That's what his old man had called him in the car when they were crawling through the A406 traffic on their way back to Barking. A right twat. You played like a fucking twat tonight, son, he'd said to him, nodding to himself as he stared at the blurred industrial estates through the drizzle running down the windscreen. This was your chance Scott, he had said, you, Ross and Jimmy, and you fucked it right up. They played their socks off, didn't they, Ross and Jimmy, they had been quality, fucking quality, but you played like a right twat.

I'm surprised they're giving you another chance, he had said, I know I wouldn't.

Thanks, dad.

Fucking thanks, dad.

Scott thought about his father again. *You played like a fucking twat tonight, son.* Scott had the CD jammed in his head and he couldn't turn it off. His father, the football expert; a pub footballer who kicked any opponent he couldn't match for skill or pace (which was every opponent), had lived in Barking his entire life and supported Manchester United. He was a glory hunter. A glory hunter not willing to put in the hard yards, the effort, the time and the dedication to make it happen; a Manchester United supporter living in East London. They were all the same, looking for immediate glory without the guts. Too lazy or inept to work for the glory themselves, they took the easy route and found it in Manchester United, or in their children.

You played like a fucking twat tonight, son.

SCOTT heard them walk into the toilet behind him. He looked down at his dick. Luckily, he'd just finished and had put it away quickly. They had given poor George a kicking in here a few weeks back while he still had his dick out, and the naked kicking was around the entire school by lunchtime. He was George "tiny prick". Most of the boys knew that wasn't true. They all took swimming lessons together. But it didn't matter. They were all happy to call George "tiny prick" for the next few weeks, all laughing together at George's expense, all thinking the same thing: Please don't let it be my turn next.

"Oh, look it's the fucking football superstar," one of them said.

Scott looked down suddenly at the crotch of his school trousers. Oh fuck. He had put it away too quickly. He had dribbled. He prayed they wouldn't notice the tiny wet patch. He was ready for the kicking. He could just about accept the kicking; it'd be all over in minutes. But the wet patch would stay with him for the rest of the year; for the rest of his school life.

"All right," Scott said nervously, still staring down at the urinal.

"Heard you got another trial at the academy tonight," another one of them said. "I don't know why, you're fucking shit."

"Yeah, yeah, I'm lucky really."

You are lucky, you played like a fucking twat tonight, son.

Scott refused to turn round. He stared down at the wet patch. Why wouldn't it just go away?

"Oi, we're talking to you, you cunt. Don't fucking ignore us."

Scott glanced across at the urinal and instinctively took half a step backwards. Urinals hurt.

"You've got no chance of making that fucking trial tonight."

Scott looked down at the small pool of his own piss at the bottom of the urinal. Why was every urinal in the school blocked? They were always blocked with, well, the usual stuff. There wasn't a lot left down there, but there was enough. Scott tried to concentrate. He must remember to close his eyes. He must remember to close his mouth. He couldn't do anything about his nose, but he must remember to close his mouth. It would be over quickly.

He noticed their outlines reflected in the tiles above the urinal. There were three of them. There were always three of them. Always the same three, lived on the Gascoigne Estate, never had a pot to piss in, dads on the dole, dirty school uniforms, greasy hair, free school dinners. No one took any notice of them at home so they made sure everyone took notice of them in school. They hated the world, but not as much as they hated Scott. Scott could play football, really play. Even they could see that. He had proper talent, a talent they would never possess, in any walk of life. There was nothing they could do about that. But they could beat the shit out of him.

Scott saw the outlines move across the tiles. He puffed out his chest. His fists clenched. He was on for a beating, but he'd fight back. His dad might accept that later.

"We're talking to you, you cunt," the leading outline on the tiles growled. "Don't fucking ignore us."

Scott noticed the outline pull back his arm, and Scott instinctively moved forwards. The punch was too slow, too choreographed; much slower than a striker turning him in the penalty box. But the reflexes that Scott had been born with, blessed with, left him out of position. He felt a dizzying sensation on the side of his head. The tiles were moving away from him quickly. He was falling. Knuckles raked across his ribcage as he went down.

As he put his arms out to break his fall, he knew his trial wasn't going to happen tonight; his second trial at the academy, his last trial; his football career all over at 13.

The kicking started as he hit the floor, obviously. He covered his head, but it was his legs. They were missing his head and his stomach. They were going for his legs. Fucking animals.

"I'll kill you, you fucking cunts," Scott screamed.

They laughed. And then they kept on kicking.

Scott peered through a crack in his fingers. He saw something moving across the tiles. Two outlines. But they were silent. Was he hallucinating? Why didn't they speak? Why didn't they run away?

Scott heard a cracking sound and a high-pitched wail. The kicking stopped. One of the outlines, the one who threw the first punch, was now lying beside Scott, clutching his nose as blood streamed through his fingers.

"You fucking want some as well, do ya?"

Scott looked up. It was Ross. His best mate Ross, his oldest friend and the funniest kid in the class. Ross was good-looking, loyal and funny. The other boys picked him first for footy games in the playground, even before they picked Scott or Jimmy. The girls gave him blow jobs behind the science block. Ross was popular because he would do anything for his mates, anything, plus he was built like a brick shithouse and loved a row.

Scott watched as Ross pushed another one headfirst into the urinal. Scott's urinal. Scott's piss. Take that, you fucker.

That's when Scott noticed Jimmy. Scott loved Jimmy. Scott shared everything with Jimmy: his home, his PlayStation, his packed lunch, his Mars bars, everything. Scott had them and Jimmy didn't. Scott even bought Jimmy some crisps on the way to training with his own pocket money, so Jimmy wouldn't be the only one without any crisps. Kids always noticed these things.

Jimmy had one pinned against the tiles, but was struggling. Jimmy was skinnier than both Ross and Scott. He had more skill on the park than both of them, but had legs like a carrier pigeon.

"You all right down there, Scott?" Jimmy shouted as he wrestled the big one up against the wall. "You wanna get up and help me out."

The pain had gone. Adrenaline took over. Scott was on his feet and pounding the prick's head into the tiled wall. Those tiles had really saved Scott today.

"Who's the cunt now, eh?" Scott screamed, as he threw another punch. "Who's the fucking cunt now, eh?"

Scott grabbed him by the throat and threw him onto the top of the other two.

Scott, Ross and Jimmy laughed. And then they kept on kicking.

JIMMY had to stop. He leaned against a brick wall and gasped for air. He glanced across at Scott and Ross and noticed they were barely out of breath, the bastards.

"Come on Jim, we can't stop here," Scott said quickly, still savouring his adrenaline rush.

"I'm knackered after all that," Jimmy muttered breathlessly. "Anyway, we'll be fine now. We're on the other side of the school now and if we keep running, we're gonna make it look well obvious."

"Yeah, he's probably right," Ross said, always the most pragmatic one. "If they see us running, they'll have us in the office. And you've got a bit of blood on your shirt."

Scott looked down at his white school shirt and smiled. It wasn't his blood. He beamed at Jimmy and Ross and they all giggled instinctively, always getting the joke together.

"That was fucking brilliant," Ross said.

"It was all right for you, I thought I was gonna get a black eye," Jimmy whined. "How could I turn up for training with a black eye? You know how the coach is always going on about how we can all fuck off back to Barking if we're not willing to put the hard work in? He already thinks I'm too skinny and don't eat enough. How can I turn up with a black eye? He'll think I'm a right pikey."

"At least you could still go training. I'd be finished if you didn't come in the bogs," Scott said sheepishly.

The three boys smiled at each other.

"Thanks."

Scott felt like an idiot saying it, but he had to say it. Ross and Jimmy knew he had to say it, but they had to ignore it.

"So are you gonna be all right for the trial tonight?" Ross asked.

"Yeah, I'm fine. It's gonna be great. It's only a few bruises I reckon. I'll just wear tracksuit bottoms. It felt like I was in there for hours, but it was probably only a few seconds before you came in."

"Yeah, we stood in the doorway for a while and watched," Jimmy said.

"Piss off."

"What? It was a good punch-up."

"Nah, as soon as we saw them follow you in there, we knew there was gonna be a row," Ross said.

"Yeah, he did," Jimmy admitted. "I didn't see them at first, but he saw them straightaway."

"Yeah, and you owe me a quid."

"Yeah, all right."

"What do you owe him a quid for?" Scott asked.

"Ah, he bet me you'd be having a row in there and I didn't believe him," Jimmy sighed. "So I've lost a quid and I'm gonna end up with a black eye."

"Stop moaning," Ross said.

"They fucking deserved it though. Scum. They're all scum over there, the fucking lot of them," Scott hissed. "They deserved a kicking. Who are they? Fucking nobodies."

Jimmy and Ross eyed each other nervously. Scott stared contemptuously at the first years kicking a ball around the pockmarked pitch that backed onto the old council houses. The first years and the council houses all looked the same. They were shit. They were all shit.

"Here, I've heard Charlie might be coming down to watch the training tonight," Ross said brightly.

"Fuck off. Really?" Jimmy asked, clearly excited.

"Yeah, one of the dads told my dad that Charlie likes to come down the academy once a month to watch the under-14s and he hasn't been for a few weeks. They haven't got a game this week 'cos of the international fixtures, so they all reckon he will be down tonight."

"That's bloody great," Jimmy exclaimed.

"Shit," Scott muttered.

"Yeah, so you better play well tonight, Scott," Ross said.

Ross raised his arms above his head and smiled broadly.

"We're on the march with Charlie's army," he sang. "We're all going to Wembley."

Jimmy laughed and joined in. Scott was too preoccupied.

"Come on Scott, join in, Charlie's a legend. The best fucking coach in the English Premier League and we're gonna meet him tonight," Jimmy shouted. "We're on the march with Charlie's army! We're all going to Wembley!"

Scott was far too distracted to chant about Charlie's coaching greatness, even if it was thoroughly deserved. He had a trial to get through first. Ross and Jimmy noticed their friend's apprehension and stopped singing. Ross stared at Scott. There was something not quite right.

"Here Scott," he said slowly. "Have you pissed your trousers?"

four

CHARLIE always took his young prospects to lunch at the players'
canteen after first-team training. It always worked. One minute
they're sitting at home in some crappy living room watching
Jeremy Kyle with their parents, and the next they're having a plate
of pasta beside an England centre-forward. It never failed. How
could it? These naïve kids just wanted to play football. They were
still at that tender age when the game itself was all that mattered.
They'd give anything to join the academy. Forget wages and
bonuses, they'd pay to kick a ball around for this club and all that
other bollocks.

Charlie chuckled to himself as he guided the wide-eyed spotty
kid towards an empty table. He saw the wonder. He remembered
that wonder. He had it once. He met them all in the so-called
Swinging Sixties, every one of the London chaps: Moore, Hurst,
Peters, Greaves, Harris, Osgood and Bonetti, he shook hands
with them all and shyly posed for awkward photographs as
he took buses and trains to every training ground in London.
Every club in the capital wanted his signature in the sixties. He
could've laced his boots up for all of them—West Ham and their
World Cup triumvirate, Chelsea's kings of Carnaby Street and
Tottenham's cup heroes—they were all his for the taking.

But all he had wanted to do was play football. It was an escape from that grey, listless drudgery. The Swinging Sixties? What a load of bollocks. They might have been for Peter Osgood down the King's Road, but for Charlie, the council house kid from Dagenham, the sixties came in sepia and frayed around the edges. Grey roads, grey shops, grey skies and grey people; that was the sixties for Charlie. The only things that broke up the grey were the dog shit and the bricks. Until Charlie bought his farmhouse in Epping, he thought the whole world was built with red brick.

He had two options. Sign professional forms as a footballer for a few quid a week or work with his old man at the car lot. His dad called it an emporium or a salesroom. Everyone else in Dagenham called it a second-hand car lot. He had it off the Fiddlers roundabout, not far from the Merry Fiddlers pub, before it became a supermarket. His dad was the best second-hand car salesman in London, untouchable. That's what they all told Charlie. His dad's mates meant it too. Charlie's dad was a special man. His sales patter was unrivalled, his gift of the gab the stuff of legend. No one could sell a second-hand car like Charlie's dad. There was an urban myth that Charlie had once sold a Morris 1100 to a bloke who'd only popped in to ask directions to the A13.

"Don't believe what you read in the papers, son."

That's what Charlie's dad had always told him whenever he asked if the Morris 1100 story was true. It had been in *The Dagenham Post* and Charlie's dad gave a playful "no comment" when asked to corroborate the Morris 1100 story. Charlie's dad died without ever telling Charlie if the story was true or not. Strangely, Charlie could never quite forgive him for that.

As Charlie got older, he realised he had two fathers. There was the fast-talking car salesman, and a bloke in a crusty armchair slagging off anyone on his portable TV who'd made a success of their life. As Charlie's career took off, he saw increasingly less of the fast-talking car salesman and more of the armchair critic.

He didn't like the armchair critic as much, but he understood him better.

Charlie's dad was the greatest second-hand car salesman in Dagenham in the 1960s. But few people had a second-hand car in Dagenham in the 1960s. There was no point having a talent that the public couldn't buy.

Charlie signed forms and became a professional footballer. He only returned to his father's second-hand car lot once, and that was just after the old man died. And Charlie sold it.

"Sit down over here, son," Charlie said warmly to the spotty kid, beckoning him towards a chair.

The kid took his seat and glimpsed across at the next table. He tried not to stare, but he couldn't help himself.

"Isn't that ..."

"Yep, England's future no. 7 and arguably one of the best midfielders knocking around at the moment," Charlie gushed. "If he stops fucking about and drifting into wide positions, and sticks between those two bloody posts as I keep telling him, he could win England the World Cup. What do you want to eat?"

"Er, I don't know, Mr Charlie. I'm not really that hungry, I suppose ..."

"Don't be silly, you gotta eat after a training session ... Tom, go and get this boy something healthy."

Tom, a slim, handsome man with short brown hair and a stubble beard, picked up his notepad from the counter and walked quickly towards the table. He took a pencil out of the pocket of his stained apron and turned over a page on his notepad.

"What do you want, Charlie?" Tom asked.

"Me, I don't want anything, mate. Just get me a cup of milky sweet tea. It's this boy we gotta fatten up. Look at him. Could be a great defender this one, but he could go missing behind a goal post. What are the first-team eating today?"

"I think they're mostly having lean grilled chicken breast with pasta."

"Get my boy a plate of that then," Charlie replied, waving his hand regally. "Whatever the first team has, he's got to have."

Tom smiled and took down the order. The boy beamed with pride.

"Good prospect is he, then?" Tom asked, genuinely interested.

"Good? By the time he gets to 18, half the women in London are gonna want to fuck him. By the time, he gets to 21, half the women in the world are gonna want to fuck him. And if he does the business for me by the time he's 25, I'm gonna fuck him."

Tom laughed and headed off into the kitchen as the boy flushed and stared down at his feet. Charlie noticed the spotty kid's discomfort and smiled. This was going to be easier than he thought. The way the kid gaped at the first-teamers, the way he almost wet his shorts when he saw an England player, the way he ignored the canteen cook completely; this kid was a textbook son of the celebrity generation. Charlie would have him signed up in 20 minutes and be back doing laps in his heated pool by 3 pm.

In the old days, kids would burst into his office after training and demand a game or a place on the sub's bench. Now Charlie dealt with their agents, who palmed them off with a slice of something nice that day. When Charlie first got into the management game, the kids all wanted to be footballers. Nothing else mattered. They still did. But now they wanted to be famous too, and that was easier to achieve. Life was so much easier now.

Charlie glanced over the spotty kid's shoulder. There they were. It was about fucking time.

"OK then, mate," he said. "It's time for you to meet my Barking Boys."

SCOTT, Ross and Jimmy made their way through the crowded canteen, nodding and shouting abuse at teammates. Charlie had nicknamed them The Barking Boys after they had signed professional forms for the club. The nickname had its downside. The other lads called them chavs and told them to bugger off back to their council houses in their Ford Escorts. Secretly, Scott, Ross and Jimmy loved the nickname. It bonded them. It made them one against the world. They were back in the school bogs again fighting battles for one another. One for all and sod the rest.

Charlie loved his Barking Boys. He always referred to them in the collective. They were from Barking. They grew up near the Captain Cook pub. He grew up near the Merry Fiddlers pub in Dagenham. They shared a London borough. They shared Bobby Moore, Alf Ramsey, Jimmy Greaves, Trevor Brooking, Tony Adams and John Terry. They shared a football pedigree. They were practically related. Alf Ramsey had Bobby Moore. Charlie had his Barking Boys, his little terriers from the same terraced streets; four men fighting to excel, to strive, to achieve, to move forward, because none of them wanted to look back.

"Come on, sit down for a minute, sit down," Charlie said quickly, his excitement growing, the sales pitch coming, his father's DNA taking control. "No tour of this place is complete without meeting my Barking Boys, is it? The good-looking one here is Ross."

Charlie always introduced the kids to Ross first. He wasn't as accomplished a player as Scott, but he was easily the best looking. He was naturally muscular, built like a middleweight boxer with blue eyes, light brown hair and two days' worth of stubble. He always had two days' worth of stubble and it drove the other lads to distraction. How the fuck do you keep two days' worth of stubble all year round? Young players were always in awe of Ross. He always attracted the most beautiful women, the most famous women, and scored the most lucrative photo shoots. These things were important.

"Hello mate, how you going," Ross said affably. "Saw you out there today, not bad, decent left foot you got there."

"What do you mean decent? This boy's gonna play for England before you do, if you don't stop fucking about in front of goal."

Ross was also a striker, and everyone loved a striker. He laughed, took out his phone and dialled as he stood up. Ross had been given a good tip and this kid wasn't a professional footballer yet.

"Well, all the best mate," Ross said, shaking the kid's hand and already turning his back on him. "Hope it all works out for you ... Yeah, yeah, it's me. Listen I've heard something about Kempton this afternoon ..."

Charlie watched him go and smiled.

"Don't take it personally," he said. "If I had a woman like his waiting for me at home, I wouldn't wait around for you either. Have you seen her in the papers?"

"Yeah, yeah," the spotty kid replied, with far too much enthusiasm.

"She's pretty tasty, no doubt about it."

Scott and Jimmy shifted in their seats uncomfortably. They didn't like Charlie's dirty old man patter. He always liked to be one of the boys, they understood that, but not all the time.

"So you could have a bright career at this club, if you keep your head down and your nose clean," Scott said, aware of that omnipresent armband. "You've got great potential, that's obvious. But it's how you apply it. Look at me, Ross and Jim. We grew up together. We trained together and now we've all made a career in the hardest professional football league in the world. The English Premier League has millions of people watching my hairy arse every week. Do you think you can handle it?"

Charlie nodded like a proud father. Scott was the most natural club captain he'd ever seen, both as player and manager. He was an English Premier League policeman, always on duty and as serious as sin. He was born wearing that armband.

"Er, I don't know yet," the spotty kid replied nervously. "I suppose I, er, won't really know until I get out there and experience it."

Scott and Jimmy looked at each other. Charlie slapped the kid on the back and roared with laughter.

"What did I tell you about this boy, eh," he shouted. "What did I tell you? He's you, Scott, 10 years ago; a wise, ferret-faced head on young shoulders. We get you both in the first team and it's Champions League football every bloody season."

Tom came over to the table and put down a plate of pasta. He wiped his hands on his apron, adjusted it and then glanced at Scott.

"Er, there's a call for you, Scott," he said slowly. "It's your wife. She says it's urgent."

"Shit, you better go," Charlie said.

"Yeah, yeah, I better," Scott replied, getting up. "Nice to chat with you mate, we'll speak again soon."

"Er, yeah, OK. Nice to meet you, Scott," stuttered the spotty kid as the captain of his beloved club followed Tom into the kitchen. Charlie watched them go before leaning across the table.

"Right then, let's get down to business," he said chirpily. "This is Jimmy, as I'm sure you know. And he's the best agent in the English Premier League."

SCOTT handed the phone back to Tom in the kitchen.

"Cheers, mate," he said. "Thanks for doing that."

"It's all right, no problem at all."

"It's just that I really can't hang around the training ground. I really do have to get home to my wife."

These plebs are so fucking thick, Scott thought. That spotty kid had better smarten up if he's going to have any chance of making the grade. He was too drippy and starry-eyed to realise that a multi-millionaire club captain might have his own mobile phone. Why the hell would his wife call the club cook? Did he work in a factory in the 1970s with one fucking phone in the building? He had his reasons to get away, but he didn't particularly want to stay to hear Charlie's spiel again. The speech itself was valid, and necessary, if that spotty kid was going to stand any chance of turning his back on the plebs, but that didn't mean Scott wanted to hear it again. Not now. This was his only chance. She would be there, waiting, in that ridiculous G-string barely covering her Brazilian. She would be there. And he would not. Scott had three hours, maybe more, but that didn't mean he could mess about listening to the dreams and aspirations of some greasy apprentice. And the dirty cow liked to take her time, insisted on it, practically ordered it. He had to get over there now and Godalming could take fucking ages if there was any traffic on the M25, all those dopey school coaches waving at him on their way to Thorpe Park.

He opened the back door to the kitchen and looked across at the training pitches. Just a couple of juniors knocking balls around in the desperate hope that one of the coaches might take notice. Don't be fucking silly, lads, they're all sitting in the canteen talking to their agents on the phone. Move with the times, boys. Since when did kids prove their worth on training pitches?

Scott closed the door behind him and took another, final look around the training complex. He took out his mobile and dialled quickly.

"Hello, it's me, where are you now?" he whispered. "Can I

come now? ... Ah, leave off, don't start all that talk now, I've got to get through the M25 and A3 first ... Yeah, all right ... I reckon he'll be away for at least a couple of hours ... Yeah, OK ... Ah, don't start talking about shaving now, you're doing my head in. Oh, and Jo, leave the door on the latch. I can't have a photo of me standing on your doorstep ... OK, I reckon about half an hour at the most, babe. Keep it warm."

Scott put his phone away and jogged to the car park. He didn't look back.

JIMMY took his coffee from Tom and made a point of over-extending his arm. The spotty kid noticed. Jimmy smiled. Of course he noticed. They always did.

"Rolex," he said indifferently. "This one's a Rolex Oyster, a GMT-Master II I think. Something like that. This one cost me about 10 grand, maybe more because it's got the 18-carat yellow gold case. Can you see that? I like that, proper quality. Most of the players I work with have got them, or something similar like a Daytona. I know I got Ross a Daytona, white gold, quality watch. I've got another couple at home still sitting in their boxes. I'll have one of them on your wrist by tomorrow, if you want."

The spotty kid eyed Jimmy nervously. He knew he was young and naïve, but he wasn't completely stupid. He knew who football agents were and what their role was in the game. His father had told him often enough and he had seen the documentaries. And Jimmy was one of the most famous in the Premier League. Not only because he handled so many contracts, but because he used to play himself; made his debut before his mates Scott and Ross did, but there was some injury. The kid was too young to remember. Jimmy was playing with

Scott and Ross. And then he was their agent.

"I'm not sure that would be right," the spotty kid muttered.

"I told you he was a bit special, didn't I?" Charlie said, before sipping his tea.

"No, no, it's not that Mr Charlie, honest. It's just that ..."

Charlie put his cup down slowly and smiled reassuringly at the kid.

"Listen, mate, do you know when I made my first-team debut here?" Charlie asked.

"Er, no, no, I think it was in the sixties, right?"

"Yep, 1966, funnily enough. Say 1966 to most people in the game and they'll tell you World Cup at Wembley, they think it's all over, it is now, three Lions on a shirt and all that bollocks, right? Do you know what 1966 was for me? It was half a quid a week, training in the morning, sweeping the terraces in the afternoons, painting the wooden stands and marking out the fucking pitch before games. Can you believe that? I used to be out there in the fucking drizzle pushing this rusty old paint roller around the pitch? Do I think it was character-building and made me the manager I am today? No, I think it was a waste of my bloody time. I should've been out on that pitch working on my weaker left foot, not painting the fucking thing.

"That's why you don't have to do any of that now. You're eating pasta at this state-of-the-art complex that cost the club 10 million quid. I used to share a bag of chips with the other apprentices under the old wooden stand when it pissed down. Do you know where those apprentices are now? I haven't got a clue, probably sitting at home and deciding whether they should skip paying the mortgage so they keep their Sky Sports going and reminisce about the good old days. But the thing is, there are no fucking good old days. It's a myth. Just a load of fat, washed-up old pros who occasionally get recognised when they're out driving their taxis or delivering the post. The game is ruthless that way. You've heard of Moore, Hurst and Peters, right? I saw Hurst and Peters at a charity game in Dagenham once, sitting on plastic chairs around a cheap plastic garden table signing a handful of autographs. I used to see Bobby Moore eating a cold bag of chips and doing radio work for some Mickey Mouse station. The game doesn't even think it owes anything to World Cup winners. The game owes you nothing, once you've gone. So my advice to you, son, is to take it while you can. Take it with Jimmy here, because you've got the rest of your life to be an ex-footballer."

"So you're asking Jimmy to be my agent?"

Jimmy and Charlie looked at each other, and both laughed.

"No, no, no, we're not saying that at all," Jimmy said quickly.

"I would not make that decision for you," Charlie added. "Bloody hell. You've got to make that decision. Agents can't use club officials to influence potential clients and vice versa. No, no, no, I would never do that. I'm just explaining to you what happens if you don't look after yourself in the game. Jimmy will do the rest."

"Like what?"

The spotty kid's scepticism made him unexpectedly brash. Charlie nodded approvingly and gestured towards the counter.

"Here, Tom, get me another cup of milky sweet tea, please mate."

Jimmy took a sip from his mineral water bottle and cleared his throat. He loved this bit. He loved the spiel. It didn't compensate for not playing, nothing did, but he still shared the lifestyle, still savoured the celebrity, the red carpets and the paps. Without that, he was just another nameless face back in Barking. Once you've had a taste, you've got to feed the addiction. And this spotty kid was about to give him another hit.

"As you probably know, I retired two years ago through injury," he said. "So I know how soon all this can be taken away. Luckily, Charlie made sure I was well looked after, insurance wise, and I was able to set myself up as an agent to help young players like yourself and stop you from going down the same path. You just met Scott and Ross, right? I represent them both. They are both on five-year contracts, but with a built-in clause that the contracts can be improved after the end of every successful season. They also have a clause where they can leave if a so-called 'bigger club' comes in with a better offer, no offence Charlie."

"I'm just waiting for my tea," Charlie muttered, winking at the spotty kid.

"So they're both sorted. They have great seasons, we renegotiate. They have crap seasons, they still have to be paid because it's in the contract. Either way, they can't lose. That's why Ross drives a Porsche and Scott drives a Ferrari. He had to have a Ferrari. He's always been the most competitive."

"Yeah, tell him what you drive then, flash Harry," Charlie joked.

"Yeah, all right. I've got a Bentley. It's a good family car."

"A fucking Bentley, he must be doing something right," Charlie said.

"And that's just the basic club contract. They've got boot deals for the rest of their careers, which will be fully paid up if injury curtails their careers; clothing deals, the car deals, watch deals and any appearance on TV or radio—absolutely any—even if it's five minutes for ESPN while they're out walking their dogs, I negotiate a fee."

"And that's how much the game has changed," Charlie interjected. "When I was playing, it was a joke, a fucking joke, the TV mob all took us for a ride. Brian Moore, may he rest in peace, would nab you for a quick word for *The Big Match* and all you'd think was, great, my old man in Dagenham is gonna see me on the box tonight. And then you'd go back in the dressing room and the lads would take the right piss out of you because you could've got 30, 40, maybe even 50 quid for that 10-minute interview. But we didn't know. Didn't have the first clue. But today, if I'm being completely honest, my first-team boys, once training's done, want serious money for everything. They won't leave their fucking living rooms for less than 50 grand, will they Jimmy?"

"It's just the way the game's gone. You watch the English Premier League. You know what it's like. Every extra camera, every extra punter, every extra jersey, every extra cable subscription means money for someone. And without you, without Charlie and without me, there is no money. There's nothing. So you've got to make as much as you can while you're playing because the real money men holding the purse strings won't give a shit about you when you're gone."

"He's right. I like my players to be protected only by people I can trust, and I count them on one hand. And Jimmy's one of them. If you go with Jimmy then I'll be reassured that you're being taken care of off the pitch, which means you'll be a better player for me on the pitch. I'm sure you've read about broken Britain in the papers. The economy is dying on its arse, everyone is skint, houses are too expensive, blah, blah, blah. As a manager, I can't have you playing like a tit because you're worrying about your mortgage and car repayments."

"No, Mr Charlie," the spotty kid mumbled.

"So go away and think about it, have a chat with your parents and then come back and let me know. You're closing in on the first team and I don't want you having any outside distractions. I like my first-team players to have no outside financial distractions or concerns. Tell your parents that."

"I will do, Mr Charlie."

"All right, then."

Charlie and Jimmy stood up in unison. Charlie offered his hand. The spotty kid stood up clumsily, knocking his chair backwards before shaking Charlie's hand.

"Luckily, he's not that clumsy in the penalty box, Jimmy," Charlie said. "Go on, mate. Get home to your parents, and let Jimmy know your decision tomorrow. And once that's settled, me and you can get on with turning you into a first-team player."

"Yes, Mr Charlie, thank you. And thank you, Jimmy."

"Don't worry about it mate," Jimmy replied. "It's what I do. Don't forget to let me know if you want one of these watches."

He jutted out his forearm to let the kid take in the wealth one last time. He gazed at the timepiece. Precision craftsmanship, exquisite design and Jimmy had never closed a deal without one.

Jimmy and Charlie watched the star-struck kid stumble his way through the living, breathing posters that had looked down on him from his bedroom wall every night. Tom strolled over with another cup of tea for Charlie. He picked up the chair and wiped it down.

"Well, that one's in the bag," Jimmy said, as they sat down again. "Piece of piss. You went on a bit about your playing days though, didn't you boss?"

"Oi, you cheeky fucker, I meant every word I said. These boys deserve looking after. I got fuck all as a player. Most of my old teammates are fucking postmen now or work on the dustbins. You've got to get every penny you can."

"Yeah, yeah, of course, boss, of course."

"So you make sure you look after this kid. He'll do a job for us. And make sure you sort me out. Four per cent on this one."

Jimmy smiled slyly as he sipped from his water bottle.

"It's usually three."

"There'll be enough to go around. This boy's special. It's gotta be four."

"Yeah, all right. Anyone else you want me to see?"

"No," replied Charlie bluntly. He swigged his tea and stood up quickly. He was already sitting in his sauna in Theydon Bois. "I wanna get home early today. There could be another academy kid in a couple of weeks, but we'll sort this one out first. I'll see you later."

"Hang on, I'm going now. I'll come with you."

Tom pushed their chairs back into place and collected the tea cups. He wiped the table down before tucking his cloth into his apron belt. He adjusted the collars of his starchy white shirt and looked around the canteen. Most of the players had left. Another tedious day was almost over. He pulled out his phone and dialled.

"Hello, it's Tom," he said. "I think we might have the old bastard."

five

TOM nodded his apology as he bumped into a red-faced guy and then wished he hadn't bothered. The BO was appalling. The Central Line really was a pain in the arse. For his footballers out in Theydon Bois and Epping, the Central Line was a dream, a jaunty day in the Essex countryside as the train trundled merrily along through medieval market towns and isolated hamlets. Not that his footballers ever used the London Underground. They hadn't been anywhere near public transport for years, unless there was a lame public initiative for them to endorse, where they had little choice but to interact with their fans for five minutes.

Tom took the tube every fucking morning. He took a tube and a bus to get to the training ground, and then he took a bus and a tube to get to White City in the afternoons. Tom had to laugh. He had always thought the football gig was going to be the easiest one yet, a bit of a giggle and a chance to slice grapefruits in half for some sportsmen he genuinely admired. Plus there was the added incentive of working on something that actually captured the public interest. This job didn't need a hard sell. Footballers sold themselves. They were The Beatles of the 21st century. That was his original pitch. Footballers were The Beatles of the 21st century.

And if they were, then there was the modern Brian Epstein staring right back at him. He had made the back pages of two of the tabloids and a single column on one of the broadsheets. He'd be happy with that. Tom arched his head as subtly as possible to make out the opening paragraphs of one of the stories. He smiled. Cheeky Charlie was banging his favourite drum again. His boys were off to Liverpool at the weekend and he was lamenting, again, how the gulf between the haves and the have-nots was destroying the game; how he had to consign himself to a decent cup run each season; how it was impossible for anyone else in the Premier League to break the stranglehold of the Big Four; how he'd love to be given their transfer kitty to give himself a real shot at the big boys.

That was his favourite violin. Give cheeky Charlie a chance and he'd be the first Englishman in years to win the English title. Never mind all these Johnny foreigners, he always said. Anyone could win the league with their budgets. Give him a budget, a generous owner and some petrodollars and he'd do it for the common man; win it for the Englishman. He'd taken the archaic Bloke In A Pub Speech and delivered it nationally for years, and the blokes in the pubs revered him. Even Tom admired Charlie's knack of speaking only in anecdotes and witty sound bites in post-match press conferences—win, lose or draw—to keep Joe Public on side. And he was undoubtedly a great coach, a classic man manager of the old school, up there with Shankly, Clough, Busby and Ferguson.

It was almost a shame really that Charlie was a greedy, devious, two-faced bastard.

TOM admired the still photographs on the wall and the awards framed beside them. He had been involved with two of them, given up 18 months of his life to be involved with them and there was the reward. Something framed from some media club he'd never heard of. He didn't do media or press clubs. It wasn't his thing, and besides his line of work required tact and subtlety, and journalists had big mouths.

"Hello, Tom. How's it going?"

Jason walked in and offered Tom his hand. Tom was shocked to see how much weight Jason had gained since they had worked on the Islamic terror cell together. Six months spent hanging out with radical Muslims in North London had taken its toll on both of them. By the end of it, even they were beginning to think that the 9/11 attacks were deserved. They had to get out and put together whatever they had. The footage had been enough because it earned them one of those framed things on the wall. They had both needed a break. Jason found his behind a desk. Tom thought he'd found his in the fluffy, superficial world of football.

"It's all right, mate, all right, bloody great actually," Tom said, shaking Jason's hand warmly. They had looked out for each other in Stoke Newington, keeping each other's spirits up while they endured warped rhetoric from would-be jihadists. Tom missed working with Jason every day.

"How's the job going?"

"Ah, great. What do you think? Making omelettes for footballers every day, it's the highlight of my life, mate. Do you know I had a Spanish omelette on the menu the other day and that Ross asked me, straight-faced, if he could just have an English omelette instead. Thick as pig's shit, the lot of them, all with Bentleys and Ferraris parked outside."

"Bit different to Birmingham, eh?"

Tom smiled. Everything was different compared to a sunny afternoon spent with the English Defence League in Birmingham's city centre.

"Do you know something? I kind of preferred it in Birmingham. There was always something happening. Always a demo with the fascists, always something on with the Muslims. Say what you like about the English Defence League and the BNP, but they were always busy."

"But you've got something now right?"

Tom took out his notepad and examined his scribbles. He had more than something this time.

"Yeah, yeah, like I said on the phone," Tom said. "I think we've got the flash sod."

"You've got him on tape?"

"I got him on tape twice. I had a mic in the apron and I had one of those cheap ones put under the table, ended up picking up almost everything. Charlie loves the sound of his own voice so much, he's never quiet. He struts about that place like he's a king in court. It was a bit of a gamble, but he usually sits at the same table right in front of my counter, so he can bark orders at me for his bloody 'milky sweet tea' and whatever his superstars want. It lets him think he's always in control when he's barking orders; too many years spent on the touchline. And do you know what the best part is?"

"What's that?"

Tom sipped his tea slowly. He leaned back into his chair and grinned at Jason.

"I've got him on camera," he said triumphantly.

"You haven't, have ya?"

"Yep, that dozy apprentice of his knocked his chair over, so I was in there like Flynn. I bent down to pick up the chair and got Charlie and Jimmy talking percentages. It was perfect."

"And they didn't twig?"

"Nah, any other time they might. I mean, it was so bloody obvious, I'm bending down over the top of this chair, wiping it for about half an hour, but keeping it at arm's length so it didn't block the bloody camera. I looked like a giraffe trying to shag a hedgehog. There I am desperately trying to stay cool, trying to make it look like I always clean a chair like that, while I'm turning slightly to my right so I can block out the sun a bit from the window behind my shoulder."

"Bloody hell."

"Ah, it was all right. I think once you've been caught in a toilet trying to adjust a pinhole camera by a BNP skinhead, everything else is easy."

"Yeah, it was a good job I came in and pissed all over the walls then, weren't it?"

"It saved me from a kicking."

"And it got me well in with the top boys. Do you know one of them told me recently that they still tell the story about that mad bastard who pissed all over the pub's toilet walls?"

"That's unbelievable."

"Great days. Great bloody days."

Jason looked out of the window. Tom shifted uneasily in his seat.

"You can always come in with me and boil pasta for Charlie's Barking Boys if you want?"

Jason turned away from the window and forced a smile.

"Nah, you're all right. So what happens now?"

Tom opened his mouth slightly. He failed to hide his surprise.

"What do you mean what happens now? We're done, mate. I've got him on tape. I've got the old bastard on camera, discussing his cut, discussing his percentage. It's an old-fashioned bung in any other name. It's the icing on the cake. We're done."

"You see, the thing is, the new boss ..."

"Come on, don't make me butter any more loaves of bread

for those muppets, please. I've been stuck in that canteen for over three months. I've been following Charlie around at night."

"I know all that, but ..."

"And me and Sarah are like ships passing in the night. After BNP and the Muslims, I promised her I'd be home more to help with the kids."

"Mate, you don't have to tell me. Why do you think I spend most of my days here?"

"Well, hopefully, to fight for me while I'm there sweeping the floors around millionaire fuckwits who don't even bother to lift their feet."

"I am fighting for you. You don't know how much I'm fighting for you. If it wasn't for me ..."

Jason stopped himself and reached for his tea. He sipped slowly. Tom glared at him.

"If it wasn't for you, what?"

"Nothing, nothing. It doesn't matter."

"Yes it does. What?"

Jason put his cup back on the table and sighed.

"The big boss wants to pull the pin."

Tom felt a tightening sensation in his stomach. At that moment, he thought of the cost of nappies. He pictured them in a supermarket with the price tag in glittery, neon letters. The image surprised him. He didn't think of his two children bouncing off the claustrophobic walls of his two-bedroom flat above a bike shop in Hornsea and the mortgage payments he could only meet with Sarah doing two shifts a week at the hospital. He didn't think about the car he sold, convincing himself that his line of work was more suited to public transport and cycling. He didn't even think about the trainers he saw Scott and Ross leave behind at training yesterday morning after wearing them once. Fucking once. Tom couldn't remember the last time he'd bought a new pair of trainers. He could only think of nappies and how bloody expensive they were.

Tom tried to ignore the burning sensation at the back of his throat. Jason had saved his job, his livelihood and his well-being on more than one occasion over the years. Tom instinctively knew it wasn't Jason's fault.

"What the hell for?" Tom asked.

Jason leaned back into his chair and exhaled deeply.

"Ah, Tom, you've read the papers. There are cutbacks everywhere. We're lucky we've still got jobs. They're giving out golden handshakes all over the place here. Well, they're giving out handshakes. There's nothing golden about them."

"The economy's turning a corner now; new government and all that. It's supposed to be a new day," Tom interjected.

"You know that's got nothing to do with it really. No one watches TV anymore. Or at least, no one watches what we want them to watch or when we want them to watch it. They Sky Plus the bloody thing, cut all the adverts out and watch it whenever they like. How are you supposed to get a ratings measure out of that? No one watches our show, if you play the ratings game, no one. I'm just hoping and praying that they are at least recording it and watching it later, or we really are fucked. Who really records a current affairs programme or a documentary in this day and age? Who gives a shit? They watch *Britain's Got Talent* and *X-Factor*. Then they skip the news and get straight to the bloody results to see how clever they are for determining the outcome of the show that they're watching. We can't do that with our programmes. We have to give them the ending that our sources give us. And they don't really like that anymore. They have to phone in their own endings now. It's reality, it's singers and ... and dancers ... and it's forgotten celebrities cooking scallops for other forgotten celebrities, but it's not what we do anymore."

"Ah, leave off, it's not like you're telling me anything we both haven't known for nearly 10 years, is it? All that shit has been around for nearly a decade and we're still making good stuff. Our BNP special was one of the highest ratings we've ever had."

Jason sat up suddenly.

"Yeah, and you know why? Old football hooligans hoping they'd see themselves on TV. The same people who watched *The Football Factory* are the same people who watched the BNP programme. We were preaching to the converted. Same people who used to watch documentaries on the Krays and the Yorkshire Ripper now watch programmes on football hooligans and the fucking BNP because there's nothing else for them to get off on. For us, it's a ... what is it ... it's a scathing indictment of the breakdown of community values. That's what we said. For them, it's a night of nostalgia. You know it. And I know it. And sadly for us, the new boss definitely knows it."

Tom stared at his tea cup on the table.

"Do you know what the most popular show in our time slot was last week, across all channels, cable and free-to-air?" Jason asked slowly.

"Oh, I don't know. *Britain's Got Talent*," Tom mumbled.

"Nope, that reality show *At Home With Jo*."

"I've never watched it."

"It's absolute drivel. It's just shots of her lying under a sun bed, catching skin cancer in a thong and telling the camera how she wants to leave behind a better world for her baby girl. Then she pisses off for a breast massage to stop them from going droopy."

"Sounds great."

Jason laughed suddenly. The mood swing shocked Tom. He was curious.

"What are you laughing at?"

"It's the worst TV show I've ever seen, mate. Terrible lighting, terrible lensing, terrible makeup and no direction at all that I can see, but it's saved our documentary."

Tom stared quizzically across the table.

"What are you going about?"

"Well, the new boss is no Bob Woodward, but he is obsessed with ratings figures. That's all he talks about. When I was telling him about our progress, I just couldn't win him over. I told him everything. The fact that Charlie tends to buy and sell players controlled by Jimmy; the fact that some of these players are sold for inflated fees; the fact that he's bought players who never played a game and then sold them on again for Jimmy; the fact that the kid from a Dagenham council estate now owns half of Epping Forest managing a mid-table side; and the fact that you had seen him introduce up-and-coming kids to Jimmy after training. He still didn't bite."

"But that was before I'd actually got any of it recorded. I've got him now. I've got them both, haven't I? We can go to the pair of them now and ask them out straight."

"Listen to me. He wasn't interested at first. Until he looked down at the ratings list on his table and saw Jo's fake tits staring back at him. Then a light bulb went off, it was like I could see the thing go off in his head. I knew where he was gonna go. It was so obvious. 'Isn't that Jo's club,' he asks. 'Yeah, yeah,' I reply quickly. 'I mean, she is *the* footballer's wife now, isn't she? Now Jordan's out of the picture and Posh is overseas, she's the main one. She's the only one.' And you could just see his face light up. 'OK, but I want to see some quick progress,' he said. And he also wants us to somehow mention Jo."

"How are we supposed to do that?" Tom asked incredulously.

"Yeah, it's very tenuous at this stage. We can't just say she's a footballer's wife, that's just sleazy and not to mention libellous, but fuck it, that's a battle for another day. We've still got the green light and that's all that matters."

"Thank god for that."

"Of course, I'll have a listen to the tapes and watch the footage. That's a massive breakthrough, that'll keep us going. Before that would've been enough, but I know he's gonna want more."

"I've got Charlie negotiating his share of a bung. What more do you want?"

"What do you think?"

Tom smiled and got up.

"Yeah, I suppose. But that's not going to be easy, is it? Not to mention expensive."

Jason stood up and stretched his legs. Tom could see he really needed to get out of the office more.

"Yeah, but they'll back us to the hilt if we can get Charlie taking the money on camera."

"I haven't got a clue how I'm supposed to do that. He's such a slippery old bastard."

"Ah, we'll think of something. We always do."

"Maybe I'll ask Jo to give him a backhander."

Jason laughed and opened the door for Tom.

"Yeah, yeah, we might even get decent ratings for that one."

six

AL-HAKIM pushed further, but it made no difference. He was bored. It wasn't about the position. He had always preferred doggy style. It wasn't about faces. He never paid for ugly women. And it certainly wasn't about his wives. He never thought about his wives. What did they have to do with anything? It was just practical. Sometimes they wore the hijab. Sometimes they didn't. Sometimes they insisted it on it, sometimes they didn't. It all depended on where Al-Hakim's servants had picked them up from. Al-Hakim had neither the time nor the patience to discuss their attitudes to the hijab or the purdah system; he was paying for their hole, not their beliefs. So he always insisted on doggy style. That way they could do whatever they liked at the other end. Al-Hakim wasn't paying to see their faces. He was paying for doggy style.

But the streets of Riyadh were not paved with prostitutes like they used to be. It just wasn't the same anymore. In many ways, Al-Hakim had a lot of time for the purdah system. It kept most Saudi women (except the most expensive ones) away from his palace. He had his wives in his palace, why would he have sex with more Saudi women on his silk oriental carpets? There was always the risk of flogging, for them of course, but Al-Hakim was a man of globalisation. Foreign exchanges and investments were so much more interesting.

Well, they usually were. This one came from Nigeria as they often did, either Nigeria or Ethiopia, and they invariably performed with a work ethic that one expected of an illegal immigrant from a poverty-stricken nation. Al-Hakim often instructed his servants to go African. They were always terrified of being deported. Even the floggings didn't scare them as much as the threat of deportation. They let Al-Hakim do whatever he wanted on his silk oriental carpets. So he did whatever he wanted.

But the Committee for the Propagation of Virtue and the Prevention of Vice was becoming such a tiresome bore. The endless speeches and crackdowns were making it harder for Al-Hakim's servants to acquire anything of real quality. And that suicide bomb attack at the Muhaya residential compound back in 2003 had been extremely irritating. Those Lebanese, Palestinians and Egyptians knew how to do the right thing discreetly. Al-Hakim and his business associates often frequented the compound, until the bombing attack. For a while, it really compromised Al-Hakim's lifestyle. Some people died too.

So he was stuck with this Nigerian mannequin. He pounded away, but he could already feel himself going limp. He had too much room. Like many whores in Riyadh, she was clearly being overworked. Damn the Committee for the Propagation of Virtue and the Prevention of Vice. Those extremists were ruining his sex life. He didn't expect this one to be tight, virgin tight—she hadn't cost enough for that—but he at least expected some effort on her part. Like all Saudi businessmen, Al-Hakim could not tolerate a poor work ethic.

"Make noise," he ordered, struggling to maintain his erection. "Make noise."

JO loved Asda. She just couldn't stand the supermarket's shoppers. All pasty-faced with their greasy hair pulled back aggressively and their black roots and their tracksuit bottoms and their fucking babies, endless fucking babies everywhere: she hated them all. Asda had stopped being a supermarket years ago. It was a fucking crèche. With its all-under-one-roof concept and three-for-a-pound specials, it was a day care centre. It was somewhere for the plebs to bring their screaming kids in out of the rain; a rubbish tip for all the chavs and scrubbers blown out of their council houses and down the windy streets.

Jo hated them; fucking hated them.

"Oh, hello, babe, I'm so happy that you turned up today," Jo gushed.

Jo had no idea who the woman in ripped jeans and a stained Gap hooded top standing in front of her was.

"Yeah, we were in the same class together at school. Do you remember?"

"Yeah, course I remember. It was a right laugh, weren't it?"

Jo didn't remember. Jo didn't care. School wasn't a laugh. It was a fucking nightmare from the day she arrived until the day she woke up with tits and gave the best-looking kid a wank under one of the lab benches in science class. The science teacher had spotted something going on at the back of the class; he wasn't stupid. Jo was Jo. She had that look that they always had in his classes. But ignoring her free wank was the lesser of two evils and they both knew it. Jo caught the old sod's eye and recognised the reaction: envy. She kept order at the back of the class. She controlled the working-class kids in a way that he never could.

"Yeah, yeah, it was a right laugh, weren't it," the stained hoodie replied. "Do you still see many of your schoolmates?"

"Not really, not as much as I'd like, babe. I'm just too busy, you know."

Are you fucking kidding me, Jo thought. Why the fuck would I still want to see you lot? What would we talk about? The good old days? Going home every night to a cold, empty house? Sitting on a freezing bench in February with purple knees and a runny nose, sharing a bag of chips and hoping the one kid in school without acne might look at us? Childhoods are for children, babe. I'm a woman now, so take your signed DVD and fuck off.

"Ah, it's great that you come back here though, innit? Come back to Dagenham and all that? Still shows you're one of us?"

The only time I'm in Asda these days, darling, is when I'm signing DVDs of the first series of my top-rating TV show, but I take your point, Jo thought.

"Well, I'm actually from Barking," Jo joked.

Everyone in the queue laughed. Jo smiled politely. It wasn't particularly funny. She knew it wasn't particularly funny. If there was one thing she had learned from growing up around here, it was real funny. She was real funny. Scott was real funny. But that wasn't real funny.

"Yeah, true, true. I moved away from Barking myself a few years ago."

"Did ya?" Jo said quickly, raising her hand to take the DVD from the middle-aged woman standing behind the ripped jeans.

"Yeah, after the divorce, I took my two boys away and made a fresh start."

"Good for you," Jo said, already signing the DVD for the woman behind. "Where did you move to?"

"Dagenham," her old schoolmate replied proudly.

Jo looked restlessly at her Rolex. Fucking hell. She still had another hour to go at least. She lifted her head up briefly and noticed the plebs stretched all the way back to her posters in the George clothing section.

AL-HAKIM stopped and pulled it out. There was no explanation and the Nigerian whore knew better than to ask for one. She remained on her knees even though the friction from the carpets earlier had rubbed the skin off her kneecaps, but she never moved in case he started again.

"Wash hands," Al-Hakim barked in broken English. It saved time. "Then you give me hand job."

He watched her get up slowly and walk across his Italian marble. He adored his Italian marble, had 1,500 tonnes of the stuff shipped over for the palace. He loved watching the whores walk across it naked, and this one was attractive. Tall, slim and very dark, she had that natural African athleticism that he was always happy to pay extra for. Her black skin made him think of something.

Al-Hakim pushed a button on his bedside table. The partitioned walls at the end of his bed parted to reveal his home entertainment system. He noticed the whore had stopped washing her hands in his gold-plated sink and gaped as the walls parted. Al-Hakim laughed.

"You not see this before," he said. "Where you come from, you lucky to see water come out of your tap. Hurry up, we start again when I find channel."

Al-Hakim admonished himself for not thinking of it earlier. MTV always helped him. Those black R&B singers in the US with their jiggling and their tight, rounded asses were enough to make him finish, no matter how good or bad the whore was.

He found the channel and it was a couple of black rappers singing about controlling their bitches. Perfect. Those gangster rappers knew how to treat their women. They were practically Saudi.

"Come here," he ordered. "I don't need hand job now. Turn around."

Al-Hakim stared at the whore as she climbed slowly onto the bed. The music video finished just as Al-Hakim positioned himself behind her. He waited. He had long ago sworn never to make that mistake again. He had once screwed a whore while watching a female singer with long blond hair in a blue leotard jump around on stage. He stopped when the blue leotard turned around. It was Rod Stewart. Al-Hakim's servants paid extra to keep the whore quiet about the Rod Stewart thing. Flogging would have been an option, but it was never practical. The other whores were less reluctant to come to the palace.

The music video showed a shot of Tower Bridge. London. He had stayed at the Tower Hotel with his parents many times in the 1980s. London's not so good, Al-Hakim thought. The singers were likely to be white. Five singers jumped around Tower Bridge to an abominable western pop song. Al-Hakim had no time for female pop bands, particularly British ones, all that pouting and sisters singing about doing it for themselves. The name of the band appeared at the bottom of the screen.

Girl Power.

That was enough for Al-Hakim. He leaned across the bed and stretched out for the button.

And then he saw her.

She smiled seductively straight at the camera. She had long, blond hair, a natural look with very little makeup on and a sweet, sincere smile. She bounced around Tower Bridge in tight hot pants wearing a T-shirt that was clearly two sizes too small for her, but displayed her firm breasts perfectly.

Al-Hakim suddenly realised he was pounding the whore again. He hadn't moved this quickly since he was a teenager. He couldn't take his eyes off the screen. Whenever there was a close-up of the blonde girl with the sweet, sweet smile, he pushed harder.

"Squeeze it," he shouted. "Squeeze it!"

She did as she was told and Al-Hakim groaned. He wouldn't last much longer. Only later would he acknowledge the obvious irony.

The whore was black. The singer was white.

JO glanced up at the Asda security guard. He was supposed to be organising the queue, to keep the plebs in order and to keep them moving. Instead he kept staring at her tits. You can't afford them on 10 pounds an hour, mate, Jo thought, so stop fucking looking.

Jo glared at the security guard. It was barely perceptible, but it was enough. He shifted his weight from one foot to the other and turned away, pretending to busy himself by straightening the queue.

Yeah. Know your fucking place, Jo thought. I'm from around here, too. I've been fighting pricks like you off for over 20 years. These corpses in the queue further my career, love, whereas your leering doesn't do anything for me.

Jo pictured setting the guy's pubic hair on fire and suddenly she felt much better. She always did. It was good therapy. Whenever a fuckwit came on strong, she told him where to go and imagined his pubic hair ablaze. She owed the imagery so much. It was one of her best stories and still did the rounds today. The burning pubic hair was her Lorena Bobbitt Story. Everyone in her game had to have a Lorena Bobbitt Story somewhere on their Wikipedia page. It pushed the feminism angle. In the early days, she had told one of the wank mags that a bloke had gotten too strong with her in the back of his motor in an industrial estate off the A13. She'd told him to stop. He ignored her. So when he whipped his tiny dick out, she got her cigarette lighter out and torched his pubes. She could still hear his screams as she dashed across the Ripple Road roundabout.

Jo loved telling that story. She had told it so many times, tightened it, embellished it and polished it that even she could no longer distinguish fact from fiction. But it served its purpose. Germaine Greer even mentioned the flaming pubes in one of her feminism columns. If one chav had to lose his pubes so Jo could get a mention in a Germaine Greer article, then that's the way it had to be. He was just another nameless character in her story, a bit like that fucking security guard.

Jo had told the story to Scott in that Soho bar. He had roared with laughter. Tears actually rolled down his cheeks, which Jo found incredibly endearing. Scott looked less ferret-faced when he laughed, attractive even. She smiled as she signed another DVD for some pleb waffling on about how she never missed an episode of *At Home With Jo*.

She might have torched Scott's bollocks before, but she certainly wouldn't now. She stared down at her photo on the DVD cover and smirked. An animal. Just like her. A fucking animal. Maybe there was something about Barking, something about those filthy streets that just made its people so dirty and feral behind closed council house doors.

Jo glanced at her Rolex again. She wanted Scott now.

And then she saw her.

"What's that you got there?" she asked, desperately hoping she'd masked the edginess in her voice.

"What's what?" replied the blushing teenager, thrilled that one of her idols had taken an interest in her life.

"There, underneath my DVD. It's a CD innit, babe?"

"Yeah, yeah, it's the new Girl Power album," the teenager gushed. "It's great. When I hear their lyrics, it's like they're singing about me. I reckon it's their best album yet, don't you?"

"Haven't heard it," she muttered.

AL-HAKIM typed in the words "Girl Power" and waited for the Google results. His friends and business clients all loathed Google. And Facebook. And Twitter. They said these search and social networking sites empowered women. Just look at what happened in Iran, they said. But Al-Hakim laughed at them. He always took the pragmatic view. Saudi Arabia had survived 9/11 relatively unscathed, so a couple of women posting diatribes to Human Rights Watch every now and then should hardly keep the Mutaween awake at night.

Al-Hakim skipped the biographies and clicked on web images. He had no interest in their life stories at the moment; he just wanted to see the photographs.

And then he saw her. She looked even more beautiful in the photographs, even more desirable. In most of the photographs, she appeared left or right of the centre or at the back of the group, so she was obviously not the lead singer, not that that mattered. She was so wholesome, so sincere and so ... so ... unattainable. That was what it was. That was the attraction. She was unattainable. Al-Hakim often thought of Alexander the Great who supposedly wept upon realising there were no more worlds left to conquer. In Al-Hakim's world, there were always worlds left to conquer. His world was capitalism in the struggling 21st century. There was always a price.

Al-Hakim clicked on a rare photograph of the blonde on her own and was redirected to the *Guardian* website. The story was in the sports section. He read the opening paragraphs quickly.

The girl's name was Nicola.

She was from London.

She was 25 years old.

She had formed the band with her best friends in a North London secondary school.

The band came in second on a TV programme called *Britain's Got Talent* and sold over two million singles and albums.

Nicola was married to a footballer in the English Premier League.

Al-Hakim read that line again. Nicola was married to a footballer in the English Premier League. Al-Hakim laughed loudly and picked up the phone beside his laptop.

"Hello, it's me," he said, scanning more photographs of Nicola. "What was the name of that football club you wanted the company to buy? The one facing bankruptcy? ... OK, it's not that one. Never mind. I have some good news for you, my friend. We are finally going to buy a football club in the English Premier League. Will that make you happy? Now I can join in those bets with the Manchester City guys at my parties ... Now my English Premier League club can take on their English Premier clubs ... What's that? ... Which club are we buying?"

Al-Hakim paused and stared at a photograph of Nicola in a bikini sitting in a wooden chair on a cold British beach. He stroked her breasts on the laptop screen.

"Nicola's club," he said softly.

This was going to be easier than he thought.

seven

NICOLA counted the steps in her head. Five, six, seven, eight; five, six, seven eight. She felt ridiculous. Her self-consciousness made her sweat under the stage lights. She struggled to stay in step with her bandmates. Well, they used to be bandmates. Now they were a glorified chorus line. Nicola wiped her forehead and cursed under her breath. Choreographers really were taking over the world. She seemed to spend entire days being shouted at by choreographers. It wasn't fun anymore. When they had sat around in her bedroom in Enfield, playing the Spice Girls' *Wannabe* repeatedly, trying to deconstruct the lyrics and understand the melody to work out what made a hit record; that had been fun. They were all skint. Nicola worked part-time in a Percy Ingle bakery, handing overpriced bloomers to old dears using the last of their pension to pay for real bread, but she was still happy. They laughed together all day long.

The band had sold over two million records. That's what their accountant had told them over lunch in Covent Garden, but they didn't laugh. They hardly ever laughed anymore.

Nicola used her right hand as a visor to peer into the delirious audience. That's what they were being told to be at the moment: delirious. They had done 'expectant applause' for the director. Then they did 'ecstatic cheering' for the cameras. Now they were doing 'spontaneous delirious'. Then the director asked them to do 'spontaneous delirious' again.

Nicola had never understood what the big deal was, playing the Royal Variety Performance at the Palladium. This was her third Royal Variety gig and she still didn't get it; it was mostly pop idols and comedians she'd never heard of making crap jokes about their mothers-in-law and cheap holidays in Spain. But the gig had made her granddad proud. He saw his favourite girl sing at the Palladium just six months before he died. It had meant so much to him, kept going on about how The Beatles had played there in 1963 and John Lennon had taken the piss out of the rich by asking them to rattle their jewellery. He couldn't believe his favourite granddaughter was going to stand on the same stage as Lennon did. Just before the cancer ripped through his vocal chords, he had whispered to Nicola. Seeing her up there in front of the Queen had been the greatest night of his life. He struggled to get the words out. He blinked through the tears in his eyes. And he asked Nicola not to see him anymore, insisted that this moment must be their final memory of each other. Nicola kept her promise. She was always the loyal one.

Nicola counted in her head again. Five, six, seven eight; point to the ceiling, point to the crowd, point to the left, step over and spin; point to the ceiling, point to the crowd, point to the right, step over and spin. Nicola stopped suddenly. This was a joke.

"What's wrong, darling?"

It was Chris the choreographer. Lovely man, gay obviously, but a lovely man. It wasn't him. It was the repetitiveness.

"Have we got this down yet?" Nicola asked.

She saw the other bandmates glare at her, and ignored them. This wasn't the place for another row. They had started off as five mates having a laugh in Nicola's bedroom, coming up with their group's name Girl Power— their tribute to the Spice Girls— and writing hits like *(I'm a) Cee-lebrity*. That song had been written in Nicola's bedroom, a piss-take on modern celebrity culture and it had went to number one in Britain, Japan, Australia and across Europe, with every teenager missing the obvious irony. They laughed all night long writing that song; five mates from school messing about with a notepad and a pen. They giggled as they sang *(I'm a) Cee-lebrity* in Nicola's bedroom. They wanted to be singers. Now they were unit shifters. When they performed their biggest hit now, the rest of the band sang the song with straight faces.

"It's coming along nicely, darling," Chris cried from the centre of the theatre. "It's looking wonderful from down here. We just need to tighten it up a little more, make sure everyone is stepping in time."

"We're not performing Mary Poppins up here with chimney sweeps," Nicola retorted.

There was some nervous laughter in the audience. Chris looked over both shoulders and then gestured towards Nicola to take the restless crowd into account.

"Of course not, we're performing as the most popular girl band in Britain," he cried triumphantly, before turning towards the audience. "Tell me guys, are these girls the best band in Britain or what?"

The teenagers in the crowd stood and screamed, waving banners and T-shirts with "Girl Power" emblazoned on the front at the stage. Their seated parents glanced at their watches.

"I'll tell you what, let's all take five minutes to have a smoothie and then we'll finish for the day, all right, girls?"

Nicola turned and stepped off the stage quickly. The rest of the band exited in the opposite direction.

LITTLE Steve saw his chance. He had deliberately picked an aisle seat near the stairs at the right of the stage. That's why he'd arrived at the Palladium so early. He had a 50-50 chance and he'd guessed right. Nicola had picked up a towel off the stage and headed towards the stairs. Little Steve's stairs. Little Steve's exit. Little Steve's aisle. Little Steve's seat. Nicola was about to walk past his seat. He reached for his marker pen and grabbed a handful of T-shirts. He stood up quickly and blocked a gaggle of screaming girls from squeezing past him in his row and stepped in front of the Girl Power singer.

"Hello, Nicola, it's me, it's me, Little Steve," he said quickly, struggling to hold back the girls behind him. He was older than the girls, but not much bigger and it wasn't easy.

Nicola stepped back instinctively. Years of practice made it a reflex action. She lifted her towel and water bottle towards her face, not enough to offend, but enough to offer basic protection. It was a reflex action. She was famous. They were not. They wanted to be in her face. She did not. But she understood. There was a degree of empathy. She had once stood with her friends outside a London hotel for over six hours to see the Spice Girls. Some of the Spice Girls had stopped and chatted. Some had not. Nicola always remembered the ones who hadn't. It wasn't right. Those friends who stood shivering outside the hotel made up the rest of Girl Power. They didn't stop and chat anymore, and that wasn't right either. Nicola did, but there had to be a line and an unspoken agreement between celebrity and fan never to cross it. Nicola hadn't. When she met the Spice Girls, she had kept a respectable distance. Most of the fans did that day.

But talent contests on reality TV had changed the rules, changed the dynamic. The balance of power had shifted. Fans asserted their perceived authority. They had voted for Nicola. They had voted for Girl Power. They had made the group. Now they were in control. Girl Power danced on the strings that hung from their remote controls. They were in Nicola's face now, all day long, and with no apologies. They called the shots. So sign their T-shirts and CD covers or they'll be straight on the phone to the tabloids.

But Little Steve was old school. Nicola loved Little Steve. He had turned up at the band's very first public performance at HMV in Oxford Street with a couple of mates. Apart from store staff, the PR team and casual shoppers, they were probably the only ones watching the band. Like most insecure boys, he was adorably shy and gangly, and looked away whenever Nicola looked at him and smiled. Nicola still giggled when she thought of Little Steve's puce face when she told him that his copy of the single *(I'm a) Cee-lebrity* was the first she had ever signed. It wasn't true. She had signed 500 units in the record company's office the day before, but it was the least she could do. Little Steve had known every word of *(I'm a) Cee-lebrity* that day and he still mouthed every word of every song when she picked him out in the front rows at gigs. He had always been interested in the songs, not the bloody dance steps.

"Hello, Little Steve, how are you," gushed Nicola.

She was always sincere with the fans, but she genuinely enjoyed seeing Little Steve.

"Oh, hello, Nicola. I'm fine, you were really good up there, really," said Little Steve.

"Ah, now I know you're just being kind."

She leaned closer to Little Steve and looked over both shoulders conspiratorially.

"You know I'm only happy when I'm singing, Steve," she whispered.

"I know. I know," he nodded keenly, delighted to share Nicola's confidence.

He lifted the T-shirts and pulled the lid off the marker pen with his teeth. A security guard in a dark suit behind Nicola muttered something into his earpiece and edged towards her. She raised her hand towards him.

"It's OK," she said firmly. "Are you sure you've got enough Girl Power T-shirts for me to sign there?"

Little Steve blushed and stared down at the T-shirts.

"Ah, just a few, if you don't mind, Nicola," he mumbled.

Nicola smiled and took the marker pen out of his hand and gently pulled the lid from beneath his teeth.

"Don't leave that there, you'll get ink on your teeth."

Nicola started to sign the T-shirts and frowned slightly.

"There really are quite a few here," she said. "Are you sure they are not going to all end up on eBay?"

Little Steve continued to look down at the T-shirts.

"Well, maybe one or two, just a couple, if that's OK."

"That's what I like about you, Little Steve. You're always honest. There's no bull with you. I hear bull all day long, so it's nice to hear a bit of honesty. Do you want me to pass them to the girls to get their signatures? You might get more for them on eBay then?"

"Nah, nah, just your autograph please, Nicola."

"OK, then. There you go."

Nicola handed back the T-shirts and the marker pen and glanced towards the exit.

"Did you see I told you on Twitter that I was going to be here? Did you see the messages I left you?" Little Steve asked.

"I did, yeah. Thanks for that. But I don't need to read Twitter to know you're gonna be here, right?"

Little Steve blushed again and busied himself tidying the pile of T-shirts in his arms.

"Anyway Steve, I'd better get going now. I've got to ..."

"For fuck's sake, how much longer are you going to be?"

Little Steve looked up and saw him grab Nicola's arm. He was wearing one of his expensive suits again and had his hair gelled upwards, which always looked shit. He ignored Little Steve, but that didn't surprise him. He'd never noticed Little Steve before. Nicola pulled his hand away.

"Don't talk to me like that here," she whispered, before turning to Little Steve. "Have you met my husband before? This is Scott."

Scott was distinctly unimpressed. Why the fuck did she waste her time with these people? They'd already bought her crappy pop songs, so what more did she want? They were in the audience. They were cheering. They had bought their tickets. Job done. It was the same in his game. They turned up in their thousands—win, lose or draw. The season tickets were in the bag so there was no need to milk it. It was a few half-hearted handclaps on the way to the tunnel and the odd kiss of the badge every now and then—just to keep them on side after a dodgy game—and then off to Soho for a night with the beautiful people. Why Nicola bothered with all that flowery bullshit with the fans had always been a mystery to Scott.

Then again, Nicola had always been a bit of a mystery. He loved her and all that probably. She was a great mother and never played away. But she had never played the game properly. The rest of the band did, and fair play to them. Scott had watched them from the wings; a quick wave to the plebs and then straight off stage and into the dressing room; no fucking about talking to Rain Man here like Nicola always did.

That's how she was. That's why she hadn't been Scott's first choice. He had always fancied the lead singer in Girl Power, the one with the legs. He'd turned up backstage one night with Ross and Jimmy buzzing after a League Cup win against Arsenal's latest batch of Spanish and French kids. It wasn't really an upset as not one of the Gooners appeared to be older than 12, but it was a rare start for Scott and he'd impressed. He knew that. All three of them had. But Scott had not only played well, he'd led well, barking orders at washed-up pros old enough to be his dad. They had disgusted Scott. Over the hill and too fucking slow, and yet still expected the boys from Barking to kiss their arses before they picked up 80 grand a week. Scott had called them useless wankers, screamed at them to get back at corners and mark up, and tore into the old club captain when he was dummied by one of Arsene Wenger's kindergarten kids.

Scott was fired up and ready to shag the lead singer of Girl Power. She had told him to piss off. She had never heard of him. He wasn't Premier League then, not really, he was still messing about in League Cup matches and playing with himself on the bench. He wasn't playing by the in-house rules. He knew the rules and now he swore by the rules, but he was pissed that night and chose to ignore them. He was man of the match and was convinced he deserved a crack at an A-lister. But he didn't. Not then. He hadn't made the grade yet, hadn't made enough appearances in their premier league to be considered a first-team regular. He was also nicknamed the football ferret by the lad mags, which didn't do him any favours.

So Scott missed out on the one with the legs and took the one with the smile; the girl next door, the safe option. Nicola wasn't even on Scott's radar. She didn't play in the premier league either, but that was by choice. She never did the lag mags, never did the sex talk for the tabloids and only wore bikinis in Girl Power videos. She didn't play the game then and she didn't play the game now.

But she did have a smile. And she was a good mother.

"I thought you'd be done by now," Scott hissed, watching

Rain Man fumble around with his fucking T-shirts as he shuffled along the row, apologising profusely to all the spotty teenagers as he squeezed his way towards the toilets.

"And why do you always waste your time with dickheads like that," Scott continued. "You know he's only going to sell them all. I mean, look at him, shuffling along to the bogs. He's only going in there to wank over you."

"Fucking shut up now," Nicola whispered aggressively, her eyes darting across the rows of seats, making sure no one had overheard, always keeping up appearances, always professional.

"What? You're never gonna get home at this rate. The kids have been with your mother all day and I'm knackered. We're away to Villa this week, six pointer, and I can't be standing around here all day with this lot."

Nicola smiled at the fans standing nearby. They were not that daft. She noticed their uncertainty. She pulled Scott subtly but firmly away from the seats and headed back towards the stage.

"Go home then," she hissed in his ear. "Go and see your daughter for a change. I've got work to do, too."

"I've missed a round of golf with Jim and Ross for this," Scott whined.

"Well go back to the bloody golf course then," Nicola snapped. "Just leave me alone to get this rehearsal done. I know you don't give a shit, but the show is Saturday night."

"And I'm away to Villa this Saturday."

"I know, you keep saying. Why don't you piss off up there now."

"I might do."

"Go away, Scott, please. You're a fucking child."

Nicola wiped her forehead with her towel and turned her back on Scott. He watched her trot up the stairs on the side of the stage and winced as the audience cheered. She waved back at the idiots in the crowd and the screams were deafening. Scott gritted his teeth. What did these people see in her? He wasn't even sure what he saw in her.

He thought about Jimmy and Ross out on the golf course. He stared at his wife on stage alone practising her dance steps. He wandered over to the exit doors and took out his phone. He hit redial and then turned away from the stage and the audience.

"Yeah, whereabouts are you in London?" he asked quickly. "BBC? Which one? ... Portland Place, nice one, I'm only across the road from you. When will you be done?"

Scott checked at his watch.

"Yeah, quality, I can make that and get ready," Scott continued, turning round to look at the stage. "I'm gonna shag your brains out."

eight

LITTLE Steve hit the backspace key on his laptop. That wasn't good enough for her. He had to get the tweet right. Little Steve spent most of his evenings on Twitter. It had its faults, but it had also allowed him to develop a number of close friendships with like-minded people in countries he had never dreamed of visiting. He stared at the flashing line in the rectangle at the top of the page and realised he was surprisingly tongue-tied. That wasn't like him, not with Nicola. Words came easily to him when he was sending tweets to Nicola; to the others it was more difficult. He spent hours fretting over his tweets to Stephen Fry, agonising over whether to make his reply witty or intellectual. He knew how many followers Stephen Fry had, so he also knew he had to be really clever if he wanted Stephen Fry to tweet back.

He never did get a reply from Stephen Fry, but he wasn't too downbeat. Stephen Fry had more than one million followers, which was even more than Nicola. Little Steve wasn't particularly offended by that fact any more. He was at first. He was appalled. How could the *Blackadder* guy have more followers than the best singer in the most famous girl band in Britain? It didn't make any sense until Little Steve understood Twitter a little better. Nicola rarely tweeted. Stephen Fry tweeted almost as much as Little Steve. If she didn't tweet, she couldn't pick up followers. That's what his friends had told him. If you wanted more followers on Twitter, you had to follow other people so that their followers could become your followers. Even famous people followed you.

Once Little Steve had started to follow others, he picked up more followers himself. Then he understood. Nicola had almost a million followers, but she only followed 16 other people. So it was impossible for her to have as many followers as that Stephen Fry. And even then, she hardly ever tweeted anything other than her latest tour dates and album releases.

She had tweeted yesterday. She tweeted at 8:27 am, according to the clock on the corner of Little Steve's laptop. Little Steve guessed that she had probably just made breakfast for her little one and then went online.

She had written: "Got rehearsal 2nite 4 royal show. Hope to see all the fan club there. Girl Power!"

Little Steve knew he had to be quick. She was a busy woman. She wouldn't have much time to sit in front of her laptop. His fingers moved furiously across the keyboard.

He typed: "I will be there, near the front. See you. Little Steve."

Normally, he stopped to count the characters before hitting the tweet button, but he didn't have time. Besides, he knew he was way under 140.

He clicked the tweet button and waited. He didn't get up from his desk, just in case.

At 9:27 am, Little Steve decided that Nicola had probably rushed out to do some interviews for the Royal Variety Performance.

He wasn't angry because he wasn't stupid. Nicola always chatted with him when they met so he knew there wasn't a problem. He never hassled her at these public events, never took up too much of her time, not like some of the others. He just asked her to sign a couple of things and left her alone. The truth was Nicola couldn't follow Little Steve on Twitter. If she followed him, then she had to follow everyone and that wasn't fair on her. She had a right to some peace and quiet too, away from the other band members. She had a right to spend time with her family.

Well, she had a right to spend time with her little girl. She shouldn't spend any of her free time with him. He was even more impolite than usual at the Palladium, and Little Steve didn't like the way he had grabbed her arm. He had squeezed hard. He had also ignored her on stage. He didn't watch her new dance routine with the other girls and he didn't even listen to her on stage, just spent the whole time chatting on the phone.

Scott was such a rude man. But then, they all were. All of the girls in the band had gone out with footballers from the English Premier League at some point in their careers—mostly in the early stages of their careers, now they went out with other singers and movie stars—and the footballers had always been rude; rude to the girls, rude to the fans, rude to everybody. Nicola was the only one who had stayed with a footballer.

She was too nice.

That was her problem.

Little Steve smiled and started typing.

"You were too nice tonight," he typed. "That's your problem."

Little Steve shook his head. No, that was too personal. He hit the backspace button again. He couldn't comment on Scott's behaviour, even if he was an idiot. It was not his business.

Little Steve noticed Scott under Nicola's list of followers and sighed. She only followed 16 people and Scott was one of them. Why? Didn't she see him all day long?

Little Steve clicked on Scott's icon. He called himself "ScottFC". Great name, Little Steve thought, it must have taken him weeks to think of that. Little Steve scanned Scott's tweets:

Tough one this week. Villa away. Going for win.
about 12 hours ago via web

Great victory against Everton. Nice goal, Ross.
10:05 AM Mar 23rd via web

Must win against Everton.
8:49 PM Mar 21st via web

Unlucky against Hammers. Everton game now crucial.
10:48 PM Mar 17th via web

Little Steve darted his eyes across the screen and saw that Scott had 856,932 followers. Scott had 856,932 followers. That was mental. Scott had 856,932 followers all clicking online so that Scott could tell them "must win against Everton". Little Steve never understood these people. They were so sad. Why follow someone who never said anything? At least Nicola gave her fans real information: where she was performing, what the name of her new single was going to be and stuff like that. Scott's tweets said nothing.

Little Steve still followed Scott though. He didn't really have a choice. Nicola followed Scott. So Little Steve followed Scott. Nicola even followed that old man Charlie, Scott's manager, and he had only ever typed three tweets about signing a new contract and they were over a year ago. But Nicola followed Charlie. So Little Steve followed Charlie, just in case.

Little Steve had 137 followers and most of them were

members of the fan club, but they were genuine followers. He knew every one of them, unlike Scott. And he actually sent tweets about real things, interesting things. He had already tweeted about the Girl Power rehearsal, commenting on their new dance routine, their costumes and their song selections, and had received several replies. He never sent general tweets about his chats with Nicola. That wasn't fair on Nicola. She had a right to privacy, too. He always sent his replies directly to Nicola. He couldn't send her private, direct messages, sadly, because she wasn't following him, but he always sent his tweets about her to @nicpower.

He was running out of time. *X-Factor* was starting soon and that was the one programme—along with *Britain's Got Talent*— that he always made a point of watching live. He loved Sky Plus, but not for *X-Factor* or *Britain's Got Talent*. He couldn't take the risk that someone would call or text to give him the results. That really would piss him off.

Little Steve sat up suddenly and thought about what Nicola had said earlier. No bull. That's what she'd said. Whenever they met, there was no bull. She had always appreciated his honesty. And she wasn't just being polite; she meant it. She never said it to anyone else and she had also said it the first time they had met.

Little Steve smiled and stared at her poster on his bedroom wall.

HE had been so nervous that day. He had waited outside HMV first thing in the morning, lined up before it had even opened. He had stood at the front and watched Nicola, only Nicola. As far as he was concerned, she was the only singer in the band. He realised that the moment Ant & Dec had introduced them to

Britain. The band should've been called Nicola and Girl Power. He had felt awkward because he was one of the only people inside HMV at that time of the morning, and he must have looked awkward because whenever their eyes met, she had smiled kindly back at him.

He was so nervous when he lined up to get his single signed that morning, so nervous. He blushed when he was nervous, and felt his cheeks. They were burning, stinging. She would not see him, not see him at all, he had thought. She would only see his red face; she would only see his eyes looking everywhere but at her face; her kind, open face. And she would laugh at him. She would laugh at him, like they always did in the office, like they always had at school. Nicola would laugh at him.

But she didn't. Instead she smiled at him. That smile. He never forgot that smile. She had smiled at him a thousand times since, but she never topped that first smile.

"Who is this for?" she had asked, still smiling. That smile.

"It's, er, for, er, me," Little Steve had stuttered.

"Shall I just sign it to 'me' then?"

Nicola giggled. That giggle. Little Steve found himself looking back at her, looking straight at her, no blushing, no burning, no stinging.

Little Steve giggled. They had both giggled together.

"No, no, it's for me, er, Little Steve."

"Why are you called Little Steve?"

"Because everyone calls my dad Big Steve."

She burst out laughing. She rocked backwards on her chair and covered her mouth with her left hand.

"Oh, I'm so, so sorry," she laughed.

"What for?"

"For making fun of your name. I wasn't trying to make fun of your name. It's just so funny."

"It's OK. Really. It's OK. I've always been called Little Steve."

"But why did your mum do that? I mean, why did your mum give you that name?" Nicola asked, as she took a swig from a water bottle.

"So no one would mix me up with Big Steve."

Nicola spat water across the desk. It sprayed across the CD single and onto Little Steve's trouser legs.

"Oh, I'm so sorry, really," she said sincerely. "I really didn't mean to get you wet. You didn't come here to get soaked did you? It's just that, your name, I mean, that's such a funny story."

"Good. I'm glad I made you laugh."

Little Steve had managed to maintain eye contact; no blushing, no stinging, no burning. He wanted to gaze at her forever.

Nicola pushed his wet CD single to one side and picked another from the pile and started writing on the inside sleeve.

"Ah, Little Steve, you have really made my day," she said. "You just tell it how it is, babe. There you go."

Little Steve took the CD slowly and read the message: "To Little Steve, I just love your name, will never forget it. Luv Nicola xxx."

LITTLE Steve stared at the flashing line inside the rectangle. No bull. Be honest.

"@nicpower Little Steve here. U great today, see you at show. U r right to be yourself," he typed.

He clicked on the tweet button and sent his message. Then he clicked on Scott's icon. He re-read the pointless tweets and clicked 'reply' on the one about playing Villa away, the most recent one.

"U don't know how luck u are," he typed.

Little Steve clicked on the tweet button before he had a chance to change his mind.

nine

CHARLIE was in charge. This was his manor, his kingdom, and they were his scribbling acolytes. The pack dogs always did as they were told. They bought and sold players for him, inflated fees, got him free transfers and jacked up his salary. He treated the red-topped hacks with all the bluff and Cockney bullshit he could muster. He was his father's son. And they were his wide-eyed punters strolling around his second-hand car lot. Charlie's old man had told him the secret to sales patter when they had wandered across to the Merry Fiddlers pub during a cold lunchtime in January, when the car lot was quiet. Always make the punter believe that he is in charge, Charlie's old man had told him. Convince him that he is the big man, calling the shots, dictating the knockdown price.

Charlie had never forgotten. Always make the hacks believe that they are in control, that they are determining the story angles, that they are coming up with tomorrow's headlines.

Charlie had his work cut out today. Villa had stolen the three points. Scott had gone off with a groin strain and they'd gone through the gap to score the winner, and now Aston fucking Villa were going to take that Europa League spot. The football had been appalling, so the last thing these pot-bellied reporters needed to talk about was the football. They just didn't know it yet.

"Do I think their striker was interfering with play before they scored?" Charlie repeated the question, playing for time. *Always play for time, son. Always have an answer ready. Never look stumped. You are a salesman, so fucking sell.*

"What difference does it make? My defenders looked like they were interfering with themselves."

The hacks in the press conference chuckled politely. It was an old Charlie joke, but it always made for good copy. Charlie always made for good copy. That's why it was standing room only at his press conferences. That's why Charlie's farming estate in Theydon Bois was recently valued at more than four million. That's why his players loved him. He never criticised them by name.

"We lost a bit of shape when Scott went off, but he'll be back next week. It looks like a mild groin strain. When you consider his missus, that's some achievement. He was gutted when he had to come off. It means he can see the whole Royal Variety Show tonight now. He's gone down in the penalty box and ended up in the royal box."

Good line, Charlie thought, good, cheesy line. The red-tops will lap up this rubbish. That's a lift-out quote right there ... sports pages and possibly showbiz pages, too. Scott will be all over the showbiz pages in the morning with his singing missus and Charlie's quote will be right beside her long legs, keeping them company.

"Will you be going along to the Palladium tonight, Charlie," a wheezing hack from a red-top shouted.

Good man. They were biting. Time to reel them in, son.

"Me at the Palladium? Look, I know we've had some problems this season, but I don't think signing Take That to fill our back four is going to do us any favours. The last time I went to the Palladium was to see *Oliver!* Now that's a show. It's set in the East End, bloody marvellous. When I first saw Fagin come out on stage, I thought it was our chairman."

Charlie smiled as he surveyed the nodding dogs in the room. That was genuine laughter. They'd pick up on the quote. That throwaway line was a story in itself.

Fagin.

His chairman was a football Fagin.

He had thought of it while he was shaving that morning.

Fagin was a tight-fisted old bastard leading his young men up the garden path. It was the perfect analogy; the perfect lead-in. They'd have to follow up. He knew Scott was going to the Royal Variety Performance to see his missus and her mates. He knew the dopey old bastards would ask him about it. They had no choice. Girl Power sold newspapers. Scott and Nicola sold newspapers. Charlie sold newspapers. Every sweaty scribbler in the room was desperate to sell newspapers, and sell them quickly before they were replaced forever by some four-eyed kid at Google.

Charlie stared directly at the fat hack from the red-top. *Ask the question, fatty, ask the question.*

"So Charlie, do you think you could've had more funds at your disposal this season?"

Good lad, about fucking time.

"Well, that is an interesting question isn't it? In all seriousness, I have been backed 100 per cent by the chairman over the years. We have a great working relationship as you all know. We all know he's no Fagin. He's one of the kindest, most generous men I've ever met. He's thrown millions into this club, millions, given everything he's got. But the trouble today is, you need tens of millions just to stay in the Premiership; hundreds of millions to even think about the top four. I mean, really, what we've done over the years, on our budget, is nothing short of a miracle. We're a top 10 side pushing for Europe. We just need that cash injection to take us to the next level."

That's enough, Charlie thought. Never show the hand. Wait to be asked. They have to retain a sense of control. Charlie sat back in his chair, rested his hand behind his head and waited for the dopey fuckers to take the bait. He was back at the Chase lakes in Dagenham, fishing with his father.

JIMMY strutted into the dressing room. It stank of liniment. When he had visited the dressing rooms of every major club in London as a kid, they all stank of liniment. Now they were five-star, luxurious affairs for the Premiership pampered, and they still stank of fucking liniment. And BO. That was the other thing. Jimmy made millions for his clients, fucking millions, but would it kill them to invest a fiver in a couple of bottles of Lynx every now and then?

Jimmy noticed Ross first, sitting in a crumpled mess under his freshly-pressed suit. Jimmy always had his clients' suits pressed during the game. He couldn't have them leaving the stadium looking like a squashed bag of chips. Ross was hunched over the bench, his head in his hands. He was still sitting in his shorts and socks. Jimmy smiled. He always was the idealist.

Not Scott though. He was already dressed and straightening his tie in the mirror. He was whistling. He had come off early with an injury, and he was whistling. Jimmy had once come off the pitch early with a sore knee and had never fucking played again. But Scott was whistling. That was his way.

"Come on Jim, I've got to get to this show," Scott moaned, slipping on his Rolex, the Daytona, white gold, the most expensive Rolex in the dressing room. It was one of two Rolexes; two Rolexes for Scott and Nicola, that was their angle. Deals were always offered in duplicate. They had to be signed by Scott *and* Nicola. They always came as a pair, like the fucking bailiffs.

"Yeah, yeah, I won't be long," Jimmy said quickly, flattening his tie. "I want to get back into the press conference."

"Are they all having a go at me in there?" Ross mumbled into his hands before looking up slowly.

"What for?" Jimmy asked, genuinely surprised.

"I missed that fucking sitter in the second half, didn't I? Set up right in front of me and I scuffed it wide."

"Don't be silly. They've not even mentioned you. This is Charlie's press conference. They won't even get a chance to talk about it."

"Well, I'll be thinking about it. I'll be thinking about it all fucking night in the casino," Ross said, getting up slowly. "Jimmy, can we do this next week? I don't wanna talk about contracts now."

"Yeah, yeah, sure, mate," Jimmy replied warmly, putting a hand on his shoulder. "Are you sure you're all right?"

"Yeah, fine. I'm gonna have a shower," he muttered.

"Where you off to tonight?"

"Ah, the usual. Mayfair."

"All right, mate. I might pop in myself for a couple later."

"Yeah, all right, nice one."

Jimmy watched Ross trudge off slowly to the showers. Scott checked his hair in the mirror, clasping his hands together to gel his fin up further.

"He didn't play too badly today," Jimmy whispered. "Is he all right?"

"Problems at home," Scott replied.

THE hacks in the room laughed. They all laughed, except the old-timers at the back of the press conference. The old-timers never laughed. They were old-school football writers, only interested in the sport itself and the romantic biographies and novels they could spin from it. They were dinosaurs. They were only Charlie's age—some were even younger—but they hadn't moved with the times. It was still sheepskin coats, "good afternoon, Mr Chairman" and Bobby Moore wiping his fucking hands before he shook hands with the Queen. The game had moved on, but they were still viewing it through black-and-white glasses with Kenneth Wolstenholme providing the commentary.

Charlie glanced up at the old-timers tut-tutting at the back of the room. He found them exasperating. They used 10 bob words where penny ones would do. They were academic and understood the nuances and subtleties of the technical side of the game in a way that the hacks never would, and yet they still lived in the old English First Division. That was their milieu, as the old English First Division had been for coaches. The English Premier League was for clowns. Clowns belonged in circuses, they had said. But they never got it. They never got the joke. There was no finer circus than the English Premier League. It was the greatest show on earth. Posh and Becks, Wayne and Colleen, Scott and Nicola—they were all global clowns, but in a positive way. They entertained. They captivated. They put bums on seats like never before. They deserved knighthoods for services to football. Fuck it, they deserved knighthoods for services to the British economy. While other sports were dying on their arses, the celebrity couples had Charlie's game covered front and back. That's exactly what it was, especially in the 21st century, a big game and that's something the old romantic prose merchants could never grasp. They still clung to Shankly's "it's a matter of life and death" bollocks. They still saw football as a sport. It was so much less than that. And so much more.

That's why the old-timers rarely asked Charlie questions at press conferences. They came to speak to the coach, not the clown, and that's why they were out of touch. The clown had to come out to play at the press conferences so the coach kept his job on the training ground; one couldn't exist without the other. Charlie knew that. Talent was temporary, in the eyes of the hacks, but character was permanent.

"So are you suggesting that the club needs to join many of the other clubs in the English Premier League and seek foreign ownership?" the fat hack asked.

Finally, Charlie thought. He was beginning to think he'd have to ask the question himself.

"Oh no, I wouldn't say that at all," he answered seriously. "Like I say, our chairman has done a magnificent job. Our working relationship is the best in the Premier League, but if he can be helped or assisted in some way financially, then that has got to be a boost to the club. I just want us to compete with the best. And to do that, you need the dosh. My old man was the best car salesman in London, but he only ever had a second-hand car lot in Dagenham because he was never given the chance to buy and sell Aston Martins in Park Lane. Like all managers, I would love to take this club to the next level."

"With the current economic climate, and if you look at the levels of debt that some of the American owners have introduced to the English Premier League," said the fat hack, "Where do you see the money coming from?"

JIMMY glanced across his shoulder to check that Ross was still in the showers. He turned towards Scott and smiled.

"You are one lucky bastard," Jimmy said.

Scott stared at Jimmy through the mirror.

"What are you on about?" he replied.

"Don't mess me about. You know what. They take you off in the second half and then 10 minutes later, Villa bang in the winner, going right through where you should have been standing. It was fucking quality, mate, quality. Anyone watching out there would know that we've got fuck all in defence when you're not there. Even the chairman. I'll be straight in there on Monday morning. We'll double the contract this time, fucking double it."

"Nice one. I do need a new car. The plebs have started to recognise me in the other one."

"You can have every car in Charlie's dad's old car lot."

They both laughed.

"He's in there now, telling the old car lot stories again, banging on about how he needs more money as usual," Jimmy continued, checking his Rolex. "I'd better get back in there soon. So, yeah, the new contract is sorted. No problem. And if there's any issue, I'll have at least two of the Big Four declaring their interest for you in the papers on Tuesday morning, easy, at least two. I might as well throw Manchester City in there too; all the other boys are doing it."

"Shame about the Europa League though. I know we've still got a chance, but it's looking unlikely now. I wouldn't have minded playing in Europe next season. Ross is gutted."

"Europa what? It sounds like a fucking gay bar in Amsterdam. Fucking Europa League. It's a Mickey Mouse league. No one in England gives a shit about it, unless an English team makes the final, you know that. I mean, Fulham made the final and no one gave a shit outside Craven Cottage. Do you even remember that final? No one remembers that final. It's got no quality. It's got no buzz. There'll be more people watching your missus tonight than there will be watching the Europa final. It's a waste of time. We want Champions League. That's all that matters. We want those Spanish World Cup boys at Barcelona. We get down to the Nou

Camp mate, and you've got the world watching you every week. And if we can't get it here, we'll be off."

Scott smiled at Jimmy.

"Fucking right we will."

They bumped fists together.

"Besides, what does this place owe you? You've given them enough back," Jimmy said.

"Oh, I'm not worried about the plebs out there. Have a blinder and they're singing, 'Scott for England'. Make a mistake and they're screaming, 'You're not fit to wear the shirt!' I don't owe them fuck all."

"Exactly, and you got to start thinking about where you need to be to get England on the phone."

"Yeah, once I get that, we're in, mate. Get that England shirt on and it's a blank slate with every twat in the country. I could break into their houses and murder their wives on Christmas Day but if I head in the winner for England ..."

"We're buying one of those world islands in Dubai."

"Yeah, we'll buy the bit of the British island that's supposed to be Barking."

CHARLIE took a sip from his tea and eyed the hacks suspiciously. Where was the question? He had a long drive through Saturday night traffic back along the M25 and he wanted to get the question in before he left. But he didn't want to push it. His chairman wasn't a punter. He was no mug. Besides, Charlie liked him. But that had nothing to do with it. He'd get a lovely payout, a tasty profit for his investment and a comfortable retirement in his Chigwell manor house. So the chairman's future would be taken care of. Charlie had to think about his own. And the club's, of course.

"Charlie, there is a rumour circulating that a property developer in Saudi Arabia has been making inquiries about the club," said a young, skinny hack near the back of the room. "Do you know anything about that?"

Charlie sipped his tea slowly.

"Yeah, I know what you're talking about and it's best to get these things out in the open, no bullshit. I've met Al-Hakim several times over the years. We both have an interest in the nags and I've seen him around the tracks a few times. As you know, I've got one or two horses and Al-Hakim has got one or two stables."

The hacks chuckled to themselves. Charlie watched them scribble furiously. *There's another quote, boys, make the connection in the papers, make the connection.*

"But there's been a link made between his property company in Riyadh and the club," the young skinny hack persisted. "Do you know anything about that?"

Charlie looked exasperated. The question called for exasperation.

"Look, in my game, you meet these guys all the time. Either here at the ground or down at the track. Al-Hakim isn't the first and he won't be last. And I'll probably see him this week at the Stakes at Epsom. Half his bloody stable is in that race. I've got my three-legged pony up against his thoroughbreds so I don't fancy my chances. But he's a football fan, too, so we might have a chat, but that doesn't mean he's about to buy the club. The trouble with you guys is every time you see any of us with an Arab, you've already sold the club for us. I know the Middle East owns half the Premiership, but it hasn't bought it all just yet."

"So you don't deny that there is an interest from Saudi Arabia?" the young, skinny hack asked.

"Look, I can't answer that question, can I? You've got to ask the chairman. All I can do is talk football and tell you that Scott has a slight groin strain so Nicola's not going to be too happy with me."

There was some respectful grinning, but Charlie knew he had over-reached with the Nicola joke. There was no need for it. The press conference had been a minor triumph and he loved the irony. He got through it without ever talking football.

The young, skinny hack raised his arm to ask another follow-up question, but recognised that the press conference was being wound up. He flicked over the cover of his notepad and checked over his shoulder. He spotted Jimmy at the back of the room, leaning on the club crest. Jimmy noticed the reporter looking back at him.

Jimmy nodded his thanks.

TOM tried to hear the press conference over his two screaming children. He loved his kids, but they were at that screaming stage. A boy and a girl, they had lost the ability to talk, whisper, sing or shout. They could only scream. In Tom's pokey two-bedroom flat, it was impossible to escape their screaming. If they were not screaming, they were running; always running. They were his adorable little bunnies, his adorable little Duracell bunnies on speed. They deserved a bit of space and a garden, not a crappy flat above a dying bike shop in North London.

"Could you be quiet please, kids," Tom shouted, as his children ran around the living room with crayons. "Kids, please, just for a minute, daddy is trying to hear the TV. Daddy's trying to do a bit of work, here?"

Tom watched his children run around the cluttered living room, dragging their crayons across his collection of newspapers, football programmes and folders. Tom picked up the remote control and turned up the volume.

"Guys, please, just for one minute, can you go into the kitchen with your mother," Tom said firmly. "Daddy has got to hear this man on TV, just for one minute, and then we'll get the crayons and draw all over the walls together, OK?"

The children stopped and stared at their father. Then they stared at their crayons. And then they ran into the kitchen.

"Thank you, thanks Sarah!" Tom shouted after them, smiling as he watched them dash off. He knew he had about two minutes before they returned to turn his living room into an art exhibition.

Tom stared at the screen, watching him go through his usual Dick Van Dyke "roll out the barrel" rubbish. The kid from the council estate turned everyone's favourite manager: the best manager never to manage England (which was ironic because he had been one of the worst players to ever play for England); the coach who always had a quote and a quip, even when he didn't have the three points.

The sixties had Shankly. The seventies had Cloughie. The eighties had Atkinson and Fergie had the rest. And now, we have Charlie, Tom thought, cheeky chappie Charlie.

Tom sat up suddenly. He saw something. It wasn't much, but it was something. It was a possible angle. If his tabloid-addicted new boss wanted something to rival the red-tops, something to drag the zombies away from *At Home With Jo*, then Tom would give it to him and kill two greedy bastards with one stone.

Tom rummaged through the newspapers, colouring books and CBeebies magazines strewn across the sofa and found his phone. It was covered in blue crayon. He smiled and started dialling.

"Hello, mate, it's me, Tom," he said. "Fancy a day at the races?"

ten

ROSS leaned over the guardrail of the private box and stared across at the parade ring. He noticed his untucked shirttail and drunkenly tried to push it behind his trousers. He swayed along the edge of the private box and began to unzip his trousers.

"Hey Ross!" he heard a voice cry from the parade ring. "Hey Ross, it's you, right?"

Ross staggered over to the corner of the parade ring and giggled. He wiped his chin and then lifted his arms in the air. His shirt opened up and the sweat on his toned abs glistened in the spring morning sunshine.

"We're on the march with Charlie's army," he bellowed. "We're all going to Wembley and we're gonna win the cup because we don't give a fuck and we're gonna ..."

Jimmy pulled him back from the edge of the balcony. He looked down nervously at the crowd gathered around the finishing straight. Luckily, the day was a relatively low-key spring meeting with only the degenerate punters braving the crisp, cool conditions of Surrey in early April.

"For fuck's sake, Ross, calm down, mate," Jimmy hissed. "We're not at the Romford dogs anymore. This is Epsom. There'll be paps everywhere."

"Ah, don't be stupid," Ross slurred. "It's a Mickey Mouse race, not the Derby. Look, there's nobody down here."

"Every newspaper in London is here and half of Saudi Arabia, you knobhead."

"What? We're having camel racing as well are we? I'm up for that. Let me get on the phone to my bookie. Hang on."

Ross tried unsuccessfully to prise his phone from his inside pocket. Jimmy smiled at his best mate and put his hand on Ross' shoulder.

"Just lay off the beer a bit, mate? It's not even lunchtime yet and you're throwing it about like a Chinese bookie."

"That's because I'm winning mate. I just put down five grand at 10-1 and he fucking romped home. Did you see him?"

"Yeah, I saw that. I also saw you put 10 grand on a certainty in the race before and he finished fourth."

"Ah, I was unlucky there. It was each way."

Jimmy peered over the balcony and noticed a photographer near the winning post had trained his long lens on their private box. Jimmy grabbed Ross roughly by the shoulders and turned him round.

"What are you doing?" Ross exclaimed.

"There's a fucking pap down there and you're stripping off up here. Do your shirt up and have a cup of coffee."

Jimmy tucked in Ross' shirt.

"Here, steady on soldier, I know we're in the Queen's Stand, but there's no need for that."

Jimmy smiled.

"Go and have a cup of coffee."

"Nope. I'll go and have a lovely cup of ..."

"... milky sweet tea," they both said in unison.

Jimmy waved Ross away and turned to look out across the downs. He could just make out London's gleaming spires and towers framing the rolling hills. He felt the sun on his face as he glanced over at the punters snarling at each other as they crawled up Langley Vale Road, hanging on their horns and sweating in their Ben Shermans, their best gear for a day on the beer. Jimmy laughed as he sipped his champagne. He noticed the pap still had his camera trained on their private box. Snap away, mate, snap away, Jimmy thought. I've got nothing to hide.

He watched as the photographer picked him out through his lens and then put his camera down. Jimmy shrugged it off. He was still part of the football club; he just wasn't part of the players' club anymore, not all the time anyway. But he had their money. He had more fucking money than all of them and was about to make a little bit more. Jimmy took out his phone and dialled.

"Hello, boss, it's me," he said softly. "I've sent soppy in to get a coffee ... I think he will, but get someone there to keep an eye on him will ya. The towelheads don't even drink, so we can't have him falling all over them stinking of Stella, can we?"

SCOTT picked up a cold canapé and sniffed it suspiciously. It smelled like rotten eggs. A waiter leaned across the table to add another champagne bucket and top it up with ice. He was hovering. They always did. Scott tapped him on the shoulder.

"Excuse me, mate, what's this?" he asked, pushing the canapé under the waiter's nose.

"That's actually a quail egg tartlet, Scott," the waiter replied enthusiastically.

Scott winced. It wasn't the quail egg tartlet, although there was no way he was sticking one of them in his mouth. It was the waiter. He had said Scott's name.

"Bloody hell, I'm not eating that," Scott said, dropping the tartlet back on the table and wiping his hands like he'd just tried a spoonful of dog shit. "Haven't you got any other snacks on the way, mate? I'm starving."

"The hot canapés are coming out soon. We've got lamb on skewers and tandoori chicken brochettes on the way, Scott."

"Ah, that's more like it. At least that's English."

The waiter laughed far too hard and had called Scott by his name twice. He had no chance now.

"I thought you were unlucky against Villa," the waiter said brightly, as he busied himself doing very little around the buffet tables.

Scott sighed and stared through the windows at the finishing straight.

"Yeah, yeah, it was one of those things," he said quickly.

"Still, three points this weekend against West Ham and you're still on for Europe."

"Well, maybe; I think we're too far behind to be honest. Is that the cheeseboard over there?"

"Yeah, yeah, over there, that's stilton and brie," the waiter replied quickly. "No, I think you can still do it. You got the three points at Upton Park earlier in the season, easy win there. You had a blinder. Almost scored with that header, almost took the top of your fin that one, didn't it?"

"Yeah, yeah," Scott muttered, clearly agitated.

Scott leaned over the table and speared a slice of mature cheddar with his fork. He turned his back on the waiter.

"Shame about the injury though," the waiter continued. "Still, it's only a groin strain, right? You'll be back for West Ham."

"Yeah, I don't know. I mean it's up to the physio, you know."

Scott pretended to take an interest in the crackers. For fuck's sake, take a hint, mate, he thought. You've had your 15 seconds of my fame, now piss off and go and haunt someone else.

"Still at least you got to go to the Royal Variety Performance to see Nicola," the waiter said breezily. "I saw them on TV. Watched the show when I got home from work. They were really good, weren't they? I saw you in the audience, too. Girl Power are really good live, really good dancers. Although Nicola was the best."

Scott turned around and stood up straight to face the waiter. Nicola, Scott, Nicola, Scott, Scott and Nicola, Nicola and Scott; everywhere it was the same. Who were these people? Scott had worshipped Eric Cantona growing up; idolised him, copied him, tried to play like him, even strutted around Barking with his collars up like him. But he didn't stalk the poor man so he could share his boring life story in Barking with him. Modern celebrity came with rules and Scott had always followed them. When he finally met Cantona at a charity event, he still followed the rules; just a brief handshake for the paps and a few football pleasantries and that was that. Scott had never been so presumptuous to believe that his uneventful life in Barking would be of any interest to Cantona. So why did the boring bastards he met always assume their tedious back story and opinions would be of interest to him?

"Yeah, she was good," Scott said, pushing the cheddar around the plate with his fork. "Look, I've gotta go, mate. I'm here with some people. You know what I mean?"

"Of course, Scott, I completely understand."

Scott nodded. *Tough shit if you don't, mate.*

Jimmy spotted Scott walking towards him. He looked furious, but Jimmy was hardly surprised. He had seen the waiter with Scott. The waiter had cornered Jimmy at the bar an hour earlier and asked him about his brief playing career. Jimmy hadn't minded. He wasn't stopped all that often anymore.

"I thought you told me no one would pester me," Scott hissed. "I fucking hate being pestered. You said this was a private box, no plebs."

"It is a private box," Jimmy said calmly.

"Private? I've got the waiter on my case within five minutes. All I want is a bit of chicken and suddenly he's on first name terms with my fucking wife. We might as well be holding this at McDonald's."

"Don't worry about it," Jimmy reassured. "I'll have a word with the manager. Make sure they keep him behind the bar."

"Yeah, either that or have the fucker fired."

Jimmy stared at Scott.

"You're not serious are ya?"

"Mate, I come here to get away from all that. You know it does my fucking head in. When we were kids, we didn't pester Tony Adams or Ryan Giggs did we?"

"They didn't earn five million quid a year then."

"What's that got to do with anything?"

"Your ugly mug is everywhere now. They think they know you. You know how it works."

"It's a joke. Got the prick saying, 'Nicola, Nicola' like he went to school with her. Who is he to call my wife by her first name?"

"She's famous. Everyone knows her as Nicola."

"Nah, it's different now. It's all changed, even from when you were playing. It's changed that fast. She was on that Twitter this morning, fucking Twitter, telling people what she's up to. You know, I had a really good shit today and this is what I thought about it. I can't just sit in the kitchen and have a bit of toast with my wife. I've got to have her million followers in there with me too. It's a joke. You know it's a joke."

"It's what we have to do now, to stay relevant."

"The Spice Girls never had to Twitter."

"They didn't have to compete with cable TV, Facebook, YouTube and digital downloads. Anyway, you're on Twitter."

"Only because you told me to. It's a waste of time. I don't even do it."

"What you on about, you don't do it? I see your updates nearly every day."

Scott laughed and choked on a piece of cheese. He coughed into his fist.

"Leave off. I don't do it, do I? They get me every Saturday afternoon for 90 minutes, that's more than enough. They are not getting me tweeting as well. I get the cook at the training ground to do it."

CHARLIE raised his champagne flute and encouraged the others around the table to join him. Jimmy held his up the highest. Scott stared out of the window at the hubbub around the winner's circle. Ross spilt his champagne over his wrist as his unsteady hand lifted his glass slowly.

"I'd like to welcome Al-Hakim and his guests here," Charlie said loudly. "And I'd like to congratulate you, Al-Hakim, on your horse beating my three-legged donkey out of sight. On behalf of the boys from Barking over here and the rest of the club, I'd like to thank Al-Hakim for inviting us here today to catch up and have this bloody marvellous lunch. Although I think we should keep our skipper away from the quail's eggs."

Jimmy laughed far too loudly. Al-Hakim smiled politely as his people, all in dark glasses and matching suits, glanced across at Jimmy. But Al-Hakim focused on Charlie. He didn't understand this football manager. He talked too fast and too often. But then, English football people always talked too fast and too often around Al-Hakim. Their tongues ran away with the smell of his money. Al-Hakim stared at his blonde partner for the day as she helped herself to some cheese and crackers. She had given a good blow job in the hotel suite while he was getting ready earlier in the morning, but she was no Nicola. No one was. Al-Hakim scanned the table and noticed that Scott was staring out of the window.

Rude bastard, he thought. He's not interested now. That's OK. That's to be accepted. Football club owners and managers always kissed Al-Hakim's ass. It was normal. Footballers paid him little attention, which he understood. He wasn't a singer or an actress. But they would listen to him soon enough. They would all listen once he owned them. Al-Hakim always commanded people's attention in the end.

He felt a tingling sensation in his groin. He glimpsed beneath the table. The blonde was now sitting beside him. She was rubbing the inside of his thigh, here, in the Queen's Suite. Al-Hakim loved the worthless pomp and ceremony of the British; it tickled his sense of humour. All pomp and ceremony and no money; he made more money in an afternoon than the Queen made all year, and he was expected to sustain eye contact and never turn his back on her every time he'd met her. It was bullshit. If this was Saudi Arabia, he could force the blonde to give him a blow job under the dinner table there and then and everyone else would busy themselves with their canapés. The thought of doing so here in the Queen's Suite appealed to his youthful rebelliousness. But he couldn't think about it. The hard-on made him uncomfortable.

Al-Hakim took the blonde's hand off his thigh and looked directly at Scott.

"Thank you for the kind welcome, but I feel I must apologise," he said. "I did not realise this was a male-only affair. I did not think I was still in Saudi Arabia."

Jimmy laughed far too loudly again. Al-Hakim eyed him suspiciously and then ignored him. Underlings always screeched like hyenas at his dinner functions. Their tiresome behaviour was to be expected. They were all whores in the end. The women screamed in the bedroom. The men screeched in the boardroom. It made no difference. They all wanted a taste.

"I brought a friend with me today because I assumed you would all be bringing your wives and partners today," Al-Hakim continued, still waiting for Scott to react. "It would have been nice to have met your families because I know this football club prides itself on its family atmosphere."

"That's true, Hakim," Charlie said. "I've been at this club for nearly 40 years, man and boy, which in the English Premier League is unheard of. When it comes to family and loyalty, there's no other club like it. That's why I brought my Barking Boys along today. These lads grew up in the area where I grew up. They are one-club boys like me. I gave all three of them their debuts before their 18th birthdays, and their loyalty to me and the club just says it all about what we're about."

Al-Hakim smiled slightly.

"They are more loyal to you than they are to their partners it would seem," he said.

Scott turned and glared at Al-Hakim. Al-Hakim savoured the moment. Under the table, he put the blonde whore's hand back on his crotch.

"I've heard lots of good things about your wife, Scott," Al-Hakim said quickly, before Scott had a chance to interject.

Al-Hakim always called celebrities and powerbrokers by their first names. Because he could. It asserted the balance of power at the outset so everyone in the conversation knew where they stood.

"I've heard she's a fabulous singer," Al-Hakim continued.

He took the blonde's hand under the table and rubbed it repeatedly against his inner thigh.

"She's all right, yeah, she's pretty good," Scott replied warily.

"That's very good. I guess you must be proud."

"Yeah I am. I'm really proud."

Al-Hakim needed to use the bathroom now.

"That's very good, I am only interested in a family club with strong families," Al-Hakim said, rising to his feet. "Now if you'll all excuse me. I must go to the bathroom. Too many canapés."

"You go for it, Hakim," Charlie said magnanimously.

"Yes, OK," Al-Hakim replied impatiently.

This Charlie really did talk too much, Al-Hakim thought. That would have to be addressed before the start of next season.

The blonde waited a few moments and then stood up.

"I might as well go as well," she muttered.

Charlie watched her totter off to the bathroom in her high-heels. He chuckled to himself.

"Bloody hell, they don't mess about these Arabs, do they? If he works that fast all the time, we'll have this thing sewn up before dinner."

Scott leaned across the table and looked at both Charlie and Jimmy. They were peas in a pod.

"Here, what was all that bollocks about Nicola," he said. "He's as bad as that fucking waiter."

"Yeah, but the difference is the waiter isn't connected to the Saudi royal family with a personal wealth of around 10 billion dollars," Jimmy whispered. "This bloke could buy the club with the change in his wallet."

"What does that mean to me?"

"It'll mean Champions League football every season," Charlie said.

"That's great. I'm all for that, but I don't want him banging on about my missus every five minutes."

"He probably just fancies her," Ross mumbled.

Scott looked at Ross at the end of the table. Ross stared into his empty champagne flute.

"What you on about?" Scott asked.

"I reckon he probably just fancies her," Ross said. "Let's face it, half the blokes in England already fancy her."

Scott turned away and stared out of the window. He watched a jockey being carried to the winner's circle by his jubilant trainers.

"Isn't it about time you put another bet on," he said softly.

SCOTT leaned on the bar and glanced across at their table. Jimmy and Charlie were deep in discussion about their next million, and Ross had staggered off to place another bet. The towelhead was still in the bog getting serviced by the slapper. There was enough time.

"What time will you be done filming?" he whispered down the phone. "Right, I'm leaving now then. Nah, they're all doing my head in. I reckon if I put my foot down and the traffic's not too bad on the A3, I'll be there in about 45 minutes. That all right? ... Yeah, the sexy silk ones. Ha ha, see you in a bit, babe."

AL-HAKIM felt so much better. They had used a private bathroom so there hadn't been a sense of urgency. Al-Hakim had hoped it might have been the Queen's private bathroom. When he was a teenager, his father had insisted on those six months at Eaton and he'd loathed every second of them; all that history and tradition, but no money or power. What was the point? There were royals in every damn classroom, titles and estates sitting around him at every meal, but what did they all amount to? A country house and a trout stream? Al-Hakim's family owned half of London and he was still called towelhead, raghead or camel jockey. Their families had history and tradition. Al-Hakim's family had a globalised economy dependent on finite resources. His time would come.

His time had come. He couldn't fuck the royal family, but he could at least fuck one of their loyal subjects in the Queen's bathroom. When he'd finished, he'd told the blonde to go and play with the horses for a couple of hours. He loved English women over a sink in the Queen's bathroom, but they had no place at the business table. The English still had so much to learn.

Al-Hakim took a sip of mineral water and examined Charlie. He was at least twice Al-Hakim's age, but ruggedly handsome in that old-fashioned, western George Clooney way. All those years spent on a training field in fresh, wintry conditions had benefited. Charlie kept himself fit. That was obvious. In many ways, he looked healthier than his sidekick. This Jimmy might have been a footballer once, but he was flabby now. Like many western businessmen, Jimmy tried to keep his appointments with the air-conditioned gym, Al-Hakim could see that, but the double chin gave him away.

Al-Hakim glimpsed the clock on the wall behind Charlie's shoulder. It was getting late. He wanted to get the blonde back to his hotel suite. MTV would soon be showing Girl Power's top 10 hits.

"OK, Charlie, how do I go about buying your football club?" he asked briskly.

Charlie and Jimmy looked at each other incredulously.

"Just like that?" Jimmy asked.

Al-Hakim ignored him. He had nothing against Jimmy. He just didn't need to expend energy on minions.

"Charlie, I'm serious about your club for lots of reasons. One, it has a long and proud history. Two, it has a respected, trusted, experienced manager in charge. Three, my accountants tell me the club is stable with a solid fan base and untapped global marketing potential. And four, I'm tired of being the only guy at my parties who doesn't own an English Premier League football club."

They all laughed. Jimmy laughed the longest.

"If you look at the other clubs in the English Premier League," Al-Hakim continued, "Among the ones that do not already have foreign owners, you definitely have the most potential. You have the London location, a good manager, a pedigree and you are stable."

Al-Hakim was rather impressed with his performance. He almost believed himself.

Charlie shifted uneasily in his seat.

"Erm, Hakim, you have probably been told that the club is around $100 million in debt. Like most Premier League clubs, we have, er, already spent next season's TV and ticket money to secure credit with the banks. Like most English Premier League clubs, I have to be honest here, we are only one relegation away from bankruptcy."

"That is no problem," Al-Hakim said dismissively. "Do you know the area in and around the stadium is prime real estate in Central London, worth at least twice that figure?"

Charlie looked surprised.

"I'd never really thought about it, to be honest," he said. "But you're not seriously thinking about moving. I mean ..."

"It's an option, sure."

"But the fans, I mean, they've been coming down there for nearly 100 years. They've got their faults, but they're a loyal bunch."

"Then they'll come with us if we move to a new stadium."

Charlie stared at the champagne in the bottom of his flute.

"Of course they will," Jimmy said suddenly. "They'll go to Scotland if we guarantee them Champions League football."

"We won't need to go that far," Al-Hakim said, addressing Jimmy for the first time. "But we may move to maximise the club's assets. Maybe. It's just an option that my property people have put to me. Nothing is set in stone. It's just an option. In the end, it's all about maximising revenue. Fans are loyal, this is true, but see how loyal they are when the team loses six games in a row. See how loyal they are when the team is relegated. Then look at Chelsea and Manchester City. Suddenly, their fans look like the most loyal in the world. They are confident. They are happy. They fill the stadium every week. Are they suddenly more loyal to football? No. They are more loyal to money. Supporters are like everyone else, gentlemen. Supporters, footballers, singers, actors, doctors, lawyers, they are all the same. People are loyal to money. Nothing else."

Charlie downed the rest of his champagne and smiled at Al-Hakim.

"You know something, Hakim. You and my old dad would have got on really well," he said. "You are absolutely right. First thing in the morning, I'll have a chat with the chairman and we'll get this thing sorted out as soon as possible."

"And I will remember all the hard work you have put in for me, Charlie."

"Ah, don't be silly. I'm sure we can sort something out among the three of us. We've all got to look after each other. It's all about the club at the end of the day, isn't it?"

"That's right," said Al-Hakim, smirking. "It's the family club."

Charlie lifted his glass for a toast.

"Right, then, to the family club," he said.

"To the family club," they said in unison, chinking their glasses together.

"Come on, let's go out on the balcony," Charlie said. "I think you've only got seven runners in this one, Hakim."

THE photographer crouched down and trained his long lens on the private box at the corner of the Queen's Stand. He was partially hidden by the punters around him, but was still aware he had to get the shots off quickly. Mother Nature was on his side. The spring clouds had parted and the afternoon sunshine lit up the white balcony. He needed a shot of them all together, talking together ideally, but at least all three of them in the frame.

They stepped onto the balcony. Jimmy first, and then Charlie, who led the Arab out into the dazzling sunshine. They looked down at the winner's circle. But they couldn't see clearly. They squinted and used their hands as visors. Charlie appeared to look at his form guide and pointed out something to the Arab. They laughed. There was some jostling, some playful banter. They were betting. They were placing a friendly bet. Charlie leaned forward and slapped the Arab on the shoulder. Jimmy giggled. Charlie pointed at his form guide again. The Arab nodded and offered his hand. The Arab had offered his hand to Charlie. They were going to shake hands. Shit. Charlie and the Arab were going to shake hands.

The photographer clicked furiously and repeatedly. He had no idea what he was taking. He clicked and prayed.

He looked through the view finder again. Charlie sipped some champagne and the Arab picked up a pair of binoculars to examine the horses being led out. The photographer eased his camera forward and pressed the playback button on his screen. He scrolled back several photographs and there it was; Charlie shaking hands with one of the richest men in the world with his dodgy agent sidekick standing beside them. They were all in focus; the sun had lit the scene in all its sleazy glory. The perfect frame. The photographer examined the image again and realised they were laughing. They were all laughing.

He dialled quickly.

"Hello, Tom, it's me Jason," he said excitedly. "I tell you what, mate, this beats sitting in that office all day, where are you now? ... Did you get the microphone in there? ... Ah mate, you are gonna love me ... I've only got 'em on the balcony, haven't I? All three of them and they are shaking hands. I have got the Arab and Charlie in the same bloody shot shaking hands."

eleven

TOM glared at the documentary awards framed around the office walls. They were awards for his documentaries; his investigative reports; his undercover work; his awards. He wanted to smash every one of the bastards.

"What more do you want us to do?"

Tom glanced across at Jason sitting on the other side of the glass table. Always the more demonstrative and short-tempered, his old friend was losing his cool. Tom noticed the protruding vein in Jason's temple. It was Jason's most obvious telltale sign of anger, but he had many others. He was an open book. That's why he rarely stood in front of a camera or went undercover. He was too easy to read.

Tom was the complete opposite. He was a blank canvas. He felt anger, frustration, sadness and fear like everyone else, but his face always remained an impenetrable mask. It wasn't through training or body language classes, just a fortunate case of genetics. His face saved him from the class bullies, who had always incorrectly assumed he was a fearless little fucker, and once spared him a kicking at a British National Party rally. The skinhead thought he'd recognised him from somewhere else. He had. They had crossed paths years earlier when Tom had worked as a cameraman on a *Panorama* exposé into the re-emergence of fascism in the UK. Tom's improvised story was full of holes and would've collapsed in any courtroom, but it was the telling rather than the story. He never blushed, never perspired, never shifted his body weight and never broke eye contact.

That's how a white man infiltrated a mosque and did his best Cat Stevens. That's how a middle-class boy from North London stood with BNP members outside Barking Town Hall and sang *White Christmas*. That's how a bloke who'd got by on beans on toast every day at university could pass himself off as a competent canteen cook at a Premier League club's training ground.

That's how he knew that Jonathan, the head of documentaries, was about to turn to him for moral support. Not for the first time, Jonathan had mistaken Tom's calm demeanour for begrudging acceptance.

"But you see where we are coming from here, Tom," Jonathan pleaded over his round, John Lennon glasses, leaning on the table for emphasis.

No, I don't know where you're coming from, Tom thought. I want to smash those fucking awards over your head.

"Not really, Jonathan, no," Tom said. "To be honest, I don't know what else you want from us. Just look at these photos."

Tom pointed at the photographs spread out across the glass table.

"There's Charlie with the richest property magnate in Saudi Arabia at the races; a man who has said publicly he wants to buy a Premier League club; a man with enough money to buy Roman Abramovich; a man who already owns most of the hotels, apartments and casinos around Mayfair and Marble Arch; a man who has Charlie in his pocket."

"They are just two well-known guys with a love of racing spending a day at Epsom together," Jonathan said.

"Ah, Jon, stop pissing about, mate," Jason interjected. "We've worked together on stuff for almost 10 years and you know that when we're this far down the road, we always deliver. We've got Charlie and Jimmy photographed and on film tapping up young players, tapping players from other clubs and now we've got them tapping up one of the richest men in the world. He's gonna buy that club for anything from £50 million to £100 million, depending on how fucked up their debts really are. Does anyone here seriously think Charlie and Jimmy are just going to get a handshake and a thank-you card? Charlie has been at it since he was picking up briefcases full of fivers in motorway services back in the eighties, and him and Jimmy have got the Premier League in their pockets. If they pull this off, then they've won the World Cup."

"We've got him primed now, Jonathan," Tom added. "We've got enough to finish him off, right now. We can either confront him or we can do it the old-fashioned way, but if we do that we've got to do it now, right now. Otherwise, Hakim's back in Saudi Arabia signing cheques and wrapping up the deal."

Jonathan took off his glasses and rubbed his eyes.

"Look, how many football documentaries have we done in the past on match-fixing and managers taking bungs and cuts, it's old hat now," Jonathan insisted. "No one will watch that any more. Viewers just want the sex and sleaze, who's shagging who, who's coked up with who and who's roasting who. Unless half the England team is shagging one teenage girl in a dentist's chair in Hong Kong, no one's interested anymore. No one's got the patience. You want an hour special on this? No one under 25 is bothered with the news anymore unless it can be reported in less than 140 bloody characters."

Jason threw some photos down on the table and stood up.

"Then what's the point, Jon, eh?" he shouted. "You've obviously made up your mind, right? Unless we can get Susan

Boyle to sing *Football's Coming Home* over the closing credits, we've got no chance of getting this made, right?"

"I never said that, I never said that at all," Jonathan said calmly. "I said we need hard evidence, something explosive and yes, OK, something a bit more tabloid. That's the new directive. That's the new ruling. And it's not even our ruling, it's their ruling, them out there; they've decided what they want to watch and it's not us, unless we make it sexy."

Tom picked up a photograph of Al-Hakim. He stared at his beard and smiled. He dropped the photo down on the table and turned it round so it faced Jason and Jonathan. He pointed at Al-Hakim's face.

"Then Jason is absolutely right," he said. "We do it the old-fashioned way."

JASON wiped his arm across his forehead and mopped up the perspiration. He glanced up at the air conditioner in the hotel room and sighed. He had already turned the damn thing down to its coolest temperature. He looked across at Tom reading some notes on the bed.

"Would you mind if I took my shirt off?" he asked.

Tom noticed the sweat rings on Jason's shirt and laughed.

"Be my guest," Tom replied. "Whatever gets you through the night. I think if two blokes are going to spend all night awake in a hotel room then at least one of them should have their shirt off."

"Piss off."

Jason turned back to the hotel desk. It was covered with laptops, notepads, mobile phones and cables leading into the back of a TV monitor. Jason peered through the monitor. He adjusted the zoom to tightly focus on a young Muslim man in a cotton thobe sitting inside a similar hotel room beside an identical desk. The hotel room was bare except for a suitcase on the bed. The young man fidgeted uneasily in his ankle-length robe.

"Where did you get this kid from again?" Jason asked, still peering through the monitor. "He looks like he's shitting himself."

"Razali will be fine. I've been through it with him all day. Less is more. I've already told him. The trick is to say as little as possible."

"Do you think he'll come through for us? He doesn't stand to gain anything from this. He knows we can't pay him."

Tom sat up straight on the bed.

"You're joking, aren't you," Tom said. "He loves us. They all do down there. After the BNP thing came out, we were overnight heroes. Razali told me they even prayed for us down at the mosque."

"No, they didn't. Really?"

"I'm telling ya. When the BNP dickheads threatened us in the papers, they started praying for us in the mosque. Razali told me."

"Well, I hope they're praying for us now."

CHARLIE stopped at a zebra crossing and watched a group of schoolchildren skip towards Hyde Park. A couple of the boys recognised him and he waved back at them. He pulled away slowly and continued down Kensington Road. Something wasn't quite right. Charlie was his father's son. He could smell a scam a mile away. But he wasn't sure. He just couldn't be sure. The towelhead was a young playboy; cocky, flamboyant, eccentric even. He screwed that Essex girl in the Queen's Stand at Epsom so he clearly wasn't playing with a full deck. But when you were worth that much money, you could play by whatever rules you liked. This didn't feel right, but Al-Hakim didn't feel right. Nothing felt right about being worth $10 billion. Charlie had a fair bit invested in properties along the south coast and lived like a king in his Epping castle. That felt right. There was nothing right about having billions in the bank accounts. All those zeroes would do anyone's head in.

There had been strange phone calls before. The first one had been a real crackerjack call. "I speak on behalf of Al-Hakim," the caller had said. "He wants to buy your football club." Just like that. And then at the races, Al-Hakim had said it again to Charlie's face, almost nonchalantly. *I want to buy your football club.* Just like that. Piece of piss. No problem. Easy.

But today's phone call had definitely been different; not quirky, just different. Al-Hakim was quirky, that's what he was. The phone calls were usually quirky, entertaining even, but this one had been straight, businesslike.

The canteen cook had handed Charlie the phone and the caller was strangely blunt. "Al-Hakim would like the sale completed quickly," he had said. "Please meet him at the Royal Garden Hotel this evening, 4.30 pm sharp. He is staying at the garden suite, but he doesn't talk business there. He will meet you in a garden room. Ask at the lobby for the room number. Then we will explain how the sale can be completed quickly. Thank you."

Charlie turned right into Kensington High Street and saw the concierge already waiting for him at the entrance. It was shaping up to be a strange end to a strange day. And that was the other thing. Why didn't the towelhead's people just call his mobile?

Charlie stepped out of his Bentley and handed the keys to his concierge. The keys were wrapped around a £20 note. Charlie never forgot his roots or the weekend hours wasted on his father's car lot polishing old bangers that would never sell. He always tipped generously. It reminded him how far he'd come. It made him feel important. The tip was always for his benefit.

"Thanks for that, Charlie, that's really kind of you," the concierge said gratefully. "I reckon you'll turn West Ham over this week."

"I certainly hope so," Charlie said curtly.

"Yeah, definitely, especially if Scott recovers in time. Mind you, if I was married to that Nicola, I wouldn't mind staying at home this weekend."

"Yeah, yeah, that's right. Cheers mate."

Charlie kept his head down and walked briskly towards the counter.

"Yep, all the best Charlie," the concierge shouted after him. "Good luck against the Hammers."

The concierge waved enthusiastically at the back of Charlie's head. He watched Charlie stroll over to the lifts. The concierge pulled off one of his white gloves with his teeth and took out his phone.

"Hello, it's the concierge from downstairs," he whispered. "Yeah, he's on his own and he's on his way up to you now."

Jason put the mobile phone down slowly on the desk beside the TV monitor. He exhaled deeply.

"We're on," he said softly.

"What?" Tom replied.

"Er, we're on," Jason repeated, clearing his throat. "He's heading up in the lift."

"Well, don't just sit there. Let's get it on with it."

Tom threw his notes to one side and jumped off the bed. He leaned over the TV monitor and pushed a button.

"Razali, can you hear me?" he said quickly. "Nod your head slowly if you can hear me, Razali."

Tom and Jason stared at the monitor. Razali nodded and wiped his nose on the sleeve of his white.

"Don't do that, Razali, mate, if you can, please," Tom said emphatically. "Please don't wipe your nose or anything on your sleeves because if you look sweaty or nervous, he'll get suspicious. That OK, Razali?"

Razali nodded anxiously. He closed his eyes and inhaled deeply through his nose.

"That's it, Razali, nice and cool. Take a few deep breaths. That's a good idea. Now remember mate, I've done hundreds of these things and they're all over in seconds. The trick is to say as little as possible. You don't really have to say anything, just do it like we said. He must take the suitcase with him. That's the key. And remember, Razali, he's from your favourite London borough of Barking and Dagenham and how many BNP councillors have they had in there?"

Razali smiled and took another deep breath. He focused on the hotel room door.

"That's it, Razali, he's a smug, arrogant prick and we're gonna have him. I'm not gonna speak anymore, but we'll be listening. Good luck, mate."

"Yeah, good luck, Razali," Jason muttered.

Tom took his finger off the microphone button and glanced across at Jason, who wiped his forehead again.

"Let's just hope he doesn't open the suitcase while Razali's still in the room," Tom said.

CHARLIE changed his mind. It didn't feel right. He didn't need the aggravation. He'd worked too long to jeopardise everything now. He hadn't come this far to throw everything away in one irrational, misguided decision. If this didn't work out, his position at the club could prove to be untenable, and that was unthinkable. He was part of the furniture, part of the football fabric. The owner's name and bank balance didn't matter in the end, because Charlie was the club. He owned the club.

Charlie turned around and headed back down the hotel corridor. He smiled. He didn't have to pitch the idea to himself. It was a wise move. He was his father's son.

Charlie knocked on the door.

"Come in," said Razali.

Razali watched Charlie step tentatively into the hotel room. That's a promising start, Razali thought. He's shitting himself. Razali was not the only person in the room out of his depth. Razali nodded his greeting, just as Tom had instructed him to. Charlie smiled awkwardly.

"All right, mate," Charlie stammered, clearing his throat.

Razali was stunned. He knew this man. Everyone in London knew this man. He was the voice of the English Premier League, the mouthpiece of modern football. Razali had read his tabloid columns and laughed at them. The old Londoner always had an opinion. After the July bombings on the tubes and buses, this football manager had expressed *his* anger for *his* people in *his* city.

His anger.

His people.

His city.

And *they*, this football manager had written, *they* had to be hunted. *They* had to be tracked down. *They* had to be hammered. This sad man had used anachronistic war imagery, so popular and yet so hackneyed in football, and applied it to real life-and-death issues he couldn't possibly understand. Razali had been made to understand. He had dealt with "us and them" distinctions and all that other xenophobic white man's tribalism his entire life. Now he had to put up with this football manager drawing lines in the sand; this football manager commenting on deep-rooted politics that were beyond his secondary modern school education. This old fossil living out with the farmers on his country estate had the audacity to express his anger about his lovable Londoners. But the city didn't belong to Charlie anymore, it belonged to Razali; *his* city, *his* people, *his* anger.

This geriatric didn't know what real anger was.

And he was a quivering wreck. Razali spotted that immediately as adrenaline surged through his body. The mouthpiece of modern football had been replaced by a jittery buffoon. Tom had been right. This was going to be easy.

"Come, sit," Razali said softly, remembering Tom's instructions. Wealthy, influential people are always listened to. They do not need to raise their voices. They do not ask. They order.

"Ah, thank you, thanks very much," replied Charlie, as he fumbled his way across the room.

He glimpsed the view through the window.

"Lovely view," Charlie said, forcing the gaiety. "That's Kensington Palace down there. Diana used to live there."

"Come, sit," Razali said authoritatively.

He pointed to the chair—Tom and Jason's chair, the chair that caught the light from the window, the chair that filled their TV monitor in the hotel room next door; the chair where Charlie would hang himself, if Razali gave him enough rope.

"Yeah, sure, OK," Charlie said, still scanning the hotel room. "Is, er, Hakim, not joining us? He usually joins us when we talk football."

"He says sorry, he is on urgent business, but he left you something to help you speed up the sale of the football club."

Charlie eyed Razali suspiciously. The kid was young and dressed like Lawrence of Arabia. Charlie knew that the towelheads dressed like that back in the desert, but not so much here.

Al-Hakim always wore designer suits in London, probably so he didn't draw attention to himself. But this kid was done up like a Mr Whippy ice-cream.

"What's in the case?" Charlie asked.

"Oh, quite a few things."

"How many?"

"Five."

Charlie blew out his cheeks and rubbed his hands along the tops of his thighs. He stared at the suitcase.

"That's a lot of things."

THE concierge ushered the party into the hotel and steered them towards the lift lobby. He hovered around the revolving doors until they had stepped into the lifts. He craned his head to make sure the lift doors had closed, and then he pulled out his phone and dialled frantically.

"Answer the phone," he hissed. "Answer the fucking phone."

Tom was transfixed. He could not take his eyes off the TV monitor. He was seconds away. He could almost reach through the hotel room wall and touch it. Months of research, months of serving pasta for carbo-loading fuckwits was all about to end. He was about to get his cake with a little Charlie on the top. He felt a vibration near his left hand. He glanced down and saw his phone sliding along the desk towards his fingers.

He picked it up. The concierge was calling.

"What the fuck does he want," Tom muttered. "I told him to call only if it was an emergency."

Jason shrugged.

"Well, you better get it then."

Tom tiptoed to the corner of the room before answering the phone.

"Look, I can't really talk now, you'll get your 50 quid all right ... What? ... When? ... Oh fuck."

Tom put the phone down and ran back to the TV monitor. He pushed the microphone button.

"Razali, stay cool," he whispered. "But you need to get out of there right now."

RAZALI felt a single bead of perspiration trickle down his back. The sweat would soon be pouring through his robe and cascading down the sides of his face. He glimpsed across at Charlie. The old man rocked slightly as he stared at the suitcase. He bit the bottom of his lip. He was making his mind up. Razali would make it for him.

"OK, then, so I leave this with you," Razali said, standing up suddenly. "I must report back and we must move this deal along much faster now."

"Here, hang on, mate, you can't just get up and leave."

"Why not? The room is yours if you want it for the night, all paid for. I need to update my boss and you need to speak to yours so we can settle quickly."

Razali gestured towards the suitcase.

"That's just there to show that my boss is a man of his word and is serious about taking control as soon as possible."

"Yeah, I know all that, but ..."

"I wish you a pleasant evening."

Razali nodded to Charlie and left the hotel room. Charlie got up quickly, shocked to see the door close quickly behind Razali. He walked over to the edge of the bed and stood over the suitcase.

"Pick it up, you bent bastard," Tom growled. "Pick it up."

Tom watched Charlie, through the monitor, as he stared down

at the suitcase. It was almost over. Charlie's greed would push Tom over the finish line. A man whom Tom had grown up admiring, a man who had created teams and developed crops of players worshipped by kids in secondary schools across the country, a man who should've had the chance to follow Ramsey's path to World Cup glory was about to fuck it all up for the biggest bung of his life.

Tom's eyes darted across the room as Jason struggled to open the front door quietly for Razali.

"Shut up, will ya," he whispered. "He's about to take the case."

Jason opened the door, grabbed Razali by the neck of his robe and dragged him into the hotel room. Jason peered out into the corridor and grinned. It was empty. He closed the door and gestured to Razali not to speak. Razali raised the palms of his hands to Jason and nodded as they crouched beside Tom in front of the monitor.

"What's happening?" Jason muttered.

"He's standing over the suitcase and thinking, 'Shall I take it or shall I wonder what all the fucking noise is next door.'"

Jason wasn't insulted. Instead he smiled at Tom. He was delighted for his friend. He had earned this moment.

Tom's eyes widened and his mouth opened. He grabbed Razali and Jason by their shoulders and squeezed hard. He rocked their shoulders backwards and forwards.

"He's picking it up, he's picking it up," he said excitedly. "He's taking the money ... look ... he's taking the fucking money."

Tom held his breath as the English Premier League's most popular manager headed towards the door with what he believed was half a million pounds in his suitcase.

twelve

THE lights were amber, but Charlie floored the accelerator. He checked his rear-view mirror and saw Harrods disappearing in the distance. He had once toyed with the idea of joining forces with Al-Fayed at Fulham, back when he still owned Harrods, but the whole Diana business had left a bitter taste. Charlie was a proud royalist.

Charlie blinked hard as he raced through Knightsbridge. The sweat was stinging his eyes. He took his hand off the wheel and wiped his brow. Screw Al-Fayed, he thought, he had Al-Hakim in his corner. He was half his age, had 100 times the financial clout and knew how to reward loyalty. The boy was special. Charlie didn't know much about him and certainly didn't have a clue when it came to his religion and politics; ignorance was most certainly bliss when it came to those two, but Al-Hakim had really come through for him. As both player and manager, Charlie had worked with some good chairmen, decent people. They were silly, naïve old duffers riding that blue-collar guilt trip, obsessed with giving something back to the dog-shit industrial community that had spat them out in the first place by blowing their fortunes on trying to turn the local football club into Barcelona. But their hearts were always in the right place.

Still, none of them were a patch on Al-Hakim. The man

exuded class. Charlie could see that now. He might be a towelhead with a thing for shagging blondes all over London, but he was a man of his word. Charlie would be indebted to him forever.

The traffic crawled to a standstill at Hyde Park Corner and Charlie gazed across at the Wellington Arch, lit up proudly in the encroaching darkness. Charlie loved Wellington, referencing him all the time in his newspaper columns and interviews; Wellington and Churchill, the Dunkirk spirit, we'll fight them on the beaches; sentiments that carried England safely to glory in '66. A spirit that foreign managers would never fully grasp or appreciate about English football; a spirit that would allow Charlie and his boys to scale the heights of Premier League success, with Al-Hakim standing beside them in the trenches.

Charlie was ready to go to war for Al-Hakim and he needed the right soldiers around him. Loyalty was paramount now. He leaned across the dashboard and reached for his mobile.

"Hello, that you, Jimmy?" Charlie shouted into his headset. "Oh, it's you … Sorry, love. Can I speak to Jimmy please?"

Charlie rolled his eyeballs. Women always slowed things down. Al-Hakim even had the right idea when it came to a woman's place.

"Hello, Jimmy, it's me … Can you talk now? … OK, I'll see you at the training ground in one hour, all right? We're in with Al-Hakim now, mate. We are well in."

JASON and Razali exchanged glances nervously. Jason shook his head and gestured towards Tom. Now was not the time for any forced jocularity or edgy jokes. Razali fiddled with a piece of cotton on his robe. Tom stared at the TV monitor, gazing at the empty hotel room next door. He appreciated their silence. He needed silence. He wanted a few moments to take in what had just happened. It had been intoxicating. It had taken his breath away and now he had to focus, to regain his senses, to determine his plan of action. Even by the devious bastard's slippery standards, Charlie had surprised him.

Tom chuckled and looked up at Jason.

"Well, I didn't expect that to happen," Tom muttered.

JIMMY stood in the car park and waited. He realised it was the first time he had been to the training ground at night. The grey complex was eerie and cheap without the primary colours of the Ferraris and Lamborghinis to brighten the place up a bit. Jimmy had never been here at night before. This was serious. It had to be about the Al-Hakim deal. No player, not even his beloved Scott or Ross, was important enough; no issue pressing enough to drag Charlie away from his farmhouse on a cold night. Deals were always done after training, when Charlie still had the smell of churned up turf all around him. It was his drug of choice and Charlie thrived on that high. Jimmy had taken nothing this evening and now wished he had. Jimmy never previously had a toot before meeting Charlie, but then he had never met him this late before. Jimmy and his missus did their partying after hours, and Charlie was incredibly Victorian in his attitude towards drugs. Jimmy found it almost twee. He hardly knew a manager who didn't need a little something to get through a season, but this Charlie got high only on football and money.

"You dozy little cunt."

Jimmy heard Charlie's voice and felt a sharp pain in his back. He tumbled forwards and felt the right side of his face smash into the roof of his Bentley. That's a few hundred quid in damages right there, he thought. That was his immediate reaction, until the fear kicked in. He felt his neck being squeezed and he instinctively swung around to free himself.

"Don't you fucking push me," Jimmy screamed. "Don't you ever put your fucking hands on me."

Jimmy pushed Charlie hard in the chest and the older man lost his balance. Charlie's legs raced backwards, but they couldn't prevent his fall. Jimmy stood over Charlie.

"I know I owe you, but don't you ever fucking bully me," Jimmy shouted. "You can bully them every day, but you can't fucking do it to me. Don't call me out in the middle of the night and then have a pop at me. I'm not some fucking punch bag to take the piss out of. Those days are over. We're not on the training pitch anymore, Charlie."

Charlie got up gingerly and brushed down his clothes with his hands.

"Oh, spare me your amateur psychology, you prat. Someone has fucked me over, all right. I'm being set up with Al-Hakim and you're the only one who knows about our deal."

Charlie's reaction surprised Jimmy. It was unmistakable. Jimmy read it in the old man's face. There was fear. Charlie was terrified. Jimmy had never seen Charlie like this before. He'd seen the bluff, the bullshit, the wheeler-dealing and the banter with the media boys—whatever the result. Charlie always had a game face—the right face—for every occasion and it was never apprehensive. Charlie's reaction scared Jimmy more than the shove in the back.

"What are you going on about?" Jimmy asked.

"Did you know I was at the Royal Garden Hotel earlier?"

"What?"

"Don't fuck me about. Did you know I was at the Royal Garden Hotel?"

"No, why would I know that? Did you go there to see Al-Hakim?"

"Yes."

Jimmy gritted his teeth and glared at Charlie.

"Well, why didn't you tell me? We're supposed to be working

together on this. This is supposed to be a 50-50 thing. I'm involved with the Arab as much as you are."

"Ah, don't get out of your pram about it, his people called me last minute, told me to get straight down there to try and push the takeover deal along."

"Well, you could have told me."

"I'm fucking telling you now. His people told me to go straight there and I meet this young towelhead who tells me they want the deal done before the end of the season and to give me an incentive."

"How much?"

Charlie stared at the floor, avoiding eye contact.

"250,000."

Jimmy's eyes widened.

"They offered you 250,000? To do what?"

"Nothing other than what we're already doing, convince the chairman that it's time to smell his roses and call it a day."

Jimmy smiled.

"That's it? That's all? Ah, mate, we're gonna be laughing by the time this thing is done."

"I don't know if it is gonna be done now, do I? Even if it is done, me and you could be banged up by the time Al-Hakim takes over."

"What are you on about?"

Charlie exhaled and looked up at Jimmy.

"Just as I was about to go, I mean when I was standing by the fucking door, my mobile rang."

TOM thought about the omelettes, the pasta, the freshly-squeezed fruit juice, the muddy footprints, the dirty training bibs left on the tables, the omnipresent smell of Vaseline, the agents, the mobiles, the phone calls from the wives, the phone calls from other people's wives, the phone calls from the slappers, the phone calls from other people's slappers, the Rolexes, the car keys; the bitching about the fans, the fans, the fucking fans, what irritants they were, what pests they were, what sad bastards they were, what a pain in the arse open training days were, why open training days should be banned, why fans should be banned from the training ground, why fans should buy their jerseys and season tickets and then crawl off quietly; the banter, the hilarious, side-splitting training ground banter, the crack, the laugh, the pranksters, the salt in the sugar bowls, the sugar in the salt cellars, the flat Ferrari tyres, the torn shirts, the paint-stained Armani suits, the dog shit in the new boy's boots, the banter, the banter, the tedious, childish, daily fucking banter.

Tom held his head in his hands.

"I've got to go back, haven't I?" he mumbled.

AL-HAKIM adjusted the belt on his dressing gown and looked down at the lights twinkling below in Kensington Gardens. He loved the Royal Garden Hotel. There were better hotels in London, but none better connected. This place had close connections with Singapore. Some of his dearest business associates from Singapore owned the hotel, and it was much like the city-state: small, quaint, efficient, courteous without being obsequious and minded its business while quietly going about the business of making money. Everyone at the Royal Garden Hotel knew Al-Hakim; it was practically his second home and he liked to know everything about his homes, so the staff told him everything.

Al-Hakim took the Girl Power Blu-ray disc off the table and chortled. The duty manager had been on the phone to his people within minutes. That football manager had just arrived, all clammy and breathless, and had been sent up to see him. That was a rather exciting development. Al-Hakim's people had expressed their gratitude to the duty manager. He preferred cash. They usually did. It was all rather easy for the duty manager after that. Check the floor where Charlie stepped out of the lift, check the corridor cameras, check the two guys hurrying out of the lifts carrying bags full of audio-visual equipment and check that buffoon scurrying from one room to another dressed like Peter O'Toole in *Lawrence of Arabia*.

It was amateur night, a textbook sting complete with a cartoon Arab in fancy dress. Only an idiot would fall for a scam that transparent in the Middle East. But Charlie had never been to the Middle East. Charlie rarely ventured past Manchester. So there was a great deal to be gained here. All Al-Hakim had to do was pick up the phone when the duty manager gave him the word and he had Charlie safely tucked away in his pocket. He would have a new pet to pat in his latest business project.

Al-Hakim pressed play on the Blu-ray remote control and watched the beautiful Nicola prance around the stage, belting out *(I'm a) Cee-lebrity*. He took off his robe, stretched out on the bed naked. He was going to enjoy this all the more now. He watched the tall blonde open the bathroom door and strut across the suite. She had shaved. Good, Al-Hakim thought, it made her look more wholesome, more western-girl-next-door, more like Nicola. He tossed her a tiny Girl Power T-shirt as she crawled across the bed.

"Wear this," he ordered. "Nothing else, just this. I want the missionary position so I can watch the TV."

JIMMY put his hands in his pockets and tried to hide the shaking. It wasn't that cold. He gave Charlie a brief glance. He was too preoccupied to notice.

"We really are in trouble, aren't we?" Jimmy said.

"No, we were in trouble when the world and his wife saw us with him at the races. Now we're fucked. We are really, really in trouble here."

"Who do you think it was?"

"Oh, I don't know, do I? Could be anybody, couldn't it? *News of the World*, *The Sun*, *The Mirror*, BBC, Channel 4, who knows? It doesn't really matter does it?"

"I know plenty of people there, I'll ask around."

"Jimmy, nobody knows more people in the media than me. I've spent more money on them than I have on my own players over the years, but if it's on camera, they can't do a thing. If the fuckers edit it right, they've got me banged to rights, suitcase in hand, heading out the door."

"You told me you never took it out of the hotel room?"

"The producer doesn't have to show that, does he? I picked up a bag of cash in a hotel room with a towelhead sitting beside me."

"Fucking hell," Jimmy whispered.

They shuffled their feet as a biting wind swept through the car park. Jimmy glanced across at Charlie.

"What can we do?"

"Well, I'm not going down that easy," Charlie insisted, standing up straight. "They can't have anything concrete or I'm sure they would've confronted me immediately. While they play with themselves in the shadows, we need a diversion; a brilliant, dazzling shiny diversion that keeps the boys distracted for a few weeks, just long enough for Al-Hakim's mob to wrap things up."

"Like what?"

"What do you think? Give them what they always want. Give them some good news, covered with some of your tits and fanny."

thirteen

JO adjusted her boobs and pouted. She loved her boobs. She adored her boobs. No one in the room had a pair like hers. They separated the women from the little girls, and they certainly separated the men from the boys. They did the business for her with the boys from Barking. They were still doing the business for her with the boys from Barking. But she was on the A-list now.

"Jo, Jo, more cleavage, Jo ... Point them this way Jo ... Can you squeeze them together Jo ... That's beautiful darling ... Ah, nice one, babe ... Did you see the two-page spread I got you, Jo? ... Did you see yourself on the *Bizarre* pages, Jo? ... I told you we'd look after you, Jo ... This way, Jo ... Need to see them Jo ... Need to see them, Jo ... This way, Jo ..."

Jo faced the paps and made love to their lenses. She knew every pap in the room by name, knew their marital status, how many kids they had and what their kids were into. She made them feel special. They made her feel special. Every time she opened up one of the daily red-tops, she felt special. She always did. From the moment she opened up her surgical gown and saw them in the full-length mirror for the first time, she had felt special, unique. There was blood and scars everywhere and her skin was green and purple, but she saw beneath the scars. She saw the bigger picture.

Once the scars healed and the swelling went down, she had the finest pair of breasts in Britain. When she showed the final product to her proud cosmetic surgeon, she was more than happy to fuck him right there in his office, with the photo of his family smiling up at them from the desk. The wife's slightly strained, smug smile said it all; having a lovely time at our mortgage-free cottage in Cornwall with our three children and two beautiful beagles, please look at this photo, darling, and try not to shag every young slut who wants bigger tits.

The photo was the wife's security, but it meant nothing to Jo. The doctor meant nothing to Jo. He wasn't bad looking for a bloke in his early 50s, lean, healthy, slightly tanned from those middle-class weekends in Europe's warmer climes with a lusty pair of balls. And he had given Jo those boobs—*the* boobs—that had changed her life. She had her boobs just as Elizabeth Hurley had had that dress. Jo remembered reading about Hurley in *The Sun* when she was a kid. She had never heard of Elizabeth Hurley. No one in her house had. She didn't make films that anyone in her house would watch. But everyone remembered that dress. But they didn't remember the dress. When it came to the tabloid media and the zombies who turned its pages, Jo had been blessed with perceptiveness beyond both her years and her intellect. Even as a kid, she knew it wasn't really about Hurley's dress. It was those boobs. It was always about the boobs.

"Jo, Jo, can you put your arms around Charlie ... Nicola, can you put your arms around the other side ... That's it, lovely, nice one ... Push them out, Jo, if you don't mind. Did you see that *Page Seven* photo spread I got you last week, Jo."

Jo scanned the press conference and hoped that no one had picked up on her sudden flash of irritation. Of course they hadn't. When did their lenses ever focus on her face?

She had seen that *Page Seven* photo spread. It was OK. She

had been shopping at Sainsbury. She knew they were going to be there. Her agent had tipped them off, even told them what she'd be wearing: a tight T-shirt and hot pants. There'd be plenty of bending over the freezers as she pondered her choice of meat. Ooh, er missus, just think about all the innuendos. She was the sweaty, middle-aged sub-editor's wet dream. Her T-shirt had a slogan on the front, right across her chest: My Child Never Goes Hungry. Yummy mummies were all the rage and Jo had always been one step ahead. He hadn't liked the T-shirt at home, said it was tacky. But he didn't understand. A footballer who dealt with the media every day, and he still hadn't a clue how to play the game. Jo had given up trying to teach him. At least Scott had found the T-shirt funny.

Scott.

The best shag she ever had.

Jo glared across Charlie and noticed Nicola smiling demurely for the media, doing her usual lost little puppy dog routine. Why the plebs lapped up that rubbish Jo would never know. She had seen that *Page Seven* photo spread all right. It was a slutty photo of her leaning right over the meat freezer to grab a leg of pork. In the early days, the caption might have been playful. Now it was double-edged. The text had been almost spiteful. Jo can't resist getting her leg over even in a supermarket. That's what those fuckers had written. Jo can't resist getting her leg over even in a supermarket. Jo can't stop thinking about getting some meat and two veg even when her kid was with her.

The tabloid boys were also playing a game. They had to gradually navigate a new course, alter the public perception slightly and get the sheep to follow a new shepherd so they could push a new storyline for the next few months. They had to gently remind their readers who they wanted to read about in the next year or so. Jo understood that. She even begrudgingly admired it.

The tabloid red-tops manipulated the plebs better than she ever could. Jo accepted her turn was slowly coming to an end. Attention spans were short. Tabloid stories were cyclical. It was inevitable. She had prepared for the eventual pedestal fall. The interest off her investments alone would take care of that. She would be all right for a few quid.

Jo knew the tabloids needed to groom someone else to succeed her. There was always a succession policy in the media; no succession, no circulation. Even Jo's fame had a shelf life. And she could handle just about anyone taking her place—anyone except that singing and dancing twat beside Charlie.

NICOLA had been right. She didn't need to be here. It wasn't arrogance. She just didn't want to be a co-star in the latest episode of that slapper's show. Jo had no talent. Jo had no dignity. Jo had nothing but fake boobs. She was a goddess to the council estates and she was welcome to them. Nicola adjusted her pink T-shirt and glimpsed the slogan on her chest. Charlie's Angels. They were having a laugh. The other girls in the band were not going to be too impressed, but then nor was she. This really was beneath her. It wasn't like she didn't do her bit for breast cancer. She had already played several gigs for cancer trusts and was a patron of those charities. She had even appeared on a couple of excruciating cover records with the other pop idols. Every time she read news of another natural disaster in Indonesia, Haiti or Pakistan, she would cringe. She knew the record label would be calling with details of her studio slot. She was usually sandwiched between Kylie and Susan Boyle. There was nothing like a charity single to underscore one's place in the celebrity hierarchy.

Nicola squinted at her Rolex. She didn't like the watch

particularly much; she thought it was vulgar. But Jimmy had insisted that both her and Scott wore them at all public appearances; the golden couple at all times with golden timepieces.

Time had stopped. This was easily the tackiest charity circus Nicola had been involved with, and it was taking too long. She smiled at Charlie and shot a glance at Jimmy. He was fidgeting nervously behind the press throng at the back of the room. Something was amiss. They were obviously up to their neck in something to pull a stunt this transparent and feeble. It couldn't be the team itself; the players were challenging for a spot in Europe and Scott and Ross were going to be called up for England any day now, but something was definitely awry. Jimmy had never dared to call and ask her to share a stage with that *Page Three* bird before. Nicola was prepared to say no, but she had detected the desperation in his voice, and she had always liked Jimmy. Besides, she had married into the footballer's culture. Her bed had already been made.

"It'd be good if you could do it, I suppose, for Charlie and the club," Scott had mumbled, not bothering to look up from his PlayStation controller when she first asked him about the Charlie's Angels stunt. "Better not rock the boat."

"What bloody boat?"

CHARLIE grinned broadly at Jimmy over the heads of the reporters and photographers. The old manager had to hand it to Jimmy. His protégé had pulled off a masterstroke in less than a week. They both knew that the TV reporters, whoever they were, would need at least a week to cobble together an investigative piece that wasn't libellous before they could put it on the air. The legal checks alone could take a fortnight. Charlie had been involved with these clowns before, and they rarely went public without door-stopping him for a quote first. He had always given them a quote in the past. And they had always ended up with nothing. They were always the same; naïve little boys trying to whitewash a man's world. When he was doing his coaching badges and getting snotty-nosed kids to run up and down a school sports hall, these reporters were getting their nappies changed. Whether it was Channel 4, BBC, Sky, ITV, *Newsnight* or *Panorama*, these idealistic parasites were all the same. If they fell into hot tub of big tits, they'd still come out sucking their thumbs.

Charlie put his arms around both Nicola and Jo and squeezed tightly. He copped a slight feel of one of Jo's. Well, it was hard not to really. He had always loved his job. Today, he loved his work just a little bit more.

"Lads, seriously, I've gathered these beautiful women here today to talk about a serious issue," he began, with all the earnestness he could muster for this serious issue.

"Breast cancer counts for more than 10 per cent of all the cancers women are struck down with. And the most important thing is, it is mostly curable. If you get it early enough, at the earliest stage, with the right treatment, up to 98 per cent of women can survive. So awareness is the key. It's all about awareness, and if it takes a silly sod like me to stand here with six of the most beautiful women I know to ram that message home, then I'm more than happy to do it."

"But why do it now, Charlie?" asked Jason, tucked in between two of the most recognisable tabloid football writers, just in case.

"There is never a wrong time to do this. But it's something that's been on my mind for a while. As you know, we went over to Australia for a pre-season tour and I watched a bit of cricket at the MCG. The entire stadium was pink; the players, the umpires, the stands, the commentators, the whole place was pink—the colour of breast cancer awareness—and they raised a fortune that day, but more than that, I bet you every woman in Australia went into the bathroom that night and checked for lumps, and that's the most you can hope for."

"Why Charlie's Angels? And why six of your footballers' wives?"

The question never came from Jason. It was too quick. Jason barely had the chance to open his mouth to get the follow-up question out before the guy in the suit in the second row jumped in. His eagerness made it too obvious to Jason, but under the circumstances Jason accepted it was a risk they clearly believed they had to take. The guy in the suit was a plant.

"That's a good question," Charlie replied. "It's all about slogans today, right? You can't turn on the TV and not come across a slogan. The lottery says it could be you. I've been doing the lottery for nearly 20 years, and I can say, 'No, it can't be me.' Simon Cowell says Britain's got talent. And I've been a coach for over 30 years and I can say, 'No, not everyone in Britain has got talent.' Believe me, I know. But it doesn't matter what I think. Slogans sell. We remember the slogans. We believe the slogans.

"Everyone remembers the original TV show from the seventies, that old git called Charlie who you never saw surrounded by beautiful women. Well, that's what this campaign will be. This old git called Charlie who you will never see surrounded by beautiful women. When you see these beautiful women in their pink T-shirts on the posters, you will check your breasts when you get home. Or you will check your partner's breasts. That's a great Saturday night after *Match of the Day* right there. Why did I ask these ladies? Because so-called footballers' wives often get a bad press. But take a look at these women here. We have six successful businesswomen, six talented women with great careers in their respective industries. Girls look up to them. Women look up to them. And now, I hope that when people think of, say, Nicola, they won't just think about all those great songs, they will also think about the importance of breast awareness."

Jason rose to his feet quickly.

"That's great, Charlie, it's a great campaign," he said hurriedly, peering across at the guy in the suit to make sure he wasn't headed off. "But some might question the timing. With your club struggling to meet its interest repayments, there is growing speculation that a hostile takeover from a Saudi consortium is imminent."

Charlie smiled and stared directly at Jason. He must be one of them, Charlie thought. And he's hit the panic button already. They've got nothing. I left that money in the hotel room. They've got nothing. They're asking desperate questions already. They've got nothing.

Charlie paused and exhaled deeply. He nodded his head in exasperation. He needed to look exasperated.

"Look lads, I know we're coming to the end of the season, which is always a time of speculation," he said slowly. "But I happen to be one of the few people to disagree with dear old Bill Shankly, god bless him. I don't think football is more than a matter of life of death. Breast cancer is still killing women and in the 21st century that is just unacceptable. So when you see the posters and ads for Charlie's Angels, don't think of me, or footballers' wives or even the game itself. Just think about breast cancer awareness and having regular checks done. That really can be a matter of life and death."

JASON watched the other journalists shuffle contentedly out of the press conference. Charlie the media master had given them what they wanted: enough boobs and bums to fill their pages for the week and a colour supplement on Sunday. Charlie had given him nothing. Jason expected as much, but that didn't make it any less painful.

Jason watched the last journalist leave the room and then checked over both shoulders. He was alone and didn't he just know it. He took out his phone.

"Yeah, it's me," he said. "You still down there? ... Yeah, I guessed as much ... What do you think? We got bugger all. No one's gonna question the timing now, not after being hypnotised by Jo's knockers. They all loved him when he was just a football manager. Now he's the man who cured cancer."

fourteen

LITTLE Steve couldn't decide if he should post another tweet to Nicola or not. He had already sent five and didn't want to come across as one of those irritating fans who lived at home with their mothers. Little Steve wasn't like that. He just loved Nicola. He knew Nicola. She never answered his tweets because she couldn't; she'd have to answer the tweets she received from the million other followers. But every time she saw Little Steve, she always made a point of telling him that she had read his tweets before leaving the house that day.

Ironically, Little Steve wasn't the biggest fan of Twitter. He thought it was a manipulative device for celebrities to control their fame and sell their latest shows, records and movies. They didn't even have to bother with the fans, didn't even have to meet and greet them. It was all there on Twitter. But Little Steve could hardly blame the celebrities. Some of the Twitterers were beyond pathetic. They were insane. He followed some of Nicola's fans and they were obsessed with celebrity, following anyone worth following. At Girl Power fan club meetings, Little Steve had been told by several Twitterers that they followed Stephen Fry even though they had no idea who he was. But the British actor did have lots of followers, so some of those followers might follow them, too. Little Steve also followed Stephen Fry, but he knew who Stephen Fry was. He was Melchett in *Blackadder*.

Little Steve only followed genuine celebrities, people he actually knew and admired. He wasn't jumping on any bandwagon. He sent tweets to most of them and he had yet to receive a direct reply, but he wasn't offended. They used Twitter to sell their products and he used Twitter to tell them how great they were. It was a means to an end for both of them.

But Nicola was the only celebrity he tweeted regularly. She had told him, on more than one occasion, that if she happened to be online and reading her messages when Little Steve's tweet came through, she would reply to it immediately. And he believed her.

So he decided to send her another tweet.

"It's me again," he typed. "Little Steve. Just wanted 2 c if u r there. U were g8 in Charlie's Angels, the best."

Little Steve sent his tweet and waited. He looked down at the clock on the corner of his laptop screen. It was late. She was probably having some dinner. He had time. Besides, he had to update his Girl Power blog.

AL-HAKIM gazed at the flat-screen TV in his hotel suite. Six beautiful women in tight pink T-shirts surrounding that ghastly old man; it was the most surreal image. But Charlie was right about one thing. They all looked like angels, except that Jo. She looked too much like a hooker. Al-Hakim didn't like his hookers to look like hookers. He didn't need to. He had money. But the other five were gorgeous. He'd have to organise a party on his yacht for all the players' families when he took over the club in the summer, and show them what real wealth was. Al-Hakim didn't have Cristiano Ronaldo's six pack or David Beckham's smile, but he always found that women in these circles still gravitated towards him. His yacht was worth more than Ronaldo and Beckham. Women in these circles usually ignored him until he had conducted a tour of his yacht. Women in these circles took their clothes off after he had conducted a tour of his yacht.

Al-Hakim checked his Cartier. Almost time to catch the jet. He was reluctant to leave London this time, which was unusual. He always enjoyed flying home, particularly when he had a couple of blondes to keep him company before he returned to his tedious world of eye slits and head dresses. He was proud of his religion, but it was awfully tiresome. He had the money to buy the finest box of chocolates in Saudi Arabia, but if he had to eat them with the wrappers on, what was the point?

Still, he could return to London in August as a football saviour, the English Premier League's great new hope. He could lead the world's greatest sporting league along the path to economic salvation. He wasn't much of a fan of the game itself; found it rather boring really, too few goals and not physical enough for his tastes, but it would take him away from property for a while. Being the English Premier League's great new hope had to be more fun than being the biggest property investor in Saudi Arabia.

London had greater pleasures. London had Nicola.

Al-Hakim stood up and gestured towards an assistant packing his luggage in another room.

"Get me Charlie on the phone," he barked.

The assistant picked up the phone and hurried over, dialling as he went. He handed Al-Hakim the phone.

"Are the girls going to be waiting for me on the plane?" Al-Hakim asked, putting it to his ear.

The assistant nodded quickly.

"Good, and make sure they are shaved like the last one. Call them if you have to, to check, I want them all shaved from now ... Ah, Charlie, how are you? ... I saw the press conference thing and it was wonderful ... No, no it is a great idea, a very good initiative. I think we should make them part of the club. That is a good idea. We are moving along quickly now with the deal, the lawyers are doing all the talking and we're moving ahead, thanks to you, Charlie. I won't forget that. And when I do take over, I want to take your initiative. I want Charlie's Angels to be our official club ambassadors ... Why not? It's great publicity. Let's have them at the first game of the season, eh? And we will have the official launch of our Charlie's Angels on my yacht ... No, no, no, it's no more than they deserve."

NICOLA bit into her toast and cringed. It was hard and cold. She wasn't the biggest fan of multigrain bread at the best of times, but her dietician had insisted on the rubbish. Nicola had pointed out, on many fruitless occasions, that she had lived on fry-ups with plenty of bubble and squeak and fried bread growing up in North London, and had never put on an ounce in weight, but it made no difference. She was a singer in Girl Power, and Girl Power singers were under the supervision of the dietician.

Nicola stared at the laptop screen as the latest messages from fans popped up in front of her. It was late, she was eating cold toast for dinner, she was alone, again, and in no mood to be sending notes out to her million followers. What did she have to say anyway? What could she say? She had spent the day with that dirty old man of a football manager—her husband's employer, her husband's biggest fan, her husband's paymaster—watching him grope that reality TV star.

What was she even doing at the same press conference as Jo?

Nicola could sing. Nicola could write the odd catchy melody and a few infectious lyrics when the mood took her. Her media appearances were usually shared with genuine talent, authentic artists; not a pneumatic, plastic fantastic tanning machine, the original brown girl in the ring.

Nicola loathed Jo, but not only for the obvious reasons. She instinctively knew that Jo might outlast her. Jo would outlast both her and Scott. Musical tastes would change; fans would grow up looking for something with more substance and fewer dance steps. Scott's mutinous legs would one day walk out on his football brain. Age could wither pop singers and footballers, but not reality TV stars. The most fake and manufactured people in Nicola's business would endure because the watching public perceived them as "real" people. Their winning personalities would prevail. Popular tastes would not give up on Jo; they would shape her. She was already busily working her way through the list, charting her course through the ever-changing directions of public opinion. Lad mag slut, *Page Three* boobs, semi-naked stunts on red carpets, joining forces with minor celebrities further up the food chain, marrying into the English Premier League, tell-all wife, devoted mother, career woman and reality TV star; Jo had signed off on all of them.

Now she was one of Charlie's Angels. That had to be worth a few photo shoots, some entertaining "ad-libbed" comparisons to Farrah Fawcett on her reality show and a few teary-eyed tales about friends with breast cancer. Jo would know someone somewhere who had succumbed to breast cancer. Jo always conjured a character she needed to reinvigorate her own storyline.

But Nicola didn't want to be a Charlie's Angel. Her management had told her not to put the tacky pink T-shirt on. Even her bandmates, who rarely spoke to her off stage these days, called her and said Girl Power shouldn't be doing humiliating shit like this anymore. Certain stunts had to be beneath them now. They had to play the fame game and this was too tabloid, too predictable and too footballers' wives. Venture too often into the world of footballers' wives, they had warned her, and you'd step out scratching yourself. Step down a rung and the impatient public—with that attention deficit disorder— would forget to let you back on the ladder.

Nicola had told the sceptics to fuck off. She was a footballer's wife because she had fallen in love with a footballer. And he had asked her to help out his manager and football club. And he had attended her gig at the Palladium, even if he didn't stop complaining while he was there. But he was there, and that was all that mattered.

But he wasn't here now. Nicola caught sight of the clock on her laptop screen. He was late again. Most days she accepted it. Boys would be boys, and the boys from Barking were inseparable, but he was taking the piss now. She had spent a day cheapening herself for a crude, disorganised campaign that had hurried cover-up written all over it for her husband, and now she was home alone promoting the event on Twitter and eating cold toast.

Nicola picked up her iPhone beside her laptop.

"Where are you?" she asked abruptly.

"I told you, I was popping out with some of the boys," Scott whispered down the phone.

"What's wrong with your voice? Why are you so faint?"

"I'm in a small drinking club full of plebs. I don't want anyone to hear my business."

"When are you coming home?"

"Soon, soon. About an hour or so."

"Well, hurry up. I don't want to be sitting here on my own promoting your career, while you're out getting pissed."

"I'll just finish my beer and I'll be off."

Scott dropped the phone beside him and looked down at Jo's head bobbing up and down between his thighs. He grabbed Jo's head by her black roots and gently lifted her up to face him. She smirked up at him.

"You couldn't stop while I was on the phone," he said, grinning down at her.

"I didn't stop because you were on the phone," she replied.

"Why?"

"I like to make sure you always remember where you are."

Jo kissed him repeatedly. Scott groaned.

"There's no chance of forgetting that, babe," he quavered.

"Bloody right there isn't. I only play in the Premier League, you know that."

Scott laughed loudly. It was an awful line. But as he looked down at Jo's head bobbing up and down between his thighs, it seemed hilarious.

LITTLE Steve had waited one hour and 27 minutes for a reply from Nicola. A response was unlikely now, but not out of the question. Nicola posted most of her messages between 9 pm and 11 pm, so there was still a little time left. She was usually very efficient and consistent in her updates and Little Steve expected her to say something about the Charlie's Angels launch.

But Little Steve understood. The press conference wasn't Nicola's finest hour. She had looked uncomfortable standing beside that manager and that tart. Obviously, Nicola had done it for him. She was that kind of devoted, loyal person, but he didn't deserve it. He treated her like shit and was too handy with her at the Palladium. Yet she not only tolerated him; she protected him and supported his career. Little Steve found her behaviour so difficult to comprehend. She was so much more famous than he was. Her songs were popular in Europe, Australia and even the Far East; just about everywhere except America. He was just a footballer; apparently quite a decent one, according to the newspapers, but that didn't mean anything to Little Steve. He only read about her husband when he was in the front pages of the newspapers.

Out of respect for Nicola, Little Steve had always refrained from getting involved. It wasn't his place. But the Charlie's Angels thing had made life very difficult for him. It made him tell a little white lie, and he had never lied to Nicola. From the first time they met at her CD single launch at HMV, she had admired him for his honesty and had always insisted on it. He had kept his side of the bargain, and their relationship had blossomed as a result.

But today, he had lied and he had to put that right. Little Steve clicked on the Twitter message box.

"Sori, Nicola," he typed quickly. "But u r 2 talented. U do not need to do that stuff 2day. U did OK, but u r better than that."

He suspected that Nicola might be shocked by the honesty, but he had to tell the truth. He loved her and would do anything to protect her.

Little Steve sent the message and waited.

fifteen

SCOTT picked up the voice recorder on the canteen table and moved it towards himself. He smiled warmly at the fat reporter sitting opposite, trying to tuck his ill-fitting Ben Sherman in behind his bulging belt.

"I'll move your gizmo thing closer," Scott said. "Make sure the interview comes out clearer for you."

Scott always opened his one-one-one or roundtable interviews with this little routine. It came from Charlie. The sly old dog had insisted on the spiel, said it never failed. Fuss over the hack, Charlie always said. Make him feel welcome, make him believe he's wanted, that you want nothing more than to answer questions you've answered 50 times before, that you'd much rather listen to him ramble on about your England chances than play 18 holes with Jimmy and Ross. Check if his voice recorder works. If it's an old tape recorder because the guy writes for the Mickey Mouse gazette, remind him to turn the tape over, particularly if he's young and gone all star struck after the first five minutes. Get him a drink. If he's a fat bastard, buy him a pork pie. If it's in the canteen at the training ground, it's free anyway. If it's not, claim it back.

Most of all, Charlie had told Scott, convince the little scribbler that you actually give a shit. The hack was your conduit, your link, to the muppets in the cheap seats. The reporter would get you a new contract, a contract extension, an extra 20 grand a week, a club player of the year trophy, an England call-up and a new club. Not only would he do all of this willingly, he might even pay you for the privilege. The English Premier League was an exclusive club for good reason. Only the footballers belonged. The hacks and the punters simply paid for the party and tidied up afterwards.

Scott needed Charlie's little box of media tricks today because he didn't give a shit. He didn't fancy this interview. He never did, but he was particularly reluctant to do this one. The groin injury was still niggling away at him and his antics with Jo were hardly helping matters. In truth, he was using the groin injury as an excuse. He was off his game, only slightly; no one had yet noticed, not even Charlie, but his anticipation and reading of the play hadn't been quite up to the mark. It was barely perceptible—he certainly didn't expect the plebs to notice, a few handclaps and a kiss of the badge always pacified the mob—but he wasn't fully focused. Having Jo wrapped around the old knob three times a week did that to a footballer. Scott was doing the one thing with Jo that he never did around the penalty box. He was taking too many chances.

"So will that work better for you, mate," he reiterated, perhaps overdoing the fawning with the fat hack.

"Yeah, that's lovely, Scott, it's fine. Call me Jason."

Jason had to admire Scott's bullshit. He almost sounded like he wanted to be here. Jason had less of an inclination to play sycophant than Scott did, but there was nothing left to lose.

"All right, Jason. Let's crack on," Scott said, gently pointing out that he was directing the interview.

"Yeah, sure, thanks for the time, Scott. I know this is the busy time of your season. Do you still think you have a chance of making the Europa League?"

"It'll be tough now. But at the end of the day, anything could happen, couldn't it? I'd like to do it for the fans. They do it every week for us—week in, week out—and they deserve a run in Europe. If we go out there and give 100 per cent every week, then hopefully the results will take care of themselves."

Even by Scott's lofty standards, that was a lot of clichés in a couple of sentences. Scott loved throwing in as many clichés as possible during interviews. Some footballers used them because they were thick. Scott used them because they killed time and revealed nothing.

"Ah, you've still got a chance," Jason reassured. "Anyway, I'm not sure if the club told you or not, but I'm doing a profile on English Premier League club captains for our network's magazine."

"Yeah, they told me, I think it's great."

"How does it feel to be captain?"

"It's an honour. It's something I never take for granted. There's a tingle every time I pull up the armband. If you go down the years, the likes of Bobby Moore, Bryan Robson, Tony Adams, Stuart Pearce and John Terry, those are some great players, great characters and great captains. They were quality, pure and simple, and you've gotta respect that. They are people to look up to, to aspire to be."

"It's funny you mention those guys because they all captained England at some stage. Did you know that of all the club captains currently playing in the English Premier League, you are the only one not to be capped for your country?"

"No, I didn't know that," Scott replied, genuinely surprised. "You really know how to make a man's day, don't ya?"

Jason blushed as he laughed.

"No, no, I was looking at it from a positive point of view. It's a good omen. I think it's only a matter of time before you get the call-up."

"That's not my decision to make. At the end of the day, I'll just keep going out there and giving 100 per cent for the fans and the manager every week. It's all about getting the three points, week in and week out. Anything after that is a bonus."

"You mention the fans there, do you think it's been hard for them, all this constant speculation that the club could be sold to a Middle Eastern consortium?"

Jason had given up on subtlety. He was bored. There was no hard evidence linking Scott to Jimmy, Charlie and the takeover bid. But Scott was club captain. He was Jimmy's best mate and Charlie's favourite player, and Tom and Jason had run out of ideas. They had decided to do something, anything, before Jonathan came downstairs to pull the plug. Interviewing Scott on the off chance that he might inadvertently let something relevant slip seemed like a good idea at the time. It didn't now.

"Well, I don't know any more about that other than what you guys tell me in the media," Scott replied, repeating a practised line. "It doesn't really matter to most players who pays their wages. Our only focus is on the next game. At the end of the day, that's the only thing we really have any sort of control over. We can only go out and give 110 per cent every week. The fans have a right to expect that."

"You seem to mention the fans a lot," Jason quipped, stifling a yawn.

"Let's be honest, mate, without the fans, me and you would be unemployed. The fans at this club are incredibly loyal. I mean, take Twitter. I didn't get it at first. Couldn't work it out. Then I get on there and before you know it I've got something like half a million fans or followers or whatever they're called. So I update it regularly, tell them about the upcoming matches and stuff. A lot of these followers are kids so it's great to interact with them ... in fact, Tom!"

Scott shouted towards the empty canteen counter. Tom pushed the kitchen swing door and walked briskly towards Scott's table, wiping his hands on his apron.

"All right, Scott," Tom said warmly.

"I'm fine. This is Jason, doing an interview with him."

"All right mate," Tom nodded quickly, barely looking at Jason.

Jason nodded back and then adjusted the jacket on the back of his chair. The trick was always to say as little as possible.

"I was just telling Jason about the Twitter," Scott said. "How many followers do we have now, Tom?"

"Er, it must be close to more than half a million now."

"You see, that's extraordinary. We only get 40,000 in the stadium. These guys are coming in from all over the world. Here you go."

In a grand gesture of benevolence, Scott took out his iPhone theatrically and handed it slowly to Tom.

"There you go, Tom," Scott said generously. "Let's say, 'tricky game this week, up at Sunderland, but one we must win if we are serious about the Europa League.'"

"Yeah, sure, you want me to do it here?"

"Nah, it's all right. Just do it in the kitchen. Bring it back when you're finished."

Scott waved him away regally and looked at Jason.

"Sorry about that. Now, where were we?"

CHARLIE stirred his milky sweet tea and watched Scott bullshit that journalist. Charlie had given his usual canteen table, front and centre, to Scott for the interview. Ordinarily, that was Charlie's table. From the main door, the side door and the kitchen counter, Charlie's table was always in view. Charlie liked to be omnipresent within his kingdom, but today he needed to watch, not be watched.

Clearly, they were clutching at straws. The only journalist to answer a genuine, probing question at the Charlie's Angels farce, the only hack to bring up the towelheads' deal, turns up at the training ground a week later to do a fluff piece on the club captain. These kids were either insulting Charlie's intelligence, or they had no place left to go. Charlie figured it had to be the latter. Reporters who had insulted Charlie's intelligence in the past usually went home with nothing worthwhile in their cameras.

The hack was a professional. Charlie had to give him that. The temptation to peer over at Charlie must have been overwhelming, but he hadn't looked over once. And Charlie hadn't taken his eyes off him.

Charlie sipped his tea and noticed Jimmy stroll into the canteen, nodding and waving to his clients as he sashayed his way through the chairs and tables. The movement was still there. For a moment, Charlie saw Jimmy with a ball at his feet again and he immediately castigated himself. Charlie had no time for nostalgia. He left that to his old teammates, earning 500 quid a night telling stories about him to misty-eyed punters after their chicken and chips.

"Where have you been?" Charlie hissed as Jimmy sat down opposite him. "I wanted you here for the interview with Scott."

"I am here," Jimmy whispered.

"That interview started over 10 minutes ago. Where you been?"

"Ah, Ross is on to me for money again."

"What now? We've just given him a new deal."

"Yeah I know, it's the usual thing."

Charlie leaned towards Jimmy and pointed directly at his face.

"I've told you about this before. You're his agent. Keep him out of those fucking cesspits in Mayfair."

"It's not just that. I actually think he's been winning lately. She's giving him aggravation at home, always on at him for more money."

"Ah, for fuck's sake. Doesn't she make enough? That's the trouble with these kinds of women; they are too high maintenance. I've been telling you boys that right from the start."

"Hey, come on, Charlie, that's personal."

"Not when it starts affecting my team, it's not."

Jimmy went to say something, but thought better of it. Instead, he twisted the lid on his mineral water bottle and swigged. He exhaled deeply and grinned widely.

"Here, we are having one hell of a result with your angels. They want photo shoots, exclusive interviews and campaigns, the lot, all of them. I've had *The Sun*, the *Star* and most of the Sundays on the phone. It's quality, it's all quality. They want to come in on the campaign, they want the pink T-shirts for their readers, whatever we want, basically."

"They are good boys most of them, known them since they were making tea for Murdoch's Aussie brigade back in the eighties. I've looked after them ever since. They're not doing me any favours here. I've given more exclusives than any other manager since Clough. They had better come through for me on this one. I've paid for their champagne and private dances at every shit hole in the West End."

"Well, whatever you did, it's working."

Charlie sipped his tea and looked up at Jimmy, shaking his head ruefully. His agent was still dreadfully callow and unaware when it came to understanding the mechanics behind their game.

"Of course, it's working," he said abruptly. "As I've told you many times before, the top football anthem isn't *Three Lions* or

You'll Never Walk Alone or *I'm Forever Blowing Bubbles.* Do you know what it is?"

"What?"

"It's *Get Your Tits Out For the Lads.*"

Jimmy choked on his mineral water.

"Ah, leave off," he croaked, wiping his mouth on his sleeve.

"Look, Sunderland could turn us over 10-0 this weekend, the punters will be calling us every name under the sun, but if they go home on Saturday night and get their end away, then suddenly the world's a brighter place, just as it will be for the players and the journalists if they all get a good shag after the game. It's all tits and arse in the end. I'm telling ya, *Get Your Tits Out For the Lads* should be the national anthem."

"You're off your head," Jimmy laughed.

"No I'm not," Charlie whispered.

Charlie watched Tom collect Scott's phone. He sipped his tea as Tom made his way back to the kitchen.

Charlie lifted his cup suddenly above his head.

"Tom ... Here, Tom," he shouted. "Bring us another cup of milky sweet tea, mate."

Charlie watched Tom put down his tea. Charlie watched Tom take his empty cup and pile it onto a tea tray. Charlie watched Tom wipe the tea stains off the table. Charlie watched and waited for Tom to make eye contact. Tom glanced up and met Charlie's gaze. Tom smiled briefly and continued to wipe the table. Charlie wanted to play poker. They always wanted to play poker with Tom. The BNP fascists, the video-making jihadists, the militants in the mosques, the football hooligans and even rival undercover reporters—they all wanted to play poker with Tom. But Tom never revealed his hand.

"How's it going, Tom?" Charlie asked, stirring his tea, staring at Tom, always staring at Tom.

"Yeah, fine, thanks, Charlie."

"Family doing all right?"

"Yeah, yeah, the two little ones are driving me mad. My little girl is into everything, drawing and colouring. I go home and there's felt-tip pen drawing all over the walls."

"I know what you mean," Jimmy interjected. "They get into everything, don't they? I'm always going home and scrubbing the walls."

No, you're not, Tom thought, you have cleaners for that stuff and your baby girl is too young, but that's OK. We're all playing a role here.

"How do you find the job here, Tom?" Charlie asked, sipping his tea, staring at Tom, always staring at Tom.

"Yeah, it's a good job. It's a great job. I used to sit in the stands watching half the guys in the canteen, now I chat with them every day."

"Where were you working before?"

"Bow Street Caterers."

Charlie eyeballed Jimmy, examining his face. Tom rebuked himself. The answer was too quick, too rehearsed. It was a minor slip, but one that the old bastard might pick up on.

"I've never heard of them before. Bow Street? That's only up the road really from where I grew up, down the old District Line on the tube, I'm surprised I've never heard of them."

"They cater for mostly private stuff, marquees, parties, VIP stuff, it was my granddad's firm," Tom said casually.

"Really? Your granddad?"

"Yeah, he was a self-made man. He came out of the War, started a greasy spoon café in East London called Bow Snack Bar and ended up with half a dozen of them. That's when he started up Bow Street Caterers to do the big events."

"That sounds impressive," Charlie said, nodding his approval.

More importantly, the story sounded authentic. Tom always told the truth whenever possible. His old granddad *had* run the Bow Snack Bar. Tom had worked there as a kid, spending Saturday mornings cleaning tea-filled ashtrays and looking at exposed, spotty arses sticking through the backs of plastic chairs. It was the truth, and the truth was enough for Charlie's amateur lie detector test.

"Yeah, he did well my granddad."

"A self-made bloke from the East End. He sounds just like me. Here Tom, before you go, you remember that phone call you took for me the other week? The one from the Arab guy?"

In these rare moments, Tom begrudgingly admired Charlie and acknowledged his talent. That was really good. Go overboard with a compliment, pander to the ego and kick off the inquisition while Tom's still digesting the fact that the football legend had thrown him an unexpected bone. Charlie was possibly a more accomplished, certainly more experienced, poker player than Tom. But Tom had a single advantage. Tom had truth on his side.

"Which one was that, Charlie? To be honest, I answer calls for you all morning."

"Yeah, I know. That's the trouble with this job, never off duty. The cheeky bastards should call the secretary, but they know I'm here most of the time with the players so they get me here. I can't even have a cup of milky sweet tea without Fergie calling up and trying to pinch one of my academy boys."

"Yeah," Tom muttered.

"He even tried to pinch you, didn't he Jimmy, until I put my foot down," Charlie boomed.

"That was a long time ago," Jimmy replied softly.

"Yeah, Fergie's always calling here," Charlie continued. "Wenger doesn't call too much anymore because most of my team are English and he's not interested. He's got no dosh anyway. Can't buy bugger all until they sell all those wanky apartments at Highbury, criminal what they did to that old stadium, bloody no respect for history and tradition, all about the pound notes with Wenger. Great coach, but tighter than a duck's arse. No, I'm talking about the Arab guy who called, who said he worked for Mr Al-Hakim?"

"Oh, yeah, yeah, I remember that one now, a couple of weeks or so ago, I think," Tom answered.

"Yeah, that'd be right. You got me straight after training, it'd been pissing down all morning and I'd screamed myself hoarse telling Ross he's supposed to shoot between the fucking posts. Do you remember how that phone call came about?"

Charlie sipped his tea slowly and glared at Tom over the top of his cup. Tom continued to pretend to recollect. Charlie's elaborate, convoluted name-dropping diversions were helping him. It was easier to feign gullibility; a certain inoffensive ignorance that had always served Tom well.

"Er, not really. I was out in the back, the phone rang and a guy just asked to speak to you, said he was with the guy Al that you mentioned. So I called you over."

"Did he say anything else to you?"

"What about?"

"I don't know, anything, really."

"I can't really remember ... I don't think so. He just asked to speak to you and that was it."

Charlie and Jimmy looked up at Tom. He glimpsed down at both of them. He had to say something. They were both staring at him. His reaction would be unnatural if he didn't respond to the staring.

"Is everything OK? Did I do something wrong?"

He looked genuinely worried because he was genuinely

worried. If the opportunity presents itself, let the real emotions play out.

"No, no, Tom, it's all fine. I just wanted to check if the guy had left any other message for me. It's OK. I'll give him a bell later."

Charlie downed the last of the tea dregs. He held the cup up for Tom to take, just to reiterate the power structure in their relationship.

"Here, you might as well get me another cup of milky sweet tea while you're there, mate."

"Bloody hell, Charlie, that's your third one in a row," Jimmy exclaimed.

"Yeah, I know. But Tom makes a blinding cup of milky sweet tea, don't you Tom?"

Tom nodded and turned, and headed towards the kitchen.

"It must be all that tea training he got from his granddad," Jimmy muttered.

Tom slammed the tea tray down on the kitchen side. He peered through the serving hatch at Charlie and Jimmy. They were laughing. They were laughing at Tom; Tom the fucking tea boy. He looked across to the left of the canteen and watched Scott gesturing wildly and pontificating about the wondrous joys of playing in front of his cherished fans. Tom noticed Jason taking down some of Scott's quotes. He wasn't taking them down properly, in the manner expected of a journalist who intended to use them in a story, but Tom couldn't be angry with Jason. Scott wouldn't notice, and Tom accepted that Jason was wasting his time and knew it. Tom was wasting his time. That nauseating milky sweet tea-swigging Cockney monster was about to make a killing on the takeover, along with his wide boy sidekick, and Tom and Jason could only watch. Quite literally, they could only sit back and watch in the club canteen.

Scott's phone beeped.

Tom had forgotten all about Scott's phone and cursed under his breath. Apart from making another cup of sugary, pissy tea for the son of a second-hand car salesman, he had to send Twitter messages to "the plebs" on behalf of captain cliché.

He looked down at the phone. Scott had received a text message. He picked it up and headed for the kitchen door, but then he stopped and turned back. If he gave Scott the phone now, he'd only get a bollocking later for not doing his Twitter updates. He had nothing to gain from giving the phone back now. And he really didn't have anything left to lose.

Tom stood in front of the serving hatch. He saw Charlie and Jimmy plotting their next bung. He saw Scott rambling on about the people who wore expensive jerseys with *his* name on their backs—his name—and yet he treated them like fucking pests. When Tom was a kid, footballers and fans still mixed together. English First Division stars turned up at family charity days at the local non-league football club or golf club and signed autographs—for free—until their hands ached. They were real footballers; real people; real men. Scott and his brethren stood behind red ropes and drug-dealing doormen and had fans swatted away at every opportunity. Thousands of supporters worshipped Scott and chanted his name when he ran to them at the end of every game and kissed the club badge. But Scott had no fans. He only had "plebs" who pestered him for mobile phone photos when he was in restaurants or filling up the Ferrari with petrol.

Tom's thumb hovered over the phone's touch screen. No more listening to Scott slag off the supporters every morning. Tom unlocked Scott's phone. No more listening to special agent Jimmy brainwash another ingenuous apprentice. Tom scrolled down to the inbox. No more listening to everyone's favourite beloved manager argue over his percentage.

Tom took one final, tentative look through the serving hatch. *Fuck you, Scott. Fuck the lot of you.*

Tom opened the message.

The message was from J.

The message read: "He's gonna be late again. Casino. So no excuses. I want you inside me in one hour."

Tom felt his stomach muscles tighten. He took a sharp intake of breath and exhaled slowly. He had to move quickly, had to stay calm, had to stay focused. He pulled his orders notepad out of his apron pocket and scribbled down the number. J's number. He peeked through the serving hatch. Good. The interview was still going. Tom considered sending a text message to Jason to keep him talking, keep him bullshitting for another couple of minutes, but there was no time. Besides, Tom would be finished by then. He craned his head around the serving hatch. Charlie caught his gaze. Tom tried to pull his head back in, but it was too late. *Shit, fuck, shit!*

"Where's my milky sweet tea," Charlie bellowed across the canteen. The apprentices looked up instinctively. Charlie had spoken.

"It's coming Charlie," Tom shouted back, scanning the canteen quickly, waiting for the kids to return to their chicken breasts. "I'm just brewing up a fresh pot now. The old stuff was too stewed."

"Yeah, all right," Charlie cried. "I bet your granddad didn't take this long to make a pot of tea."

Tom smiled weakly and heard the arse-licking Jimmy laugh loudly. *Ha fucking ha.* Tom glanced across at Scott and Jason. Nothing. No reaction. Jason still had his interviewee lost and isolated in Scott's world. Tom pulled his head back in and turned the kettle on. He really had forgotten all about the milky sweet bloody tea. He took out Scott's phone and scrolled through his numbers. He found 'Nic'. There was no other 'Nic' in the address book, other than 'Nic – home' and 'Nic – mobile'. He checked both numbers. They didn't match his scribbling in the notepad. They were different numbers.

They were different numbers.

Tom saw his left hand take out his own mobile phone. He noticed that he was dialling quickly, dialling the number in his notepad. He realised that he was listening to the ringing tone, waiting for someone to answer. He worked out that the noise was his heart pounding through his chest.

"Hello, who is it?"

It was her voice. It was the voice of J. It was not Nicola's voice. It was the voice of J. It was not Nicola's voice. There was only one J in Scott's address book. There was only one J.

"Yeah, hello, is that Jo?"

Tom's voice was breaking. His throat had dried up.

"Yeah, it's Jo. Who is it?"

Tom saw himself hang up the phone.

sixteen

JASON pushed the papers across the table. Jonathan caught them under his hand and looked up at Jason. He sighed.

"Read them, just read them," Jason said, stubbing the top of the papers with his forefinger.

"I've read them before," Jonathan replied quietly and slowly.

Jonathan cast his eyes on the framed documentary awards on the wall behind Jason. Those documentaries belonged to another time, another audience, another country. They were cutting-edge documentaries. Now they were quaint relics from an earlier golden age of television.

"Read them again, read this bit," Jason persisted. "Read this bit here. The bit about St John's Ambulance, can you see that? Do you know what St John's Ambulance does?"

Jason knew what St John's Ambulance did. He had been a willing volunteer. Thirteen years old, self-conscious and uncertain, he had never been more proud than the day he was handed a St John's Ambulance uniform for the first time. He had taken part in all the accident scene simulations. He had loved the day trips to the countryside, playing a "victim" in a Hertfordshire barn, being covered in fake blood and acting out the symptoms for his particular ailment. Most of all, he had loved puking up the fake vomit all over Heather Smith as she attended to his "injuries". No one had liked Heather Smith at school.

Jason had completed all the simulations, attended the first aid classes and passed every test. He was an advanced first aider who knew how to use an automated external defibrillator. Then he had been handed the uniform and the match fixture; his first match fixture. He had polished his black shoes three times the night before, dressed in the mirror, checked and rechecked his first aid box, even practised what he might say to the fans; the ones squashed behind the fences, the kids with bruised ribs after crowd surges. He even mimed running along the touchline holding his end of the stretcher as the crowd roared its approval.

In the end, the clash between Enfield and Barking FC proved to be something of an anti-climax. There were no serious injuries. There was hardly anyone at the game. No one had told him that the Essex Senior Football League didn't attract big crowds. The only wound of the night came when Jason accidentally scalded himself, collecting a cup of tea for Old Man Bill, his St John's Ambulance partner. Old Man Bill had been working the football stadiums around Greater London, Essex and Hertfordshire since just after the War. Jason loved spending time around Old Man Bill, listening to his stories about treating a young Jimmy Greaves or an impudent Charlie George, giving them the old magic sponge and seeing them on their way, and sharing a fag with Greaves at half-time. Jason had never been sure if half of Old Man Bill's stories were even true, but he always enjoyed hearing them.

When Jason thought of football today, he still saw himself sitting beside Old Man Bill, checking his first aid box and tapping his foot against the handle of the stretcher. He had never really attended any of the matches at the highest levels, unlike Old Man Bill, but that didn't matter. At the non-league matches, fans handed him cups of tea and Bovril over the whitewashed wall and the club gave him and Old Man Bill a pie at half-time. Jason had never felt so welcome, so needed.

But those days were gone. They were part of another simpler century. This is the modern world. It was there in front of him in black and white.

"Look at those figures closely," Jason continued.

"I told you, mate, I've seen them," Jonathan said firmly.

"They owe St John's Ambulance almost five grand, five bloody grand. They can't even pay a bunch of volunteers a few quid to keep an eye on the fans with their first aid boxes."

"That's the English Premier League. What do you want me to do?"

"But it's human interest. You said you wanted human interest. This is human interest. Look at this. According to the last audit, the club owes almost 150 million, right? And yet Charlie is still paying huge fees in image rights to players signed by Jimmy, players who barely played for the club, players who are not even at the club anymore. It's crazy."

"It's disgraceful. It's immoral. It's obscene. It's the modern game," Jonathan replied irritably. "But that doesn't make it good TV, does it? There are stories like this on the *Guardian* website every day. How many hits do they get online? You read the story. I read the story. Regular *Guardian* readers read the story. They post their educated, indignant reactions underneath the story. That's it. A hooker sells her story about shagging half of Manchester United and the story tops every news website in the country. What do you want me to say?"

"But this is beyond the pale, Jon. Look at this here, right. They owe St John's Ambulance almost five grand, five poxy grand. So what? Tough shit. If the club goes into administration, St John's will be lucky to get any of that back. They even owe the fan club almost £1,500, the bloody fan club. They are spreading their legs and shitting on their own fans; their own fucking fans. They don't really have to give anything back, look, because these poor sods are listed as unsecured 'ordinary' creditors.

"And here's the best part. This is the part that blows your mind. Look how much they owe to players. Look at this bastard here. He left the club last August, a shocking striker, hardly got a game. But thanks to a deal negotiated by Jimmy, the club owe him two million in image rights, it's insane. And they will have to pay the cash to his registered tax haven in the bloody Virgin Islands. They can't pay the kids and pensioners working voluntarily for St John's Ambulance, but they can top up a millionaire's nest egg in the Virgin Islands."

"Well, if they go into administration, they won't be able to pay him either, will they?"

"But they will. That's the point. They've got no choice. Any transfer fees and outstanding wages must be paid in full. It's English Premier League and the Football Leagues' rules. If they don't pay, they can't continue as a club, in either league, so they'll pay all right. If the Saudi guy comes in, the first thing he will do, the first thing he will have to do, is pay all these players their outstanding money, these multi-millionaires, they must get every penny. St John's Ambulance will be told to get fucked, the poor sods sitting there on wooden benches with their first aid boxes, freezing their balls off in February will be told to piss off, but at least the players will get that extra zero in their bank accounts."

Jason leaned back on his chair and clenched his jaw. He had always been hot-headed, but the audit had really pushed his buttons. He wanted to throw the fucking thing out the window.

Jonathan flicked through the pages of the audit. "I know what you're saying, of course I do," he said. "But how do I put this on TV?"

"It's there. It's all there in black and white. You've got the human drama. You can't pay the poor St John's Ambulance kid holding the plasters and the bandages his bus fare home, but you can pay Charlie five million quid a year. The audience will lap that stuff up. We've got all that footage of Jimmy and Charlie together. We've got Charlie at the hotel. I even got fresh footage at the training ground this morning."

Jonathan looked surprised.

"Did you? Why did you do that?"

"Oh, I don't know. We had nothing to lose, did we? We thought we might as well get some footage of Jimmy and Charlie talking together in the training ground for the voiceover. It was pretty decent too, had the camera in my jacket on the back of the chair. Had to sit through a piss poor interview with their captain to get it, but at least it's there now."

"Did he say anything?"

"Scott? No nothing. What do you expect? A load of clichés about how he wanks over his fans, nothing of any value, knew nothing about the Saudi consortium, or he said he didn't; a waste of time really."

"Did he mention Nicola at all?"

Jason rubbed his face in the palm of his hand.

"Ah, we're not going down that path again, are we? Yes, he mentioned Nicola. He said she was a great wife and mother, but she's working part-time at the club, doing the accounts and keeping two sets of books; one in the office and the other one in her knickers. Of course, he didn't mention Nicola. Fucking hell, Jon."

"Now look, I'm not the bad guy here. But you know the new directive, you've read the e-mails. It's gotta be more commercial, more mainstream and yes, all right, more fucking celebrity. We're in the news business, but the business just isn't real news anymore.

You don't like it. Tom doesn't like it. And I don't like it. We can all not like it all the way to the dole queue because if our department is even still here in three years I'll be amazed."

"So, what are you saying, no more documentaries?"

"I don't know what I'm saying. I don't know what's gonna happen. But the way things are at the moment, unless they sack Charlie and replace him with Russell Brand, I don't know what the public interest is going to be."

CHARLIE watched Jimmy sip the wine. He anticipated the reaction, the awe and compliments in quick succession. He waited for the refined appreciation, but it never came. Jimmy sipped from the wine a second time and stared at some papers on Charlie's desk.

"Not a big fan of the wine, then?" Charlie asked, clearly disgruntled.

"No, it's all right, nice drop, Charlie," Jimmy enthused, but not convincingly.

Charlie leaned across his mahogany desk and rolled his eyes at Jimmy. These kids, these fucking uncouth, uncivilised kids, he thought. They grew up on the same council estate as Charlie, practically next door, but they had no social aspirations, no desperate search for the next rung on the ladder. Crass had replaced class. For Charlie's generation, nothing else mattered. Everyone was in the same boat. They all wanted to be a different class. They all clamoured to get off at the next stop on the line, move a little further east along the District Line, away from the London boroughs and their red brick giveaways, towards the Essex countryside and their green paddocks, gated communities and gravel driveways. It was all about small steps, making inroads, moving through the postcodes, hanging out the Shangri-La signs and playing the pyramid game all the way to the top. These kids thought the pyramid game was obsolete. They didn't bother with social structures anymore. There were only two classes now: those who had money and those who didn't. Jimmy had money, shit loads of it, probably more than Charlie, but he had no class. Thatcher really had created a classless society; classless, but tasteless.

"It's not a nice drop, it's not a nice drop at all," Charlie insisted. "Spend a fiver at Tesco and you'll get a nice drop, a bottle of Jacob's Creek and a bag of peanuts. This isn't a nice drop. This is the finest glass of wine you'll ever hold to your lips in your life."

"Yeah, it's really nice."

"No, it's not. Strawberries and cream are nice. This is a Romanée-Conti, vintage 1978. I got this in an auction, phone bid, cost me a small fortune."

"It's really good, Charlie."

Charlie sighed in exasperation.

"Look at that photo up there."

Charlie pointed to the framed black-and-white photograph of himself on the wall behind Jimmy. Jimmy sipped his wine and turned to examine the blown-up photograph, lit up softly by an overhanging light. In the photograph, a teenage Charlie was shaking hands with a middle-aged man with oily hair parted down the middle. Charlie was beaming in the photograph, his short back and sides opening up his handsome face, revealing his impish grin. He was happy, deliriously happy. He was standing in the same office—Charlie's office—he was leaning across the same mahogany desk—Charlie's desk—the oily-haired bloke was sitting in the same leather chair—Charlie's chair.

Charlie's office; Charlie's desk; Charlie's empire.

"I was 15 in that photo," Charlie said proudly.

"Yeah, I know, Charlie."

"It was the happiest day of my life. When I signed on as an apprentice, my dad took me up the road to the nearest fish and chip shop, a proper fish and chip shop, not just an old takeaway with a bit of ropey cod shrivelled up in the glass cabinet; a proper place, knives and forks, napkins, waitresses, everything. I had plaice and chips, my old man had rock and chips and he bought me a cup of milky sweet tea, freshly made out of the urn, never tasted tea like it, still haven't. I was just finishing up when my old man said I had a chance. I had a real chance. That's all he said. I had a real chance. He didn't say what, but I knew what he meant. He meant I didn't have to sit in that fucking armchair and moan at the TV all day. He spent his whole life arse-licking punters in the car lot and he never owned his own car. Can you believe that? He never owned his own car. He was a light ale man his whole life, a rock and chips man. And now I'm sitting here drinking a bottle of Romanée-Conti worth more than 20 grand. I had a chance and I took it. Without that chance, I'm fuck all. Without that chance, that kid in the photo doesn't sign to play in the First Division. That kid in the photo signs ownership papers for other people so they can drive out of his dad's car lot with an Austin 1100."

Charlie's red face betrayed his anger as he sipped his expensive wine. Jimmy stared at his former manager and mentor and wondered what to say.

"Yeah, I know that, Charlie," he muttered.

"So these TV wankers have got no chance if they think they can take all this away from me now. I've worked too fucking long, too many years, too many relegation battles and fights with the chairman to come this far and have it taken away by a couple of soppy kids running around with video cameras."

"Yeah, I know, Charlie, but it's not over yet. They could still go public. Al-Hakim's people haven't finished going through the books yet. What if they find something?"

"What are they going to find? What are they going to learn? That we're skint? We've been telling the towelheads that from day one. That's why they're getting the club so bloody cheap in the first place. I spoke to one of his henchmen today and they're very happy. He's very happy. It's a done deal."

"But there are so many debts for them to clear."

"Ah, he'll take care of that out of his back pocket."

"I hope so. I hope it's settled up quickly too. If this TV documentary thing does come out before Al-Hakim takes over, he might get cold feet."

"What are they going to come out with? Me sitting in a hotel room and having a chat with one of the towelhead's mates? It was just a friendly chat with a bloke I thought was with the Arabs, mistaken identity, they all look the same in their dressing gowns anyway. I came in with nothing and I left with nothing."

"They might have other stuff, some of the players on my books."

"Which is all written down in black and white. They've got nothing. It's finished. They had their chance, but unlike me, they didn't take it. They fucked it up. It's over. We won. And by the end of the season, we'll have a new owner, a nice few bob and a chance to show the Big Four what I can really do with a decent budget. I'll show City that if you've got that much talent, you really should play with two strikers up front and you should be challenging for the title every fucking year. This club will show them all, don't you worry about that. So drink up. And this time, Jimmy, drink it properly. Savour the taste of luxury."

JONATHAN looked up at the clock on the wall. He was late. He had to attend a meeting on the latest round of redundancies. He suspected it was only a matter of time before he was handing them out to Jason and Tom—two of the most industrious, reliable reporters he'd ever known. Their work on the trainee jihadists in North London really had been exemplary. Now they were a misstep away from being sidelined. The Charlie investigation was a misstep. It wasn't a year ago, but it was now. That was the fickle, precarious business they worked in. English Premier League managers taking bungs was old hat. Find a manager who wasn't taking a backhander and there might be a story. Find a manager in the jungle willing to eat a kangaroo's testicle in a bushtucker trial on national television and there might be a story. Jonathan checked his watch.

"Look, mate, I can't keep going round in circles," Jonathan said finally. "I know what you have contributed. That's why we're still here. I have fought for this programme for months out of loyalty. You have delivered so many times for me before, but this one is beyond even me. I just can't sell them on the idea of a bent football manager in bed with his bent agent. It's been done before."

"But not on this scale," Jason pleaded.

Jonathan pushed his chair back and stood up.

"I'm sorry, Jason, I really am. But they want to cut their losses and pull the plug."

Jason glared up at Jonathan.

"You're joking, right?" he said.

"Sorry mate, but no. They said we've taken this as far as it can go. The sting failed, and we don't have enough content to fill an hour and Charlie's lawyers would rip us to pieces with what we have got."

"So three months of work, gone, just like that? Poor Tom making pasta and fucking chicken salads every day, it was all for nothing?"

"It wasn't my decision, Jason."

"You couldn't even wait for Tom to get here before you told us?"

"I've got to get to another urgent meeting."

"Oh, I'm fucking sorry to put you out."

Jason folded his arms and glanced over at the documentary awards hanging on the office walls. They meant nothing.

Jonathan saw Jason's anger and sighed. He had always liked Jason and Tom. They were committed and loyal, always dependable in the field. Jonathan sat down again.

"Look, Jason, we will make sure you and Tom are fully paid up for this project. I mean ..."

"Bollocks," Jason snarled.

Jonathan started to speak again, but the office door flew open, slamming against the office's glass partition. Tom stormed into the office, smiling manically and waving his mobile phone in the air.

"There is a god," Tom roared. "There is a fucking god!"

seventeen

ROSS scratched his stubble and examined his cards again. He had 14—a king and a four of diamonds. There were too many other picture cards on the table. There had been too many picture cards in the last hand. The dealer had him beat. With two cards, the croupier had him beat. Ross watched the croupier's hand hover over the shoe. The young bloke was better than competent. He was Asian. He was Asian-Chinese. He was practically unbeatable, just like the casino. The Palm Beach might be in Mayfair, but it was as Chinese as a plate of Singapore noodles. The Palm Beach catered to high rollers, because it was owned by Malaysian Chinese. The Palm Beach employed the finest croupiers, because it was owned by Malaysian Chinese.

Ross watched the scrawny Chinese kid. His hand still floated over the shoe, but not obtrusively. Ross smiled at him. He did not reciprocate. He had been well-trained. Ross recognised the training from the first hand of blackjack. The kid's handling and stacking of the chips and the way he lifted his card was pure class. An ant crawling under the dealer's hand wouldn't have been able to read his cards. But Ross fancied his chances. Too many picture cards had been drawn already, and there was a chance the dealer had another one. Ross scratched his stubble again and noticed a vase of orchids on a nearby coffee table. Flowers were a good idea.

He was late and well down on the night. A bunch of flowers were a shit peace offering, but they might get him through the door at least.

Ross felt the exclusive eyes of the other faces in the Gold Room on his cards. He knew some of the faces, by name or by sight. Like every VIP room in London, there were only three types: celebrities, Asians and mugs. Quite often, the punters might be both. Ross had met a couple of faces who were all three. Apart from Jimmy and Scott, Ross never came to the Gold Room with other footballers because they were all mugs, throwing their money about like it was the Romford dog track. They dropped thousands, but that wasn't always enough to pacify the Asian owners. Exclusivity and discretion were more important to their clientele than a couple of pissed English Premier League footballers dropping a few thousand on the roulette wheels. Some of the Asian businessmen and politicians that Ross had shared a blackjack table with spent more than his soppy mates fuelling their private jets. They could not afford to be recognised because some footballer had pissed in a plant pot, dropped a million quid and then cried for his mummy. Footballers attracted the paparazzi and those photographs reached stockholders and voters back in Asia, and that was never acceptable.

Ross had been in the casino the night that twat lost a million playing roulette and poker, a right fucking mug. A multi-millionaire in the England team and he was losing a million playing roulette and poker, right in front of all the major faces in London. Ross was appalled. Only a mug played roulette and poker; there were fewer angles, and the probabilities were harder to calculate. Ross was a striker. His game thrived on probability, anticipating the defender's turn, waiting for the keeper to make his move, looking for the angle. Ross' game wasn't one of bluff. It was one of calculation. And when he got it right, he scored. That other dick not only missed, but he broke down and cried like a child in front of the entire casino. The croupiers had never moved so fast to grab their phones. They were loyal to the casino, but they were also Asian. Their game was also one of calculation and probability. The tabloids simply paid more. Ross had barely enough time to cash in and slip into his car before the snappers arrived. He wasn't happy. The tabloid boys then staked out every decent casino in London for the next fortnight, and Ross was forced to stick with the horses, which didn't give anything like the same buzz.

Ross touched his finger softly against the table.

"Hit," he said finally.

The croupier slid a card out of the shoe and across the table to Ross in one brisk, fluid movement.

Ross inhaled and bit the inside of his lip. He paused before lifting the card. It wasn't a picture card. He knew that. But he had no way of knowing if it was going to be a high card. Ross lifted the corner of his card with his thumbnail.

Four of spades.

Ross had 18. He never reacted. He put his hand over his cards and gestured towards the scrawny Chinese kid in the bow tie. He was done. The croupier flicked over his card.

Seven of clubs.

He had to go again. Ross stole a glance at the croupier's passive face. Nothing. He was really good.

The croupier pulled himself another card and turned it over.

Nine of hearts.

The croupier never reacted. Ross never reacted. He heard some people laugh over his shoulder as the croupier counted out some chips and pushed them over.

Thirty thousand.

Ross now had about 65 grand in his stack, which was handy. He only had another 130 grand or so to claw back.

JONATHAN looked out at the twinkling lights of White City. The floodlights of Loftus Road glowed in the distance. Queens Park Rangers must be at home tonight, Jonathan thought. He stared at the floodlights. They were strangely hypnotic this evening. He saw them most nights, barely paying them any attention. But tonight, he was mesmerised by them, captivated. Football had been dead this afternoon, but the English Premier League had just been resuscitated. Jo had given the game the kiss of life.

Jonathan turned back to face Tom and Jason. It was late. All three had families to get home to, but no one wanted to leave.

"Well, this changes everything," Jonathan said.

"Of course, it does. We get our documentary back," Tom declared. "You wanted sex and sleazy celebrity and we got it for you. We're at home with Jo, mate. We can put the two together."

Jason frowned and sipped his coffee. He wasn't entirely convinced.

"We've got them, we've got the whole club now, corruption, bungs, aggressive takeovers, probably an illegal takeover, and the country's most famous celebrity banging their captain," Tom continued excitedly. "It's in the bag. The only thing we've got to worry about now is not what we put out, but when."

"I don't wanna be the prophet of doom or anything, but how are the two connected?" Jason asked.

Tom's eyes widened. He frowned at Jason and checked Jonathan's reaction.

"What are you on about? This is a massive story," Tom insisted.

"Yeah, I know it is," Jason agreed. "It's huge. But how does it really help us? Jo shagging Scott is wonderful, but it's not directly linked to our corruption story. It's just the same club. We've got no evidence to suggest either of them are involved with any of the backhanders."

"Jason's right," Jonathan said solemnly. "There is no direct connection between the two."

Tom looked up at the ceiling. He laughed in exasperation.

"So what are you saying is, you wanted celebrity shit, but now you don't want it," Tom said. "You just said it changes everything."

"It does change everything. We've just got to work out how," Jonathan reassured. "We're not *The Sun* or the *Daily Mirror*. This is not our thing, not directly anyway. But I agree with you, this is the breakthrough we've been looking for. I can get the green light for the documentary now, I suspect, we've just got to work out a way of using this stuff."

ROSS wiped his nose with the cuff of his shirts and sipped his lemon tea. Fucking lemon tea. He'd had the cold for over a week now. He'd told Charlie and the boys that there was a bug going around. They hadn't believed him. No one else in the dressing room had gone down with the flu. Besides, it was coming to the end of the season, and it was the wrong time of year to be coughing and sniffing. Charlie had nodded and smiled at Ross. He knew the score. Conditioned athletes didn't really pick up colds after Easter. Conditioned athletes getting by on three hours of sleep because they'd spent all night in the casino did start snivelling. Charlie had let it go this season, just as he had in previous seasons, because Ross had delivered for him on and off the pitch. He scored goals and kept up the banter in the dressing room. Every dressing room needed a class clown—the team practically insisted on it—and Ross had been happy to play the village idiot since primary school. There were no self-esteem issues because he had always been the good-looking one, both in school and in the dressing room. He could take it, so he could most certainly dish it out.

But the banter hadn't been forthcoming of late. That was the first sign. The slight dip in form came later. The moment Ross had stopped slashing tyres at the training ground and putting dog shit into the apprentices' boots, Charlie sensed something was awry. And Charlie needed Ross. Not only was he one of his revered Barking Boys, he also had a specific role to play. Scott was team leader, Jimmy took care of business and Ross was the class clown. Charlie took the crack in the dressing room extremely seriously. Happy campers went out and did the business at the weekend. Happy campers didn't ask questions. Every one of Charlie's squads had needed a class clown—he'd go out and sign one if there wasn't one—and Ross had been given the elevated position in the current team.

"I'll stick," Ross muttered to the croupier, wiping his nose again. He was sticking on 17, which was a beatable hand, but the head cold was playing havoc with his judgment. His nose kept tingling and his eyes were sore. Every time he sneezed, his eyes filled up and his blurred vision struggled to focus on the cards being dealt around the table.

The croupier turned over his second card. He had 18. The second card was always going to be a high card, but the constant sniffing was a distraction. Ross watched the croupier rake his chips in. That's another 20 grand to make back.

Ross checked the Rolex—Daytona, white gold, classy, thanks to Jimmy—and thought about phoning home. He glanced around the Gold Room, just the high rollers left now, mostly Asian businessmen and a couple of guys he recognised from the music industry. It was a quiet night. The regulars had already slipped out through the private exit and into the sobering, early morning air of Berkeley Street. But Ross was going nowhere. He had money to recover.

Ross pushed 30 grand across the table and admitted to himself that he was bullshitting. It wasn't about recovering money. He'd get it back eventually; a week in Vegas would take care of that. He had picked up $250,000 in one weekend at a blackjack table at the Wynn Casino. The money was a secondary concern. He was fucking around with his career. That England muppet who cried into the roulette wheel after dropping a million had at least made his point already. The Three Lions had already strutted across his chest. He'd been handed the England cap, seen the brass band march out at Wembley, sang the national anthem, savoured the goose bumps. He left the casino weeping about his mother finding out about the missing million, but what did he really have to sob about? He was an England player. The image rights could recoup a million within three months.

But Ross was running out of time to be an England player. Time was on his side, but form wasn't. He was knackered. He loved a night out, particularly with the boys, but she expected catwalk appearances, the nightclub stuff and movie premieres, and he no longer had the energy to say no. He had never turned her down. That had been his problem in the first place. Now she was fucking around with his career.

"Excuse me, Mr Ross, can I get your autograph, please?"

Ross looked over his shoulder to check if it was a sincere request or an eBay auction. A 30-something Chinese guy held out a piece of paper with the Palm Beach Casino letterhead and a borrowed casino pen. His suit was crumpled, his hair dishevelled and the deep, dark rings under his eyes betrayed his intentions. He had lost everything. He was desperate. The autograph was a pitiful bid for eBay cash.

"Sorry, mate, I'd love to, but I'm in the middle of a hand here," Ross whispered. "Maybe come back when I've finished at the table."

"Yeah, sure, I will come back."

He would not come back. They both accepted that. Ross wasn't going anywhere until he'd made back at least 50 grand and the Chinese guy had nothing left to offer the Gold Room. His unsightly appearance meant it was only a matter of time before security told him to fuck off. The Chinese guy trudged slowly towards a fellow Chinese face behind the bar. They shared a culture, but that was all. There would be no sympathy.

Ross glimpsed down at the corner of his second card. He had 19. The croupier might beat him. He suddenly thought about Jimmy and Scott. If they were here now, they'd tell him to call it a day. They had always looked out for one another, fought battles together. If they were here now, they'd force him to see reason, to consider his England chances. But they were not here now. Ross was alone.

The croupier turned over his cards.

Ross nodded as the croupier leaned across the table and took his chips.

TOM fidgeted in his chair. Under the table, his heels were raised and his legs jerked up and down repeatedly. He smiled nervously at Jason across the table as Jonathan opened the office door and walked in.

"Well?" Tom asked.

"We're on," Jonathan exclaimed triumphantly.

"Yes!" Tom shouted as he pumped his fists.

Jason leaned forward and patted Tom on the shoulder.

"It's got to go how I said it would," Jonathan added calmly. "If there's public interest in the club, then there's public interest in the documentary. I will work full-time with Jason now on putting all the footage together. Tom, you will work on getting the story out there. Now, we don't want the whole story, not a full leak, we don't want the bloody plumbers called in. Just a teaser, don't tell them anything more than they need to know, all right. This is our story, not theirs."

"Yeah, yeah, of course, no problem," Tom said.

"Start putting the feelers out in a couple of days, and when the shit hits the fan, we'll be ready to go."

"Terrific," Jason chirped.

"And thanks, guys, really," Jonathan said. "I'm really pleased we could see this through, you deserve this."

Jason picked up his coffee cup and stood up suddenly.

"I'd like to make a toast," he said. "To Jo and Scott, thanks for shagging each other's brains out."

Jonathan and Tom laughed and picked up their coffee mugs.

"To Jo and Scott," they chorused in unison.

They swigged the cold dregs of their cups and winced.

"You know something. I still can't believe it," Tom said. "It's amazing when you think about it. It's gonna go crazy. There hasn't been a football story like this since, I don't know. I mean, they went to school together. They're best mates."

eighteen

ROSS tried to focus on the front-page headline, but the tears blurred his vision. The tears surprised him. He hadn't cried since he took a kick in the balls against Birmingham City in the FA Cup, but that hardly counted. Before that, Ross hadn't cried since, well, Ross couldn't remember the last time he had cried. Ross didn't do tears. Ross did jokes, banter and piss-takes, but he didn't do tears. Ross was ruggedly handsome, boasted a toned physique and was born with Robbie Fowler's instinctive awareness of where the goal was over his shoulder. What did Ross have to cry about?

He gripped the sides of newspaper and wept loudly. He was shaking uncontrollably. The tears and snot flowed over his mouth, past his chin and dribbled onto the front page of *The Sun*. He never wiped his face. He didn't notice. He didn't care. His stomach muscles tightened and he suddenly felt the urge to vomit. He reached over for the dustbin in the kitchen cupboard, but there wasn't time. The vomit splattered across the Leicht Orlando worktop and trickled down the Leicht Orlando cupboard doors. She would moan about the kitchen appliances later, remind him that Leicht were the best kitchen designers in Germany and tell him again how much the kitchen project had cost. She told everyone how much their kitchen project had cost.

Ross' parents never had a kitchen project. They just had a fucking kitchen. The vomit stench would have her straight on the phone to the cleaner, screaming abuse at Ross while she dialled. But he didn't care what she would say later. Right now, he didn't give a fuck about her.

Ross slumped over the Tennessee Walnut island in the middle of her light wood Leicht Orlando kitchen. He felt the lumps of vomit on the side of his face pressed against the worktop. Through the tears, he noticed a photograph of him on the wall above his built-in plasma TV. A younger Ross was smiling down at him, with the ball under one arm and a trophy in the other. He was 14 years old in the photo. Charlie had just handed him the trophy, told him he had a turn of pace and natural upper body strength to make the first team, told him that he had Fowler's poaching potential and Alan Shearer's power. Charlie had ruffled his gelled hair and told him he could play for England. His name would one day appear on the electronic scoreboard at Wembley. Ross had believed him. Charlie was rarely wrong when it came to unearthing little gems from the council estates of South-East England. Charlie had produced England players before. Ross and Scott were going to be his new crop.

Ross sobbed as he looked up at the photograph. He'd fucked up any chances of an England cap now. The England set-up had changed since he was a kid. It wasn't like the old days when you could be tied to a dentist's chair and drenched in tequila on the Friday and then bang in a couple on the Saturday. England had suddenly gone all puritanical in its values; drink, drugs, women and gambling were out. If the players wanted a bag of crisps on the plane home, they had to ask permission first.

Ross stood up slowly and reached for the kitchen roll. He wiped the worst of the vomit off his face. He was still crying, but he was beginning to focus. His chances of an England cap had gone for the foreseeable future. England was too strait-laced on such matters and he had no intention of becoming a laughing stock. New kid on the block or not, if they poked fingers and giggled at him in the dressing room, he'd punch their fucking lights out.

England was gone, but Ross still had to salvage his club career. He blew his nose and picked up the phone. He wiped it with kitchen roll and dialled. The cleaner could take care of the kitchen. He heard the phone ring and took a deep breath.

"Hello, Jimmy," he said. "You've seen the papers right? I'm fucking devastated. I don't know who I want to fucking kill first. Better get round here mate before I smash up the place."

JIMMY surveyed the damage in the kitchen. There was vomit across the bench top, the sink and the hobs. He noticed some smashed crockery on the floor and a blood-stained cup. He stared quizzically at Ross. His best friend smiled as tears streamed down his face. There was dried snot under this nose and lumps of vomit stuck to his cheek. When they were at school together, Jimmy had secretly wanted to be Ross. Everyone in the school wanted to be Ross. He was the David Watts of their secondary school. But Jimmy didn't want to be him today. Jimmy didn't want to be here today.

"You haven't done anything stupid, have you?" Jimmy asked slowly.

"Like what?"

"I don't know. There's blood down there on the floor."

Ross laughed.

"Yeah, I know. The first cup was bloody smashed by accident. I had a go at cleaning up the puke when the bastard cleaner told me she couldn't come in early, and I knocked a cup off the side.

It kind of summed up my day really, so I smashed a few more to keep it company."

Jimmy wanted to hug his oldest friend. He really did. But he had to maintain a professional distance; one of them had to remain rational.

"We can sort this out, mate, you know we can," Jimmy said.

He was desperate to help.

"How can I fix this? Everyone is gonna think I'm a joke. You know what it's like out there, you played the game. The fucking shit abuse we have to take every week. They already say I take it up the arse every week because of that bit of modelling work you got me and the fucking Hugo Boss stuff. They already think I'm a bit of a joke. But this will finish me off. I'm a proper fucking joke now."

"You're not being fair on yourself, mate. This isn't your fault, is it?"

"Of course, it's my fault. I should've stayed at home more."

"All I'm saying is, don't do anything hasty. We can find a way out of this."

Ross glared at Jimmy and wiped his mouth. He was incredulous.

"Are you fucking kidding me? Did you read the front page? Did you see it? Look at it for fuck's sake."

Ross picked up his damp copy of *The Sun* and shoved the front page under Jimmy's nose.

"Go on, read the fucking headline," Ross shouted. "Say it out loud! Go on, say what every fucking pleb in the country is saying over their cornflakes this morning. Read out the fucking headlines!"

Jimmy eyed Ross nervously. Ross had always been the most laid-back of the three of them; that was a natural fringe benefit of being the best-looking one. He was also the most physical, the strongest, but he rarely lost his temper. Jimmy was scared.

"I'm not going to read the headline," he whispered. "I'll sound silly if I ..."

"Read the fucking headline ... now!" Ross screamed.

Jimmy looked down at the newspaper. He saw the photograph and cringed. He closed his eyes. He didn't need to see the headline. He had it memorised. He had read and re-read the fucking thing a hundred times already this morning.

"Gone to the Dogs," Jimmy murmured. "Striker Owes Bookies Over Two Million."

JIMMY waited for the kettle to boil and stared out of the kitchen window. He watched some cattle grazing in the distance. England really was a green and pleasant land at this time of the year, particularly through the window of Ross' Georgian farmhouse in Godalming. Jimmy had watched Ross' dumbstruck face when they turned off Highfield Lane and onto the gravel drive for the first time to admire the property. Jimmy had lined up the sweetest deal for Ross, an interest-only loan with lower repayments. Ross didn't even notice the monthly interest coming out, but he'd notice the difference when he eventually sold the bloody thing at the end of his career. He'd also notice the 12 acres, swimming pool and tennis court. Jimmy was there when Ross had been handed the keys for the first time. Ross didn't have to say what the property meant or express his gratitude. They had grown up on the same street. They had shared the dog shit on the pavement.

"Do you want any sugar?" Jimmy asked.

He looked over his shoulder at Ross, who was still slumped on a La-Z-Boy, staring at the front page.

"How do they know?" Ross muttered.

"Do you want any sugar?" Jimmy repeated, trying to distract his friend.

"What? Yeah, all right, three."

"You're still taking three sugars in your tea, bloody hell, how have you got any teeth left?"

Jimmy stirred the tea and took it over to Ross.

"Put that bloody paper down, for God's sake," Jimmy said. "You've read the story 20 times, it's not going to help, is it?"

"How do they know?" Ross muttered again, sipping his tea and staring straight ahead.

"Who? What are you on about?"

"Do you know how much I throw about at the races every month? I reckon I dropped about 50 grand at Epsom the other week. And I signed so many autographs that day I felt like Ronald fucking McDonald. There were kids pestering me all day long, getting me to sign their shirts, school bags, wallets, whatever."

"Yeah, I know, it's always like that."

"That didn't get into the papers. I was throwing it around like confetti, and when the Arabs came down that time I was pissed, there were cameras all over the place, and the paps didn't bother with those photos. And I was hammered that day, fucking hammered."

"Come on, if they had a pound note for every time a footballer popped up at the races," Jimmy said, blowing his tea. "There's no story in that, is there?"

"Look, you know I'm not a mug. I've been doing this since my old man used to take me down Walthamstow dogs on a Friday night after school. You remember? He used to always stop off at Ladbrokes on the way to training and have a bet."

Jimmy laughed at the memory.

"Yeah, I remember. Top bloke your dad, a proper character," Jimmy said.

"He is what he is. He loves a bet. Horses, dogs, football, that's my family. I always remember going round my old granddad's and being told to keep quiet when there was a big race on the radio. My dad's the same now with the Sky Racing channel. I could've smashed in a hat-trick at Old Trafford, but if I call him when he's got that racing channel on, he'll tell me to fuck off."

"Yeah, well, you're not far behind, mate. Can't get a word in when you've got a race on in the car. How many times have you buggered off to the bogs to call the bookies?"

Ross shrugged his shoulders.

"Yeah, I know, but I don't apologise for it. It's who I am. I don't hurt anybody, it's my money and I'm no mug. I don't lose that much when you balance it out over the year because I'm not a mug."

Jimmy gestured towards the newspaper on Ross' lap.

"Two million though, Ross. Fucking hell, mate. I knew you were getting a bit carried away. I'm your agent, too, here, but I never knew it was anywhere near that figure."

"It's not," Ross said bluntly.

"Really?"

"No, of course not. It's about one, maybe one point two, tops. I'm going over to Vegas, back to Wynn's, and I expect to get at least half back. You know it's not a problem for me. You know I can afford it. I don't spend my nights crying into the roulette wheel and I don't waste my time bluffing with poker. I play blackjack and nothing else; any other game is for muppets."

Jimmy pointed at the newspaper.

"It's obviously serious enough to get this far."

Ross sat up suddenly. His eyes widened.

"Exactly. That's my point. I've been going down to the races, all the big meets, since before I made the first team. After I made my debut, I went down the track the next week and blew a week's wages. When I scored for the first team, I went to the casino that night, buying champagne for half of Mayfair. There isn't a croupier, waiter, cleaner or punter who doesn't know who I am at the Palm Beach and I never get aggro. That's why I go there. It's owned by Asians, discreet, calm exteriors. They don't fuck about. They've got no time for bad publicity. They don't give a shit who I am. It's never about the celebrity bollocks with them. It's always about the pound notes."

"Well, someone must have tipped them off. A cloakroom kid, someone cleaning the bogs; it's easy money for a couple of phone calls."

Ross shook his head.

"Nah, it doesn't work like that. Yeah, those fuckers call the tabloids up every night. But unless I'm falling out of the casino with Kate Moss, where's the story? And even if I have dropped a bundle, the red-tops have to get it verified and they just will not give out that kind of info at the Palm Beach. They won't tell anyone how much someone owes the casino. That stuff is too valuable to them. They don't want a competitor knowing, let alone the fucking newspapers. As it is, they will have an internal investigation down there. I know how they work. Someone will get fired, just to send a message out to the rest of the staff. But it wasn't the casino. I know that."

Jimmy put down his tea cup and sighed.

"I can't lie to you, mate. We don't need this right now either. I've already had a few missed calls from Charlie. I'm putting him off for as long as possible. He's not gonna be happy."

"Well, he's got no room to talk. He loves a bet."

"Yeah, but not now. He wanted everyone to keep a low profile now, no negative publicity."

"Why?"

Jimmy shifted uneasily on the sofa and stared down at the floor.

"You know why. The deal with the Arabs. Everyone knows it's

on, but these Arabs are a bit sensitive. Who knows how they will react? They are right conservative bastards over there. We know the main man puts it about a bit, but not publicly. Gambling is tricky. It's verboten over there, isn't it?"

"I'm sorry if I put Charlie out," Ross growled.

"No, no, I didn't mean that. It's just that we've got to be careful. Charlie has to be careful."

"Well, he better not take it out on me. I'm in no mood for his bollocks. I've got to take it from her, whenever she decides to come home from wherever the fuck she is."

Jimmy noticed the time on Ross' Rolex. He really didn't want to be here.

"Charlie will look after you," Jimmy insisted. "He's always looked after us three, right? Look at me."

"I hope so, mate," Ross said. "I just want to play my way through this."

THE flashes distracted Jimmy. He tried to point out a favoured reporter, but a photographer stood up in front of his guy and snapped Jimmy, just as he was about to take the question. A slim guy in a London Fog trench coat took the opportunity to cut in.

"Don't you think you are overreacting a little here," the person in the trench coat shouted over the other journalists, all jostling for attention.

Jimmy surveyed the press conference. This wasn't right. This wasn't Jimmy's press conference; he hadn't orchestrated it. He had little chance of controlling it. There were too many unfamiliar faces, too many designer suits in the room. The broadsheets had brought out their biggest bylines. Every facial tic and gesture would be dissected in the morning's papers by the country's finest columnists and humorists. Like Charlie, Jimmy always preferred the tabloid populist scribblers. They were hungrier. They were malleable. The broadsheet boys in their trench coats were different. The trench coats were famous in their own right. They had their own celebrity to think about. They no longer had to play Charlie's games. They took the piss out of Charlie's jingoistic anachronisms for the amusement of their more discerning readers.

Jimmy gazed across the table at Charlie, desperately seeking refuge.

"No, no, I'm asking you, Jimmy," the Trench Coat persisted. "You're his agent. You're his best mate, apparently. Don't you think the club is overreacting a little?"

"I really can't comment on the measures the club have taken," Jimmy said slowly. "But you're right, I'm gutted for Ross. We've known each other since we were four years old. What do you want me to say? As his agent, he's well looked after financially. As his best friend, I'm choked for him. He's got a problem and we're helping him deal with it. But I won't have you fucking sit there and tell me that ..."

"What Jimmy is basically saying is that we have to acknowledge that there is a problem," Charlie interjected. "It is a society problem. How many of us play the lottery every week? We are all hypocrites to a certain degree. That's not to underplay the seriousness of Ross' problem, or to excuse it, we're just trying to understand it. And that's why we are giving Ross the time and space he needs to get the kind of expert help that obviously we cannot provide."

"So you are suspending Ross," a reporter shouted from the back of the press conference.

"No, no, no, I'm not saying that at all," Charlie replied firmly. "I want to make that clear. I don't want any misunderstanding here. Ross has not been suspended. Ross has not been fined or docked a penny from his wages. We just want Ross back to his best and doing what he loves best on the park, I think we all agree with that. When I first saw that boy spin away from the entire defence and score when he was just 13, I said he would play for England. I said I now knew what Alex Ferguson must have felt like the first time he saw a skinny kid called Ryan Wilson messing about on the left wing. I still believe that. Ross can play for England, but to do that he needs to focus on his football, and his football alone. And no other distractions. There are only a few weeks of the season left, so we thought it was better for Ross to take a time-out, get the treatment he needs and come back fresh next season."

"But you still have a chance of making the Europa League, Charlie," a reporter said. "Don't you think ..."

"... This represents a wonderful opportunity for the rest of the squad to help their teammate out by working their balls off to give him European football next season. What a wonderful way to welcome Ross back into the squad."

"No more questions," Jimmy mumbled into the microphone, still seething.

AL-HAKIM stared at his plasma TV, utterly engrossed. He watched Charlie gently push his underling out of the press conference. The minion was not short on self-assurance, but it bordered on defiance. That flash of anger in the press conference betrayed both his loyalty and his inexperience. Those weaknesses needed to be addressed next season.

Al-Hakim picked up his drink and headed towards the lounge doors. He pulled them apart and stepped out onto the deck of his yacht. The hypnotic, crimson sun was setting over the South China Sea. Apart from the humidity, Al-Hakim always enjoyed conducting business in Southeast Asia. The Chinese efficiency and their subservience to money meant his meetings were usually finished by mid-afternoon, and he had time to take a couple of Malay girls back to the yacht. He had thought about picking up a couple of western backpackers, assuming it might help, but he suspected that wasn't the way to go. There was only one Nicola. There was no point pretending otherwise.

Al-Hakim watched a handful of Indonesian fishermen set their *kelong* fishing traps for the night and took out his phone. He had been impressed with Charlie, not so much with his actions, but with his decisiveness.

"Hello, is that Charlie," he said loudly. "Yes, sorry about the line, I am using a satellite phone from my yacht ... yes, some business in Singapore and Malaysia ... just a few days. Look, I wanted to thank you for doing that for me. I hope you understand that some of my business partners are very old-fashioned when it comes to gambling. We are a conservative country. The hypocrisy can be really tiring, but some of the older guys do consider gambling to be a sin, so I do appreciate what you did for me today. I think it will also calm things down and allow us to buy some time to tie up a few loose ends before completing the purchase. So thank you, Charlie, goodbye."

Al-Hakim rarely bothered with small talk. He didn't have to. He sipped his fresh lime juice and stared at the fishermen balancing precariously in their rickety, rotting wooden boats as they fixed their nets. Al-Hakim chuckled. He couldn't help himself. His business partners didn't care about gambling. They bought English Premier League clubs so they could win friendly bets during the weekends. Besides, Al-Hakim didn't have business partners.

No, it wasn't the striker's gambling scandal. That was a trifling concern. It was the principle.

Al-Hakim owned several casinos in London. But he didn't own the Palm Beach in Mayfair.

nineteen

NICOLA and Scott couldn't take their eyes off the screen. Nicola had tears in her eyes as she took the milk cup out of their daughter's mouth and handed her over to the nanny.

"Are you OK?" the nanny asked tenderly.

"I'm fine, I'm fine, really," Nicola replied, sniffing and wiping her eyes. "I'm fine. If there are any problems with her, just shout out and I'll come up, OK."

Nicola watched the nanny carry their daughter slowly up the stairs, then shot an angry glare at Scott sitting in the armchair.

"Did you know about this?" she hissed.

"What?" Scott replied innocently.

"This, this here look," she pointed frantically at the TV, which was airing a montage of Ross scoring goals. "You're always out with him in the casino, the poor bastard, you knew he had a problem."

"Yeah, I knew he liked a bet, but I didn't know he had put down this much. I didn't expect any of this to happen, did I? I didn't expect the club to bloody drop him like this."

Scott meant it, too. When the story broke, he had suspected that Charlie might give Ross a benign rebuke to keep up appearances; a playful slap on the wrist to silence all the soapboxes. The plebs, who spent all their weekends in Ladbrokes, would expect nothing less. But he never anticipated Ross being dropped. They needed Ross' goals if they were serious about their Europa League push. There was still time, but only with Ross' goals. They were fucked now. Charlie had sacrificed his favourite striker and their European aspirations for a few quid lost on the blackjack tables. It didn't make any sense.

"You know who's to blame, don't you? His bloody missus," Nicola said, clearly angry.

Scott felt his cheeks burn. He was blushing. He looked down at the floor.

"What are you going on about now?"

"That bloody woman drives him mad. Dragging him all over London for crappy photo opportunities. He doesn't need that. He never used to be interested in all that shit, the poor sod. I used to love Ross."

"Yes, yes, we all know how good-looking you think he is."

"Oh, shut up, he's a lovely bloke. He's so easygoing, he just wanted to play football. You used to be like that, you know."

"Yeah, all right, no fucking lectures now, eh?"

"You were all like that when I first knew you, all three of you. And then she came along and that was it for Ross. He had no chance after that, doing all that rubbish with her. He didn't need all that. He was better than that. He was better than that."

"It was up to him, wasn't it?" Scott mumbled.

"And you know what really pisses me off. She'll be off now, you watch. If he's out for the rest of the season, no chance of making the England squad, that silly cow will be off. He'll have no further purpose to serve. Their photographs at the Ivy won't be worth as much anymore. You can't sell a photo shoot if your bloke is playing in the reserves, no matter how many goals he scores."

"I'd better phone him," Scott said abruptly, getting up quickly, eager to change the subject.

"Yeah, give him all our love won't you," Nicola replied.

"Yeah, of course," Scott whispered. "The poor bastard."

Scott strolled purposefully into the kitchen. He checked over his shoulder and closed the kitchen door quietly. He took the phone off the wall and dialled quickly, still glancing over his shoulder at the kitchen door. He scanned the framed photographs all over the kitchen wall: his under-13 championship with Barking Juniors, his first senior appearances, a rare headed goal away at Goodison Park, lining up with the England under-21s. They were all there; all his memories, most of them shared. Then he saw the photograph of all three of them taken by Charlie's favourite reporter—their first big interview with a national newspaper—caked in mud but smiling, arm-in-arm during that freezing training session, united, unstoppable, the boys from Barking; all for one and sod the rest.

Scott turned his back on the photographs.

"Er, hello, it's me," he whispered. "I need to see you now. Yeah, I know all that, but I don't care. I'll see you in half an hour. This is getting out of hand."

TOM knocked on the door. He was more than a little anxious. The meeting could go either way. Everything could go either way at the moment. Why couldn't English Premier League footballers just do as they were told? They were one spanner after another in his works. BNP rallies in East London were a doddle compared to the complexities and vagaries of the English Premier League.

"Come in," Jonathan said sharply.

Tom took a deep breath and opened the door.

"All right, mate," he said.

"Sit down, Tom," Jonathan instructed.

"That was all a bit weird, wasn't it?" Tom said as he sat down and noticed the newspaper headlines littered all over Jonathan's desk.

"I don't know if I'd call it weird, bloody unexpected maybe, but not weird. Did you talk to your mate in the *News of the World* like we agreed?"

"Yeah, of course I did. We were all set up and raring to go."

"So where did he get this rubbish from," Jonathan said, lifting up some of the pages before throwing them back down again. "We could have done with some of this stuff before. This clown is in casinos, this guy is dropping millions at the races. This is perfect for us."

Tom relaxed a little. At least Jonathan wasn't angry.

"Yeah, it certainly puts them all under the microscope."

"It does, but what's it got to do with Scott shagging that Jo, apart from the obvious connection. How did your mate go from Scott shagging Jo to Ross being a degenerate gambler?"

"He didn't."

"What are you on about?"

"This is not his story. That's what I came up to tell you. I thought you knew that already. He was still doing a few background checks on Scott and Jo, the last time I spoke to him. He told me he was aiming for a Sunday job, four-page special and all that."

"So who told them about this stuff then?"

Tom smiled at Jonathan.

"I haven't got a clue," he said. "Bloody good though, isn't it?"

SCOTT eased the Ferrari into his parking space at the training ground. He peered through his windscreen at the gloomy training complex. He thought about his second visit, his second trial, his second and last chance to make a favourable impression. He thought about Ross. He had made it happen for him, characteristically unselfish as always. The academy coach had thrown yellow bibs at Scott and Jimmy. Same side, as always. But Ross had been handed a red bib. Ross against Scott, striker against defender, best mate against best mate. Ross was already in; Scott still had everything to prove. Scott could still see Charlie, standing at the side of the gym, arms folded, already checking his watch, clearly bored and wanting to get home to his very big house in the country. Scott could still see Ross thundering towards him, his tree-trunk thighs somehow moving like pistons, the yellow futsal ball being jabbed aggressively towards goal, towards Scott. On that squeaky gymnasium floor, defenders turned slower. They always looked lumbering. Scott always heard his father's voice over the squeaking gymnasium floor.

You looked a right fucking twat tonight, son.

But Ross did something that saved Scott's career. It was barely perceptible; only Scott and Jimmy would have spotted it. Ross knocked the ball a fraction too far forward, not enough to be recognised as deliberate, but enough for Scott to make his mark. Head down and running at goal, Ross always had the most immaculate ball control, but not this time. It was a matter of inches, but it was all that Scott needed. He intercepted the ball with his right foot, and dragged it from right to left, across the front of Ross, and strode imperiously away from him before laying it off to Jimmy on his left foot. He had stayed on his feet. He had launched an attack. He had pulled off a textbook defensive interception. Bobby fucking Moore couldn't have done it any better.

And then he saw the wink. Unable to resist, the joker in their pack had smiled and winked at him before turning and running back to help out in defence. Scott then stole a glance at

Charlie. He was no longer looking at his watch. He was nodding approvingly.

Scott's daydreaming was shattered by a tap on his car window.

"Come on then," Jimmy said. "I haven't got all fucking night."

Jimmy was irritated. There was no point in concealing his frustration. His oldest mate had taken a fall today; his future international career was in serious jeopardy—that would cost a couple of million in itself, international strikers were easier to stick on a box of cornflakes—and his club career was uncertain at best, so he was in no mood for a lecture. He scowled at Scott as he got out of the Ferrari and then slammed the car door behind him.

"Do you want to go inside?" Scott asked. "It's freezing out here."

"No, it's all right. I said I wouldn't be long. What's up?"

Scott stared at Jimmy in disbelief.

"What's up? Are you having a laugh? Ross is gone for the rest of the season. Didn't you see that coming?"

"No, I didn't. I didn't have a fucking clue."

Scott kicked at the gravel beneath his feet.

"Jesus Christ, you're his agent. You're Charlie's agent, too."

"No, I'm not," Jimmy stressed. "Charlie doesn't have an agent. He represents himself."

"Oh piss off, you know what I mean. I'm not interested in all that bollocks that you two get up to now, but you must have his ear on this."

Jimmy gritted his teeth. He had always liked Scott; he was one of the finest footballers of their generation and they made plenty of money together, but he had always been an irritating pain in the arse.

"I don't pick the fucking team, Scott," he shouted. "If I did, Ross would be in there, up front and banging in the goals every fucking week, but I don't pick the team. No one picks Charlie's team, except Charlie. He'd rip my head off if I even tried. I just do their contracts, but it's his team. His team, his squad, his suspensions, his punishments; it's all down to him."

Scott hesitated. Jimmy rarely lost his temper. Scott was the hot-headed one. That's why he privately acknowledged that Ross and Jimmy had always been the closest. They were more lackadaisical. That's why Jimmy was out of the game, Ross was suspended and Scott was club captain.

"I understand that, of course I do, but it's still a bit harsh," Scott reasoned. "I mean, let's be honest here, if every club in the Premier League banned every player who had a gambling debt, they wouldn't be able to put a team out every week."

"It's still Charlie's call, no one else's. I'm sure he had his reasons."

"Well, I think it's fucking out of order. You don't suspend a bloke just because he likes a gamble."

Jimmy felt his stomach muscles tighten. The unexpected anger was overwhelming. He took a step forward. To Jimmy's surprise, he had squared up to Scott.

"Well, what the fuck did you expect, Scott," Jimmy shouted. "What the fuck did you think would happen? When you asked me for help you must have known that this was a possibility? You must have realised that this might be on the cards? You're not an agent, but you're not fucking stupid either."

"Of course I didn't. Jesus Christ, who do you think I am?"

"I don't know, Scott, do I? You tell me. You're the one who was caught with your dick hanging out again. I told you that I'd been tipped off, that's all. I wasn't the one shagging around. If you hadn't fucked half of London in the last three years, none of this would have happened."

Scott laughed contemptuously.

"Oh, and you're fucking innocent in all this, are ya? You told me I needed a diversion. You told me the plebs needed a distraction. Distract and confuse, you said. One of the oldest tricks in Charlie's book."

"I didn't expect you to grass up our fucking best mate, did I?"

Scott eyeballed Jimmy.

"I didn't," he hissed, poking Jimmy in the chest. "You did."

Jimmy sighed and focused on his Armani shoes. He had scuffed them on the gravel.

"We always do it," he said softly. "Me and Charlie have been doing it ever since I started out. Charlie reckons he's been doing it for 30 years, robbing Peter to pay Paul. You hear they're hungry for a story; you feed them something else to keep the packs at bay. They either forget about the first story or it goes away."

"And you told me to give you another story."

"I didn't think you'd give up our best mate."

"You bloody used it though. You gave it to these scavengers. Neither of us expected any of this. I just thought it'd be a couple of page ones, the plebs getting outraged, a bit of slagging off on the phone-ins. Give it a week and he'd make it all back by selling his story to the red-tops. 'I've learnt my lesson,' he'd say. 'I've seen the light and I will help others out of the darkness,' and all that bollocks. He could've got his midnight gambler autobiography out in time for Christmas, all the juicy rehab stuff; football's Elton John. They love that rubbish. He would've been laughing six months from now."

"He won't be now," Jimmy retorted.

"Nah, I never thought Charlie would suspend him. Never."

"Neither did I."

Scott and Jimmy turned away from each other and stared up at the training complex. They could barely see it in the darkness. Scott peered across at Jimmy.

"Still, at least the gambling stuff has killed off my story," he said.

twenty

ROSS dropped the phone clumsily onto the Axminster. He had expected to feel guilty after calling the reporter, but was shocked by the surge of adrenaline. He felt relieved after the call. He knew the euphoria wouldn't last, but it was almost like scoring a goal; not quite, but almost. The moment that ball bulged the net, the best sex did not come close, did not come into the picture. That's what women never understood. That's what the fans never really understood. When the away mobs said he took it up the arse, called him a fat cunt and told him he'd never play for England, they never got it. Ross didn't care. He really didn't give a fuck about their abuse. It was all about scoring. When he scored, he was untouchable, impregnable. Sticks and stones never reached him when he was on song. Even the money didn't matter, the goal bonuses an irrelevance; just another few quid for the blackjack tables.

Even the media didn't get it. The hacks spewed out their puritanical values and moralised to the masses about the perils of gambling addiction, typing out their patronising paragraphs between gin and tonics. How could a man with both the ball and the world at his feet throw it all away in casinos, the hysterical headlines cried. Because he scored goals for a living. That's why. That's also why the old, retired pros held back in their weekly columns, particularly the old strikers. They had slagged him before for missing sitters, not tracking back enough, not providing enough assists and all those other clichéd criticisms that the uneducated plebs needed to be fed every now and then. But they didn't really get at him for the gambling. They couldn't. They had played the game themselves.

The old pros empathised with Ross' predicament. They remembered the feeling. It was unique to them. Where did you go after a goal? The only way was down. Women did it for some, a few lines did it for others and gambling took care of the rest. Nothing else came remotely close. The view from the top was so exhilarating; the mind lacked the logic to slowly descend again. Revealing an ace beneath a picture card would never beat the ball smashing into the top corner, but it was the best that Ross' simple psychology could come up with. Blackjack was his methadone. He had to come down somehow.

Ross rarely gambled heavily when he wasn't scoring. That was the other thing that the hacks could never comprehend. If he wasn't scoring, he didn't need to feed the buzz. The blackjack table wasn't an escape or a refuge; it was a place to extend the high, to sustain the orgasm. The trouble was, Ross had been scoring since his dad threw him a plastic football at Barking Park when he was three years old. On their way home, his old man had then popped in the betting shop.

Scoring and gambling were Ross' life. He didn't know how to function with anything else.

And they had taken them both away from him.

Ross swigged from an almost-empty bottle of vodka. He coughed until his eyes watered, and then he picked up the phone again. He wasn't a vindictive man usually. It wasn't part of his makeup. But they had crossed a line that was beyond his comprehension. And it really was beyond his comprehension.

All the lads saw him as the clown, and he was always content to play up to the circus. That was his party piece. It was why they always had him on *Match of the Day* after games. It was why the lad mags always paid him the most. It was why Charlie always worshipped him. He had Charlie's impudence. Scott had Charlie's drive and calculated ambition, Jimmy had the old man's business acumen and media savvy, but Ross had the brashness and sense of loyalty. Ross loved the dressing room banter because he loved being around his mates. Women always looked better naked—and Ross' women were exceptional when naked—but you couldn't have a laugh with them afterwards in the same way; couldn't take the piss out of Manchester United supporters with them afterwards. They meant well and they smelled good, but they just didn't belong. They could never fully be a part of Ross' world.

Only the lads got the jokes. That's why there was a camaraderie that the women didn't appreciate. The chaps stood together as a collective as 40,000 dribbling beer bellies called them useless cunts through gritted teeth. That forged a bond that their women, the plebs and the hacks could never fully grasp; a bond that made any betrayal all the more unexpected and distasteful.

"Hello, darling, it's Ross," he said cheerily down the phone. "Yeah, I know, babe ... Thanks, mate ... Yeah, it'll be fine. Honestly, I'm fine, really ... Yeah, I know. I appreciate that. If there's anything, I'll give you a shout. Look, is he in? ... Yeah, all right, cheers babe."

Ross polished off the rest of the vodka and waited for his best friend to come to the phone.

CHARLIE stood on the touchline and watched the kids go through their paces. He pulled his collars up, but they were no defence against the driving rain spitting against the side of his face. He used to enjoy keeping an eye on his boys. Both Charlie and Ford came from Dagenham. Both had their production lines. Charlie liked to think that his made him a little more money. Ever since the late 1970s, when the old farts in the boardroom stopped choking on their cigars long enough to tell him he could help out with the youth team for a few extra pennies a week, Charlie had taken on their challenge with a fervour that surprised even himself. He examined every kid in microscopic detail. Their favoured foot, their balance, their pace, their ability to turn and track back, their temperament, their diet, their family background; Charlie needed to know everything. He became obsessed with the failures. He spent more time dissecting his flops than he did his successes. There were kids at 14 blessed with a natural-born talent to rival Best or Cruyff. By 21, they were playing non-league football and cleaning windows. And then he came across mouthy little bastards with two left feet, who spent their days mixing cement and their nights banging slappers. By 25, they were getting international call-ups because their Cockney granddads had shagged an Irish nurse during the war. In the 1980s, the paradox pushed him to the brink of insanity.

By the early 1990s, Charlie had it down. Even Alex Ferguson said publicly that the man made in Dagenham had an unrivalled gift when it came to plucking kids from the tree and turning them into £30-million transfer targets for Manchester United. Charlie always said his crystal ball could conjure a positive or negative reading within six weeks. That's all he needed. Just six weeks spent watching and talking to the boy and—more importantly— talking to the boy's family and seeing his home environment was enough to know whether he'd be playing for England or a Sunday morning pub team in six years' time.

Charlie was rarely wrong. He surveyed the malnourished, pasty-faced kids huffing and puffing and drowning in the drizzle. He knew these kids. They were the kids he saw most seasons now. They had overly-developed thumbs, but calves like pieces of string. They were world beaters with a game controller, but only saw a training pitch once a week when their dads dragged them down to the local team's training session. They dazzled in those sessions and got their daft old dads giddy with excitement and blinded by dollar signs. But they only excelled against other kids from the PlayStation generation. Take away their thumbs and they're all fucked.

Charlie knew what these kids were. They were wasting his time.

"Come on, lads," he shouted half-heartedly, his eyes blinking through the rain. "Make your decisions before you get the ball, not after. That's the difference. The first two yards are always in the brain."

One or two of the kids near the touchline nodded, but the other lads didn't hear him. Charlie knew they barely acknowledged his presence. He wasn't a real person to these teenage vegetables. He was an animated character inside a computer game.

Charlie peered over his shoulder and spotted a couple of reserves warming up nearby. The reserves always warmed up near Charlie. They liked to remind the old man that they still existed.

"All right, lads," Charlie called out at them.

The reserves smiled eagerly. He had noticed them.

"Go and get me a cup of milky sweet tea," Charlie continued. "I'm freezing my bollocks off out here."

A reserve trudged off back to the dressing room, his shoulders slumped.

Charlie heard his mobile phone ring. Normally, he loathed being disturbed during a training session, but he was delighted for the distraction now.

"Hello, Charlie, it's me," a voice crackled down the line. "It's me, Matty from the *Guardian*."

Charlie brightened suddenly. He always enjoyed taking calls from the hacks, especially the educated hacks. They invariably wanted something. But Matty was different in any case. He had ghost-written Charlie's second autobiography a couple of years ago and they had become genuine friends. Theirs was a relationship of mutual benefit. Matty had never done a hatchet job on Charlie because Charlie only handed him the hatchet to use on other people.

"Hello, Matty, my son, how are you, mate?" Charlie boomed.

"Yeah, yeah, I'm fine, Charlie, I'm fine."

"How's that missus of yours? She had the baby yet?"

Charlie always remembered, always. Births, marriages, christenings and deaths of all the media's big fish and their families; his secretary regularly updated a file for him and left it on his desk.

"She's got another week to go. They're both doing well, thanks," replied Matty, quite astonished that Charlie had remembered.

"I wish I was," Charlie groaned. "I'm standing here in the poxy rain watching the youth team. I'm getting too old for this bollocks."

"Any good ones?"

"What do you think?"

Of course not, Matty thought. If Charlie had unearthed another gem, the kid's story would've been on the Sky Sports loop by now.

"Look, I'm sorry to call you like this, but I've heard a whisper about your boys," Matty said.

Charlie rolled his eyes.

"It's not Ross again, is it? For fuck's sake, he's been taken care of. They can't possibly get any more mileage out of him now.

The story's already out there and we've slapped him on the wrist, end of."

"I have heard he's sold his story, not to us, obviously. But it's just starting to filter through to us now. He's spoken to one of the Sundays."

Charlie smiled in spite of himself. Ross had always been a cheeky little bastard.

"He's a little fucker. He's already been told about that. Between me and you, Matty, he's still getting paid his full whack, even win bonuses, over 60 grand, we promised him that. But he couldn't go public about the gambling."

Charlie heard Matty sigh down the line.

"It's … er … it's not about the gambling," Matty stammered.

"No? What the hell's it about then?"

ROSS rolled drunkenly towards the edge of the sofa and reached for another half-empty bottle of vodka on the glass table. He stretched out an arm, but he couldn't quite touch the bottle while holding the phone with the other hand. He dropped the phone on the Axminster and snatched the bottle.

"Hello, Ross, hello … Are you there? Ross, are you all right?"

Ross heard Jimmy's voice through the receiver. He giggled. Let the fucker wait. He'll get what's coming to him. He unscrewed the vodka bottle lid with his teeth and spat it across the living room.

"Get in there," Ross said.

"Ross, I can hear you there. Are you are all right, mate?"

Ross smiled and swigged from the bottle, forcing the alcohol down until his cheeks flushed. He pulled the bottle out of his mouth suddenly and gagged. The room was moving around him. He was struggling to focus. He made out the outline of the coffee table and slowly guided the bottle towards its edge. He let go of the bottle and watched it topple off the side of the coffee table, spilling the vodka all over the Axminster.

Fuck it. She bought the fucking carpet in the first place.

He sat up slowly and took a deep breath. He picked up the phone.

Ross was ready.

"Hello mate," he said cheerily. "You all right?"

"Yeah, I'm fine, mate, I'm fine, you all right over there? You sound a bit funny."

Ross heard the uncertainty in the voice immediately, the apprehension; the anxiety. He closed his eyes and inhaled, taking it all in, savouring the moment, getting high on the consternation coming down the line. Revenge was the drug now.

"I'm fine, Jimmy. Are you all right? I mean have you fucked over any other mates of yours today?"

The pause gave Jimmy's game away. Ross could taste the trepidation.

"What you on about, Ross? I didn't fuck you over. Did you see me at that press conference? I backed you up all the way. I didn't want you suspended. I begged Charlie not to suspend you. It's not in either of our interests for him to suspend you. You've been flying along this year, I'm finalising all kinds of deals and once I can sell you as an England striker, then we can all take our ball home and retire. Believe me, mate, the last thing I wanted was for Charlie to suspend you for the rest of the season."

"Then why did you shop me to the papers," Ross said evenly.

The pause was excruciating. Jimmy couldn't find the words to say. Charlie's boy had no words.

"Why did you grass me up to the papers," Ross continued.

"Who told you that? That's a load of bollocks, Ross, fucking hell. What could I possibly gain from giving you up like that?"

Ross felt his vocal chords tighten. He swallowed hard. His sentimentality would not betray him now.

"They told me it was a distraction. You see, the paper that called me told me that the paper that called you had a different story which you didn't want them to print. So you do them a favour and they do you one. You give them one client to save another, that about right?"

"No, Ross, listen mate, you don't understand. That's bollocks. I work with these fuckers every day. I know every one of them. I know all their faces. They tell you A, so you tell them fucking B. That's how they do it. It's textbook stuff for these bastards. I've been dealing with them for years. It's how they operate. They tell me that you're struggling for form. I tell them that Manchester United have expressed an interest. You get a new contract and an extra 20 grand a week. It's all bullshit. But that's how it works."

"It's a good little speech, mate. You always did have the gift of the gab. Even in primary school, you could talk a fucking glass eye to sleep."

"Fucking hell, Ross. How many people see you at that casino? How many people see you at the races? How many people work at your bank? It only takes one of them to pick up 50 grand by telling the papers how much debt you've got."

"Yeah, it's true. Normally, I'd believe you. I'd ignore the fact that the story knew all the specifics about where and when I go and how much, and you're the only person who really knows the state of my finances and I'd still probably believe you. But you fucked yourself this time mate, you and Scott. You fucked yourselves because I already knew."

"What are you on about?"

"I already knew, mate."

"I don't know what you're trying to say."

"I already knew, Jimmy. And I've just been on the phone to the bloke who tipped me off and I thanked him by telling him what I knew. He reckons I'll get at least 100,000 for this, maybe more. It's the story of the year, Jimmy."

There was that silence again. Ross had Jimmy on his knees now.

"What story? What do you know?" Jimmy asked, his voice breaking.

Ross thought about their friendship. He saw the three of them playing football tennis up against the breeze block wall on the side of Barking Football Club. He saw them sitting around his mother's table eating pie, mash and liquor together, fighting over the last drop of Ribena. He thought about the betrayal. It was too big for him to comprehend, too absolute. There could be no way back after that. Ross wiped the tears from his eyes.

"I know about Scott. I've always known about Scott," Ross said slowly, his hand shaking, struggling to hold the phone. "He's been fucking her for ages, Jimmy. He's been fucking her for months. He's been fucking Jo for months and I didn't even try to stop it. He's been pounding away at her, getting those dirty blow jobs, licking those enormous tits. And she's your wife, Jimmy. She's your fucking wife."

twenty-one

SCOTT struggled to keep up with Jimmy. He eyed the crowd walking towards him; a disagreeable mix of pissed locals, Aussie expats and tourists. He had never liked Covent Garden at the best of times. He had been up on a school coach trip with Ross and Jimmy to go to the London Transport Museum and had been bored shitless; a load of old buses and tubes, and then a Punch and Judy show in Covent Garden. He never came this way for a drink, too many Asians with those bloody Pentax cameras taking four weeks to get the zoom right. The meal in the Savoy had been pretty decent, and they'd managed to ditch the rest of the team and drop their wives, and were up for a nightcap in Soho. Jimmy had insisted on walking, through the streets of London, fucking anarchy. It was all right for Jimmy. Only the anoraks bothered him now to sign their retro DVDs and jerseys. But walking was a nightmare for Scott. He never walked the streets anywhere. Streets belonged to the nameless.

"Jim, where are we going?" he asked impatiently, as Jimmy turned into Maiden Lane.

Scott looked down the congested street in disbelief.

"What are you bringing us down here for," Scott whined. "There's that bloody Aussie expat pub down here. You know what they're like when they've had a few Fosters and they're waving their flags. They'll drive us fucking nuts. It's late. They'll be pissed. I'm not going in there."

"No. We're not going in there," Jimmy replied firmly.

Jimmy spotted a dimly-lit side street by the Thai restaurant. Lumley Court. Jimmy peered down the empty alley and glanced over both shoulders.

"This will do," he muttered. "Let's take a shortcut."

Scott stopped by the side street. He squinted down the narrow, eerie walkway and noticed a single, archaic lamp barely lighting the street.

"Who are we going for a beer with? Jack the fucking Ripper? I'm not going down there. We'll get stabbed."

"We need a private place quiet to talk, and we need to talk now."

"Couldn't we have done this at the Savoy?"

"No."

"Ah, for fuck's sake."

Jimmy marched ahead down Lumley Court and Scott reluctantly followed, his hand sliding along the small, white tiles, acting as a guide. Jimmy strolled down some steps and craned his head. He saw the Strand up ahead. No one was coming. The theatre crowds had already side-stepped the homeless and scurried into the safety of their black taxis, and it was too early for the clubbing crowd. He turned and glared at Scott.

"Who have you been shagging?"

Scott instinctively took a step backward to get Jimmy out of his face, moving away from the glare of the solitary street lamp, and buying himself some time.

"What are you on about?" Scott retorted, clearing the fog from the Savoy beers.

"Scott, I know you've been shagging around, all right. Please don't fuck me about. Someone at the papers told me. That's what they do for me. This is my job, all right. I know you fuck about.

We've all fucked about. But it's different now."

Scott was now relieved that Jimmy had bundled him down a caliginous West End back alley. He felt his burning cheeks redden in the darkness. The sweat was making its way through his hair. That could be explained away by the gel and the beer, but not for long.

"Look, Jimmy, I can't say ..."

"I'm not interested, you know that," Jimmy said. "I couldn't give a shit. But the club is going through a tricky time now, what with the Al-Hakim thing. And Charlie's told me straight. No dodgy publicity of any kind until it's all done and dusted. So we have to keep a lid on this, if it's at all possible. So are we talking a one-night stand here, a long-term shag or are you deadly serious and about to divorce Nicola?"

Scott tried to read Jimmy's eyes in the shadowy street.

"You don't know who it is then?"

Jimmy shrugged his shoulders.

"Why should I give a shit? I don't care who you shag. That's between you and your conscience. And who am I to talk, especially after that away game at Wolves."

Scott forced a laugh.

"Yeah, that was a good night," he recalled.

"It was a great night. I still get at least a semi just thinking about it."

Scott laughed, genuinely now. He felt his stomach muscles loosen. He had stopped sweating. Jimmy didn't know. Jimmy didn't fucking know. He wasn't out of the woods yet, but he could at least see the clearing.

Scott cleared his throat.

"So what do you think we should do?" Scott asked.

"Well, that depends on her, more than you, doesn't it? I mean, if she decides she wants to ... ssh."

Jimmy held his forefinger to his lips and peered over Scott's shoulder. Scott turned and picked out two young backpackers, a man and a woman, draped in an Australian flag staggering down the murky steps of the alley and towards them.

"G'day mate, how's it going," the tanned, bleach-blonde Australian said to Scott.

"All right," replied Scott quietly, staring down at the floor.

The Australian guy grabbed his partner's arm and stopped. He stared at Scott. Scott winced as the smell of cheap booze slapped him across the sinuses.

"Here, I reckon I know you, mate," the Australian said, looking at Scott and then across at Jimmy. "Are you two famous or something? You're two sportsmen, right?"

"Nah, not me, mate, I wish," Scott said briskly. "I work up the road in your pub, the Aussie pub, you must have seen me in there."

"Yeah, all right," the Australian replied, clearly not assured.

"Come on," his partner drawled. "I wanna get a pizza."

"Yeah, all right. See ya, fellas."

Jimmy nodded at the two Australians as he stepped aside to let them pass. He smiled approvingly at the girl's vest and cut-down khaki shorts. She had long, tanned athletic legs. He looked back at Scott.

"It wasn't her, was it?"

Scott laughed.

"No, I wouldn't mind having a go at her."

"No, nor me."

They both watched the Australians stagger through to the Strand before disappearing.

"Right, is the woman gonna get her tekkers out for the papers or not," Jimmy continued, his focus immediately recalibrated.

"No, definitely not, out of the question," Scott said.

"How can you be sure? They always go to the papers in the

end, you know that," Jimmy insisted.

"She won't. She doesn't need to," Scott muttered.

Jimmy frowned.

"So she's either rich, famous or both. Fucking hell, Scott, do I need to know who she is?"

"Not really. It was nothing really."

"But it's probably better for all concerned if it doesn't make the papers."

"It can't make the papers."

Jimmy might have been mistaken, but he was positive that he picked up on something in Scott's voice. He sounded vulnerable, cowed even.

"All right, then it can't make the papers," Jimmy said. "Do we need an injunction?"

"I've told you, she won't open her mouth."

"They always do in the end."

"She won't. She can't."

"I'll look into the injunction anyway. It's insurance. This is your private life. The plebs have got no right to your private life."

Scott stamped his feet against the concrete. He was getting cold.

"Either way, that won't stop the papers if they've already got the story. How did they get it anyway?"

"Fuck knows," Jimmy said angrily. "I'd love to know who it was though."

The possibility flashed across Scott's mind. It was only fleeting, but it was enough.

Jo.

There was always an angle for Jo, always an "in" with the media that she spotted long before anyone else. But there was no mileage to be gained from this, not even for Jo. The plebs wouldn't tolerate an infidelity of this magnitude. She would have seen that without being told. There were children involved on both sides. And the plebs lost the faith every time when there were children involved.

"We can worry about that another day," Scott said. "For now, nothing else matters. This cannot go public, not now."

"Have you been discreet?"

Scott frowned at Jimmy.

"I'm always discreet. I have to be discreet."

Jimmy nodded thoughtfully as Scott tried to read him.

"How do we stop it from going public?" Scott asked finally.

Jimmy grinned slightly and shrugged.

"The way we've always done it. We need more sex, more drugs or more death. Anything that draws attention away. Remember your red card for the two-footed tackle at White Hart Lane? I called Big Pictures straight after the game and had the paps waiting for Tottenham outside the Punk Club that night, just as a bit of security. That's all we need now, any sort of distraction, a bit of a diversion, the bigger, the better."

Scott looked up at Jimmy.

"What about gambling?"

Jimmy's eyes narrowed.

"Are you serious?"

"Do you think it will be enough?"

Jimmy found himself nodding, already calculating the media scales. Would this story be enough to counter-balance Scott's shagging? Would the hacks be pacified?

"It might be, yeah, it might be," he admitted.

"It'll certainly give you the distraction," Scott said.

"Yeah, it would. But fucking hell, Scott, we shouldn't even be saying this out loud. We shouldn't even be thinking it."

"Yeah, I know. I know all that. Jesus. You don't have to tell me, but we're desperate. I mean, have we got anything else on the table?"

Jimmy adjusted the belt buckle on his trousers.

"No, nothing. Nothing as strong as that anyway. If nothing else, it would buy us plenty of time to think it through. By the time the dust settled, the Al-Hakim thing would probably be over anyway."

"He'd never know it was us. No one would ever know it was us."

"Yeah, but ... I don't know. It's just not right, Scott. Fucking hell, do you know how many times I stayed over his house after my parents split up?"

"Yeah, of course I bloody know. I was there too. But we've got nothing else, right? You said that yourself."

Jimmy bit the corner of his lip. He stared transfixed at the single, hypnotic street lamp and nodded to himself.

"When you make the England squad, I want 15 per cent of your image rights," he said flatly.

"What?"

"Fifteen per cent to get you out of this shit, and I don't want this conversation ever mentioned again."

Scott shrugged. There was nothing to think about. Neither of them had any choice.

"Yeah, all right," he said.

"He can't find out," Jimmy insisted.

"Of course he can't fucking find out," Scott retorted. "Bloody hell, Jim, give me some credit please ... What do you think Charlie will do?"

"It doesn't really matter now, does it? It's the lesser of two evils."

"Yeah, all right, all right. I know what I've done. But it should be all right for him, shouldn't it? I mean, he does need help. We both agree on that. Something positive could come out of this."

Jimmy glared at Scott.

"Who's he? His name's Ross. He's our best fucking mate, remember?"

twenty-two

JO raised her arms over her head and swayed erotically from side to side. She was missing the beat. Kylie Minogue's *Can't Get You Out of My Head* always packed the dance floor at the Embassy because of its easy beat, but Jo couldn't catch it. Jo couldn't really dance. White girls couldn't really dance. Jo had always known that. She also knew it was irrelevant. White boys couldn't dance either, and they always made dicks of themselves pretending that they could; all wiggling arses and hips and out-of-rhythm handclaps. For men the moves mattered. Men didn't have boobs to jiggle. A tight vest and hot pants masked any shortcomings on the dance floor. Even Kylie knew that.

Jo jutted out her hips and rocked sexily. Her tacky moves belonged around a pole, but it didn't matter. She was Jo. And she owned the Embassy club. If the club was the heart of Mayfair, then she was its breasts. All eyes were on Jo. She smiled seductively at the wealthy plebs dribbling around her and wiggled her arse at them. They got excited. She got them out of her face. She was not wriggling around on a club podium in Romford. They were not her people anymore. They were not famous enough.

She fleetingly saw her reflection in the antique mirrors and laughed. God, she was an awful dancer. There were some gifted dancers in the members' club tonight, she noticed, but they danced alone. Her days of partying alone ended in Essex years ago.

Jo peered across at her glittery table gathering in the VIP lounge. They were all there—the glamour model, the TV host, the singer, the soap actor; all that was missing was the bloody candlestick maker. They were raising another drunken toast with champagne; her champagne, her private table, her Embassy membership.

The actor, Shaun, stood up and waved at her. He had been angling for a shag for weeks, but Jo had brushed aside his puerile advances. He was handsome with short, cropped black hair and a warm smile, but what use did she have for a soap opera actor now? Jo's eyes narrowed. He was holding up her phone. The cheeky fucker had answered it. He had overstepped the mark. He was out.

Jo made her way across the floor as the dancers parted for her. She jogged up the stairs and snatched the phone.

"Don't ever answer my fucking phone," she shrieked, putting her hand over the phone.

Shaun looked hurt. He glimpsed across at the rest of Jo's party sitting around the table and looked down at the floor.

"It rang three times," he whimpered.

"What? I can't hear you over the music, can I?" Jo yelled.

"I said it rang three times."

"Then it rings three times. If it's anyone important, I'll call them back."

Jo glared at Shaun and put the phone to her ear.

"Hello, who is it," she shouted. "Oh, hello, Pat, what are you doing calling me at this time of the morning?"

Jo adored Pat. She had been her agent since her first glamour model shoot. Pat was a council house girl from Essex, too. She had grown up in the same fish tank. She had always understood

Jo's drive and ambition. It wasn't only about the money, or even the fame. They were by-products. They gave Jo, and by association Pat, the only thing their birthplace had denied them: Respect.

"Where are you, Jo?" Pat's voice hollered down the phone.

"I'm at the Embassy. I thought I told you that already. I got some great pap shots coming into the club, standing beside one of those giant plant pots. Look out for them in the morning, Pat."

"You need to go home now, Jo," Pat cried.

Jo laughed for the benefit of the hangers-on looking up at her.

"What are you on about, Pat?" she said, failing to hide the uncertainty.

"We've already seen the early editions of the paper. You're all over the front page, Jo. You're everywhere."

"Ah, yeah, that's all right."

"You and Scott," Pat said, her voice dropping abruptly.

Jo noticed she was walking. She was walking quickly. She was nodding at the doorman, gesturing towards the door. He was winking at her. She was smiling back at him, always flirting, on auto-pilot, never able to turn it off. He was whispering in his earpiece, saying, "Jo is coming out, Jo is coming out." One name; always one name. She had worked so hard to be just one name. The door was opening. Jo examined her tanned legs. They were moving so fast, gliding through the door and into the streetlights. There were so many lights—more than streetlights. They were London lights. They were Jo's lights. These lights had given Jo her freedom. Now she was trapped by them. She was blinking, staring, but she couldn't see; too late to spot the ambush.

The paparazzi had been waiting.

LITTLE Steve rubbed his ears vigorously. She wouldn't want him to cry. She was much tougher than that. He stared at the headline on his laptop. The headline was scorched into his brain. He closed his eyes, but it was still there: SCOTT AT HOME WITH JO. The sub-heading was no better: Footballer Scores With Best Mate's Wife. Little Steve had no interest in the best mate. He didn't even know who Jimmy was. Little Steve loathed football. There were only so many times he could be left leaning against the fence as the two school captains picked up sides; always giggling nervously, feigning indifference, the last man standing.

Little Steve had no time for football or Jo. She had ruined everything. Her kind always went with footballers. They deserved each other. Her behaviour was encouraged in the English Premier League; it was almost expected, practically celebrated. This was what people like Scott and Jo were supposed to do in the English Premier League; recording their sex videos, sleeping with hookers, organising secret abortions and taking part in those sickening roastings with other teammates. Little Steve had read about them in all the newspapers and scanned the photographs; disgusting, simply disgusting. The more he stared at the photographs the more repulsive they became. Nicola didn't deserve to see that sort of stuff. Nicola was pure. She was the most popular singer in Girl Power, even though she wasn't the lead singer. Nicola's band sold millions of records because of Nicola. She was the reason why Little Steve's Girl Power website got thousands of hits every day. The site's popularity wasn't because of Little Steve's graphics and web design, even though he constantly moderated and updated the content and layout, sometimes on a daily basis. It wasn't even Girl Power. It was because of Nicola. She was a loving wife and mother, and easily Britain's most talented singer.

Nicola had once been pure and unblemished. Now she was tainted. Jo had left her slightly dirty, forever contaminated. Nicola did not deserve this.

Little Steve blew his nose and re-read the breaking story on his laptop.

THE image of Scott and Nicola filled the screen of Ross' plasma TV. There was a crude, ragged cut down the centre of the image, splitting the photograph in two. The camera cut back to the Sky Sports News studio where the host, Tony Donald, was sitting beside Trevor Bonds, the former Newcastle and England fullback.

"It's still hard to take in, isn't it, Trevor?" Tony asked.

Trevor adjusted his ill-fitting tie strangling his bulging, perspiring neck and took a deep breath. It was early in the morning and he looked exhausted.

"I'm still trying to get my head around it, Tony, I really am," Trevor mumbled, clearing the frog from his dry, early morning throat.

"Now, Trevor, don't take this the wrong way, but you're a good person to bring in on this because ..."

"Ah, thanks very much," Trevor interjected.

"No, no. I mean, when you were playing there were some incidents and scandals at the clubs you played for and, let's be honest, one or two of them involved you, but did anything like this ever go on?"

The now-obese, sweating Trevor Bonds shifted uneasily in his seat. He smiled, but under the unforgiving studio lights, it came across as a sneer.

"No, that's true. I think my problems have been well documented, both in the UK and in Asia. Footballers messed around, they always did. I'd be lying if I said otherwise. And yes, footballers occasionally slept with their teammates' wives. I know this is not what you want to hear, but footballers are human and in any walk of life, whether you're a professional footballer or an office guy or a security guard, people have affairs with their colleagues' partners."

"But if the allegations in the early editions of this morning's papers—and I must stress that they are allegations at this stage, we are trying to speak to someone at the club as soon as they arrive—this is more than just an affair, right?"

"Ah, Tony, this is beyond anything that I ever saw when I played. I mean, if it's true that Scott had an affair with Jo, his best mate's wife and then leaked a story about Ross to try to divert attention away ..."

"According to the newspaper report," Tony interjected.

"Yeah, of course, according to the newspaper report, but this newspaper report is supposed to be based on an interview with Ross, which I find extraordinary, and you have to wonder what's gone on there. But the idea that a footballer and his agent, a former footballer himself, grass up their best mate and teammate just so they can cover the tracks of the first footballer's affair with his agent's wife, I mean what can you say? We're gonna need diagrams to explain this one."

"But if it all happens to be true?"

Trevor sighed, blinked the perspiration from his eyes and shook his head slowly.

"If it's true, Tony, then, I don't know, it's the way the game is going I suppose, isn't it?"

The programme went to a commercial break and the show's theme tune flooded through Ross' surround sound system. His living room walls were now bare. She had taken all her catwalk shots and magazine covers down before she left. They would be better served elsewhere now. A broken-down footballer, even a handsome one, had little value in such a competitive market.

Ross stirred and curled into the foetal position. He continued to snore on the sofa.

NICOLA sat on a kitchen stool and watched her daughter—their daughter—play on the tiled floor. She smiled dreamily at the girl and stared. She was empty. There was nothing left inside. She had been hollowed out. She pictured the old guy in the white jacket tearing away at her insides with an ice-cream scoop. Daft really, but that was how she felt. She saw the old guy in the white jacket on Brighton pier scooping her insides out. She had loved that old guy in the white jacket, always smiling as he handed her a double scoop of mint choc chip. He always gave her extra. Everyone always gave her extra. She never asked for it, but it was that angelic smile, that wholesomeness. She had captivated people since she was a kid, not intentionally, but she did anyway.

Nicola watched her daughter—their daughter—push a pink car along the kitchen tiles, lying alongside the car, keeping the vehicle at eye level and making the engine noises. Nicola had wanted to take her daughter—their daughter—to Brighton pier, just once, to walk along the creaky timber planks, hear the waves smash against the rusting iron girders underneath and taste a mint choc chip from the old guy in the white jacket. But Scott had never wanted to go. He moaned about being pestered, about the plebs never leaving him alone. So she hadn't seen the old guy with the white jacket again; she only had the memories and Scott had defiled even those now, too. She could only see the old guy in the white jacket leaning over the curved, plastic counter and ripping her insides out with an ice-cream scoop.

She was a plastic shell. She had become that fucking whore. For the first time, they were both the same, a pair of plastic shells. Maybe Scott would find his wife alluring again, not that it mattered now.

The little girl picked up two plastic figures and delicately sat them in the front of her pink car.

"Mummy," she said cheerily. "And daddy."

She looked up at Nicola.

"Where's daddy? Daddy house?"

"No, daddy's not in the house," Nicola replied slowly. "Daddy's at nanny and granddad's house."

"Daddy house?"

Nicola swallowed hard. The burning sensation at the back of her mouth made her angry. Don't you dare, she thought. Not for him; never again for him.

"No, daddy's not coming to our house tonight. Daddy is staying at nanny and granddad's, but he might come and see you later, OK?"

The phone rang and Nicola picked it up quickly, eager for the distraction.

"Hello," she said.

She gritted her teeth.

"No comment," she hissed. "Yes, right, OK, understand all that. No comment, OK, bye."

She slammed the phone down and it immediately rang again. She snatched it back.

"Look I just told you, no bloody comment," she shouted.

Her face softened.

"Oh, hello, Jimmy," she whispered. "How have you been? No, he's not here? ... Yeah, I know, I know how you feel, but that's not going to solve anything is it?"

CHARLIE marched up and down the pool house in his dressing gown. He reached the end of the pool, turned on his slipper heels and went back again. He had normally swum his daily 20 lengths by now. He had normally had his scrambled eggs and mushrooms by now. He had normally had a go on the missus by now. He was normally on his way to training by now to beat the traffic on the M25. He was going to be late for training. Fuck training. They could stew in their own piss for all he cared. He couldn't concentrate on training anyway. His mind was racing. The phone hadn't stopped ringing since 5 am and his wife had ripped out the TV plug, claiming he was getting too stressed and raising his blood pressure. He stared at his reflection in the still water of his lap pool. That bastard had really screwed him over.

Charlie turned his mobile back on and the beeps started immediately. They wouldn't stop. He had no time for the missed calls or the text messages. He dialled quickly before someone got through to him. He paced around the edge of the pool as he waited for an answer.

"Ah for fuck's sake," he screamed, stamping his feet and preparing to throw the phone in the pool. He gritted his teeth and thought better of it. Instead he waited impatiently to leave his message after the tone.

"Listen to me, you little cunt. You can turn off your phone from them, but don't ignore me. I don't expect you anywhere near the training ground today, but if you haven't called me back within one hour, me and you are gonna have a serious fucking falling out.

"What the fuck am I supposed to say to the towelhead? How am I gonna explain this one away? Of all the women in London you could've shagged, why did you pick her? I can't defend you on this. I can't protect you. Everything's fucked now. The deal could be fucked, my job could be fucked, even the Charlie's

Angels could be fucked. Well, of course, they're fucked, what am I thinking? You've already stuck your dick in most of them, you fucking little twat. Every camera in the world is gonna be shoved up our arses for the rest of the year. If you, me, or Jimmy farts, they're gonna be in the toilets waiting for us to take a shit. They're gonna expect me to fix this, do you understand? The whole fucking world is going to expect me to get you two in the same room together and kiss and make up. How am I going to get you and Jimmy in the same room? Jimmy will rip your fucking head off before he sits next to you."

twenty-three

JIMMY stared at the TV screen. That fat old footballer Trevor Bonds was telling Britain what Jimmy should do, how he should handle the delicate situation of his celebrity wife sleeping with his best friend and most profitable client. But the fat man on TV was wasting his time. Jimmy already knew what to do.

Jimmy stood up suddenly and picked up the remote control. Unexpectedly, he thought about his mother. His poor old mum. She was always there for him after his parents divorced, England's first soccer mom. She stood on the sidelines at most youth games, making her voice heard over the testosterone, shouting words of encouragement above the male battle-cries to bruise, batter and maim the other scrawny kids on the field. She was there with her ex-husband when Jimmy signed his first contract in Charlie's office. She was there when he made his debut. She was there with him, holding his hand, fighting back the tears, telling her boy to be brave, when the surgeon had fixed his gaze on the X-rays, unable to look either of them in the eye.

She had ordered him not to cry in his beer. She had helped him settle his insurance payment. She had badgered "Mr Charlie" to look out for him. She had saved Jimmy's life and career.

But she couldn't save him from Jo.

"She's not your kind of girl," she had said, sitting up in her old, flea-bitten armchair that she refused to replace in the Barking house that she had refused to leave.

"What's my kind of girl?" Jimmy had retorted.

"Oh, you know, Jimmy. I know what you do. I know what you all do, you, Scott and Ross. I read the papers. They're practically falling at your feet and I know you three are randy little buggers. But Jo is, well, loud. You know where she's from."

"Hey, don't be an old snob, mum. I'm from Barking, too."

"Yeah, I know that, but you haven't got the big chip on your shoulder like most of them around here. You're comfortable in your own skin. She's not. No one even knows what her own skin is."

"Hey, come on, mum, I think she's great."

Jimmy's mum sat up and glared at him.

"What's so great about her then?"

"She makes me laugh."

And she did. Jo had her role to play in public and Jimmy had tolerated it benignly, if he had never really accepted it. But his Jo was private, self-conscious, uncertain and a great piss-taker. Ironically, he had fallen in love with the Jo that everyone else was eager for her to leave behind, including herself. He had loved the awkward, slightly insecure Barking girl with the tied hair and the harsh face. But Jimmy hardly saw that girl anymore.

Jimmy turned off the TV and headed into the hallway. He grabbed his car keys and picked up his phone. He thought about the football tennis. It was all they ever played. Every night after school, a tennis ball up against the ruins of Barking Abbey, only one touch allowed. The rules were simple. First shot with the right foot, second shot with the left, the tennis ball couldn't stop moving and if the ball missed the wall, the player was out. They played until dusk. Their parents wouldn't allow them to walk from Barking city centre at night and Barking Abbey was too eerie after dark.

Jimmy always won the football tennis. He had the most natural skill. Ross was certainly more accurate and Scott the most dedicated, but Jimmy was Barking's answer to Steve McManaman.

Jimmy saw himself in the hallway mirror. The grey hair was now sprouting around his ears. She had wanted him to dye it, but she could get fucked now. She would never be allowed to tell him what to do ever again. He smiled at himself in the mirror as he pressed the phone to his ear.

"Hello, Charlie, it's me," he said flatly. "Yeah, all right, I don't really want to talk about it now over the phone."

Jimmy exhaled deeply.

"Look, I know how this works. This fucking thing will not go away until there is some sort of resolution; we've been doing this long enough to both know that. I'm not going into hiding for anybody. I've got a job to do and clients to look after and I'm not having fat cunts like Trevor Bonds pontificating on TV about what I should and shouldn't be doing now. We put the speculation to bed and we get this settled ... Yeah, I'll be fine. I just want this fucking thing to go away. If that means I've got to shake the bastard's hands for the cameras, then so be it. I want my life back, all right? ... Where is he now? ... There's still enough time then. Get him home first, make sure he gets changed and let's get this over with."

Jimmy slipped the phone inside his jacket pocket—Armani jacket pocket. He wasn't going to give them the satisfaction of turning up in rags. Ross had always been the best-looking, but Jimmy was the smartest.

Scott was the ugliest. Jo had always joked about him in their living room; mocked him on *Match of the Day*; took the piss out of him; said he had a face like a ferret. They had laughed together.

It didn't bare thinking about.

Jimmy checked himself in the mirror one last time and put on his Ray-Bans. The paps were outside, and he had no intention of looking like shit.

He opened his front door and the cameras clicked furiously. He still had enough time. He had to end it now.

CHARLIE stormed down his gravel drive and frowned at his lawn. The gardener had cut the grass too short and there were yellow strips along the edges. Charlie tutted. His shoebox front garden in Dagenham had been perfect. Charlie now boasted a koi carp pond bigger than his front garden in his parents' old house, but his father had maintained an immaculate lawn with a rose bush in the middle. No one had the inclination to get their hands soiled anymore. No one had any pride left. They had swallowed it years ago. Even Jimmy had disappointed him.

Charlie adjusted the phone earpiece and dialled as he unlocked the Bentley.

"Ah, you're in this time, are ya," he shouted. "Look ... look ... I'm not fucking interested in your excuses now, all right. Get home first and hope Nicola doesn't kill you before I fucking do. Just get your best suit on and have a shave. Don't turn up looking like a fucking tramp. You'll just give them more ammunition. Get down to the training ground and we'll work on this bloody press conference before they're burning effigies of you outside the stadium all right ... Yes, he's just called me and he's said he's willing to be there. He's already on his way so you'd better get off your arse ... Of course not, he probably wants to kill you. I want to kill you. Half the fucking country wants to kill you. What did you expect? ... No, you've burnt all your bridges with Jimmy, but he wants to finish this and so do I. He's being mature about this. Shame you weren't, innit?"

JIMMY pressed the volume button on his steering wheel as he accelerated and swerved into the fast lane. Oasis had to be played at full volume or not at all. Everyone else had moved on from Oasis, the band itself had disintegrated, but Jimmy always went back to *Definitely Maybe* when he was alone in the car on the M25. Besides, it was their song; it belonged to them, at school, playing football tennis, going to training at the academy, making their debuts, everywhere. It was their song. It was about their lives. *Live Forever. We'll see things they'll never see.* The three of them sang that line together on the way home from school. It was their line and it had proven prophetic. *We'll see things they'll never see.* And they did. Scott, Ross and Jimmy had seen more women, more money, more clothes; the game had allowed them to fly.

We'll see things they'll never see.

Scott, Ross and Jimmy had always understood that. There was a profound understanding, even off the pitch. They could never cross the only line left. They had sprinted across every other line—there were no restrictions once you signed on as a member of the exclusive English Premier League—everything was on the slate, everything was on credit, just a signature please, sir, your autograph on this jersey please, sir, and everything I own is at your disposal; what's mine is yours.

So they had taken everything. It was their right. They spent money that belonged to the punters. They shagged women who belonged to the punters. There were no self-imposed limits to what they could take. The punters were given 90 minutes on a Saturday, and that was more than enough. Everything else was up for grabs.

But their world had to be protected if they wanted to fly. They could take from everyone else, but not one another. That was the unwritten rule. That was the only rule if they wanted to live forever. Fuck another man's wife and there was something to talk about on the training ground on a Monday morning. Fuck another footballer's wife and the bubble would burst, and the expense account swiftly withdrawn. There had to be a calm exterior to protect the status quo within.

That was why Jimmy had no choice but to do this. Publicly, the other lads in the English Premier League would be forced to castigate Jimmy's actions, lamenting his loss of dignity and self-respect. Some of the lads might even call it disloyal; a corruption of their secret code; a betrayal of the brotherhood. He accepted that. He'd trot out a similar line if he was still playing. Privately, of course, the chaps would celebrate his statement. The matter would be closed. Order would be restored. The VIP section would be roped off again and the velvet curtains drawn. The private party would continue.

Jimmy parked the car down a leafy street about a mile away. He didn't want the paps in his face the moment he opened the door. They would already be here. They were everywhere today and he needed time to think. He had to consider the statement he was going to make. The cameras would be rolling, and every word and gesture live on that bloody Sky Sports News—the damn channel that transmitted 24/7 and was always scrambling for fresh content. They would dissect everything. They would replay everything for days and weeks to come.

Jimmy crossed the road and peered into the parked cars. They were all empty. The paps had parked closer, which made sense. With a story this big, parking tickets and fines were irrelevant. No one could miss the chance of "papping" the elusive Scott, who had been in hiding since the story broke. Jimmy took out his phone.

"Hello, Charlie, it's me again," Jimmy said. "Yeah, I'm almost there. Yeah, I know it's early, but I want to get this right. He's already made a cunt of me once; I won't let him do it again. Are you at the ground yet? He's not there yet, is he? ... Good, he can't get there before me. He's got to go home first, get a decent suit ... Yeah, she'll let him in. She won't talk to him, but she'll let him in. She's stronger than all of us that girl, she's got more dignity than the lot of us ... Yeah, all right, I'll see you soon. I'm almost there."

Charlie sat in his office and stared up at the photograph of him signing his first contract with the old man. Charlie usually had no time for nostalgia. He didn't do whimsical.

Today was different. Today, he couldn't take his eyes off the boy with the short back and sides in the photograph. The boy who once kicked a tin can all the way along the Heathway, through the spine of Dagenham, from one end of the world's biggest housing estate to the other, without breaking stride or losing control; the boy who had stared down at Charlie every morning for over 20 years.

Charlie didn't recognise him anymore.

He stood up, straightened his tie as he focused on his reflection in the photo frame and headed out for the hardest press conference of his career.

TOM scanned the room, examining the fidgeting journalists checking their notepads and voice recorders. The tension was palpable. His brethren lived for moments like this. This was their Watergate. All the President's men would soon be trotted out for slaughter; Charlie and his bloody Barking Boys were about to get what was coming to them. The English Premier League was about to get a little payback from its downtrodden, forgotten paymasters. The neglected fans were going to see what they had long suspected: the emperor really didn't have any new clothes. These were the real men behind their cola commercials and sanitised sound bites; solitary, nasty and brutish.

Tom struggled to contain his pride. He had made this possible. It wasn't quite Woodward and Bernstein, but today's revelations would affect just as many people.

"This is unbelievable."

Jason elbowed Tom in the ribs excitedly.

"I mean, it's fucking amazing," Jason continued. "We couldn't have dreamed of this a few weeks ago—Ross' gambling and suspension and this bloody Bermuda triangle of shagging."

Tom smiled back at Jason.

"I know, well, what goes around comes around."

"This is gonna be one of those 'where were you' moments. JFK and the grassy knoll, John Lennon outside the Dakota, walking on the moon, Ali's Rumble in the Jungle, I'm telling you, this is right up there."

"Oh, leave off," Tom laughed.

"I'm telling you, never mind Ali and Frazier or Federer and Nadal, we've got Jimmy and Scott and it's gonna happen right here, right in front of us. The whole fucking world is gonna be watching Jimmy and Scott and it's happening right in front of us. They should be selling bloody tickets for this."

"It's certainly going to work well for us."

"And the best part is, I don't know what I'm going to enjoy most. Watching Scott and Jimmy's reactions towards each other, will they shake hands, will they talk to each other, will they even look each other in the eye, will Scott apologise to Jimmy, will Jimmy tell him to fuck off, there're just so many scenarios. And on top of all that, I want to make sure I clock Charlie's face when he sees you with that notepad beside the camera crew."

"Yeah, I can't lie. I'm looking forward to that, too."

That was an understatement. Tom had thought about nothing else. He had barely slept the night before and when he did, Charlie haunted his dreams; the old man spotting him across the press conference in slow motion, time standing still. Even in his dreams, Tom had savoured the euphoria. There wasn't even a pressing need for Tom to attend the press conference. Jason and the camera crew could handle it without him. Besides, they had more than enough material, and this was just a little bit of frilly tabloid window dressing to decorate the edges with. But Tom had to be there. Charlie was his target, and Charlie had spat in his face. Leaving that case in the hotel room was one thing, but posing and giggling with those footballers' wives in a pink T-shirt was taking the piss. Fuck it, Tom thought. This was personal. He was only human. Charlie had been fleecing players, agents, other clubs and the fans for decades, and buried it all beneath his media patter and bullshit. But the old bastard was finally going to get what was coming to him.

Tom surveyed the room. They were all here: BBC, Sky Sports, CNN, ESPN; even Fox Sports in Australia had a camera set up in front of the top table. Tom had invited the world to the unofficial soft launch of his documentary. He smiled and nodded gently. He was coming home.

Charlie entered the room slowly. He looked shrunken and old. He made his way ploddingly to the middle of the long table— clearly he would sit between them; a handshake was looking highly unlikely—and pulled out a chair. The scraping of the chair's legs along the timber floor echoed around the otherwise silent press room.

Charlie took in the wide-eyed journalists in the room. He paused as he spoke, not for dramatic effect, but because he had no idea what to say.

"Ladies and gentlemen, thank you for coming today," he said. "I've spoken to both Scott and Jimmy and they will both be attending today's press conference."

Charlie watched his audience fidget excitedly as the murmurs filled the room.

"If I'm being honest, whether they both turn up at the same time, I cannot say. Scott will be a little late, I think, but Jimmy has just told me that he has parked his car."

JIMMY pushed his way through the throng. They were jostling for space to get off a few frames, but there was a definite sympathy there. The paps were doing their jobs, but they were being respectful. He had always maintained a good relationship with the paps. They were straight shooters. He gave them the odd exclusive tip-off, so they could "spontaneously" catch Scott or Ross buying a copy of *The Big Issue* down the King's Road or slipping a few quid to a homeless geezer in Soho. And they gave his clients the odd night off at the casino.

"All the best, Jim," one of the paps muttered, still snapping away, but from a dignified distance.

"Good luck, mate."

"Do the right thing, Jimmy."

"Yeah all the best, mate."

Jimmy nodded politely at the paps, but kept walking with his head down.

"I hope you cut that fucking bastard's bollocks off."

The paps all laughed. Jimmy looked up and saw a black Ford Focus pulled up in the street and a middle-aged, tubby bald guy fist-pumping his support towards Jimmy and tooting his horn. Jimmy waved back at him.

"I'm a Chelsea fan, Jim, but what that little shit did was bang out of order," the bald guy shouted. "He's took a right fucking liberty, Jim!"

The guy tooted his horn again and his Ford Focus roared off down the street. Some of the paps applauded him. They had stopped taking photographs of Jimmy to applaud his outspoken supporter.

But the bald bloke was on the money.

He's took a right fucking liberty, Jim.

Jimmy had no alternative but to go through with this. He stopped outside the two-metre tall iron gates and took in the vast country pile in Godalming.

Scott's house.

Jimmy punched in the security code on the alarm box on the stone pillar, and the gates swung open. The paps thought about following him inside and took a couple of tentative steps. Jimmy turned towards them and nodded his head solemnly. They stepped back as the iron gates swung towards them. This one was going to be played behind closed doors.

Jimmy marched purposefully along the curved, gravel drive towards the house—the five-million-dollar house with its own lake, the five-million-dollar house that Jimmy had helped to finance, the five-million-dollar house where Jimmy and Jo had gone over for dinner, the five-million-dollar house where Jo and Nicola had pretended to like each other for the sake of their partners.

They were best mates. And that was what the partners of best mates were supposed to do. They behaved themselves. They did not take liberties.

Jimmy marched towards the door and thought about the oblivious Charlie at the press conference. His mentor had to understand. They were in the business of shit clichés and sound bites. Footballers were programmed to give nothing away in interviews; words were reckless weapons of self-flagellation to be used sparingly, if at all. Actions always shouted the loudest. That was ingrained; instinctive even. Retired footballers, like decommissioned officers, never forgot their basic training.

Jimmy peered up at the bay windows, tastefully decorated by Nicola along with the rest of the house, and thought about his old best mate.

Scott.

Inside.

He's inside the house right now, putting on his Armani suit, another Jimmy deal; slipping on his Rolex, another Jimmy deal; picking up the keys to the Ferrari, another Jimmy deal; and heading to the front door, where Jimmy would be waiting.

"Jimmy! Jimmy!" the paps suddenly shouted at him. They were waving at him, frantically holding up their phones through the iron gates, beckoning him to come back.

But Jimmy only heard the bald bloke's words.

He's took a right fucking liberty, Jim.

Jimmy rang the doorbell.

He's took a right fucking liberty, Jim.

Jimmy banged the door repeatedly.

He's took a right fucking liberty, Jim.

THE incessant ringing and door banging was getting out of hand. It was obviously one of the paps chancing his arm on an exclusive doorstep photo. They had been trying their luck all morning, tapping the window tentatively; sneaking up to the doorbell and then scurrying away again like bloody schoolkids. Enough was enough. Their daughter was trying to sleep.

Jo opened her front door and the exploding flashes forced her to shield her eyes. The paps jostled for position, shoving one another violently, desperate for one full, clean frame.

"You guys are taking the piss now," she screamed. "Stop knocking on my fucking front door. I've got nothing to say to you bastards and if you ..."

Jo felt something trickling down her stomach. She looked at the jittery kid with the camera round his neck. He was fiddling anxiously with his hands, not taking her photo, obviously star struck; too distracted by the money shot; a fucking amateur. Just like the boys back in school messing around with her bra; dribbling, submissive amateurs, all of them; minor characters in her story. Nothing had changed. She still captivated a cowardly crowd, even now. Jo found herself giggling at the scrawny kid. She still had it. She still controlled the game.

Little Steve shook the sweat out of his eyes and blinked quickly. He gripped the handle tightly and twisted his right hand as hard as he could.

Little Steve stared at Jo.

Her face looked funny.

twenty-four

THE funeral procession passed slowly along Ripple Road. The streets of Barking had come alive to see the death of Jo. They were once her streets, but she was the only girl who had got away. She took her bottles of peroxide and spray-on tans and flew to the moon. They had begrudged her fame when she was alive, but she was dead now and no longer a threat. She had pushed buttons they didn't want pressed. She had championed their anti-intellectualism on her reality shows. She had made being thick a great British virtue. She had shown the rest of the country that people like Jo could slam the council house doors shut behind them, step over the dog shit and embrace the world. She had shown the rest of the country who people like Jo really were.

And they had hated her for it.

So they had to come out for her now. They had to fly their flags. They stepped out onto the kerbside in their thousands— from the funeral home in Barking Town Centre, past Vicarage Field where she had stacked shelves when she was that hard-faced teenager with tied-back hair, past the Gascoigne Estate where she had lost her virginity—and followed her along Ripple Road.

Jo was everywhere. Every red-bricked and plastered house in Ripple Road seemed to open its paint-chipped front door to one Jo after another, strutting along the garden path in their grey tracksuit bottoms and white vests and cropped tops, weeping, crying their eyes out; the granite, sneering, fuck-off veneer stripped away. They took shit from no one; they were fucking well hard, just like Jo had been. They were all Jo until they reached the edge of the kerb; until they saw the funeral procession crawling past; until they gaped at Jimmy, the former English Premier League footballer and multi-millionaire celebrity agent, sobbing in front of the world's media; until they stared at him clutching his baby daughter, squeezing the air from her lungs as his tears soaked her face. They peered into the hearse and saw the gold-plated coffin surrounded by wreaths. The biggest one read: "JO." Just Jo. No other name required. Only gangsters and footballers made it out of East London with one name, but Jo had been the exception.

And they had hated her for it because she had found her wings and taken flight. It was no coincidence that music from Tchaikovsky's *Swan Lake* was chosen for the funeral service. Jo had always claimed that *Billy Elliot* made her cry every time she watched it; the boy from the council estate who had discovered a talent and the will to make it happen. But the vitriol went beyond superficial envy. Jo had once been the face in the funeral crowds. She was every woman. She had been spat out wearing those baggy tracksuit bottoms and scuffed trainers. She had been born an ugly duckling, but she died a swan; a manufactured swan, but a swan nonetheless. The girls with the tied-back hair and harsh faces watching the celebrities stroll past in their dark shades and Hugo Boss suits would not escape. No cosmetic surgeon was going to pluck them from their fish tanks.

So they had dismissed Jo as nothing more than a footballer's wife. Slagging her off had made them feel better when they swigged their cans of Stella on Saturday nights. Even better, when Jimmy was forced to quit the game, she became the ex-footballer's wife. That was most palatable with a kebab and large chips on the way home.

They had wanted nothing to do with her because they were her. She was leading their lives, speaking their words, magnifying their ignorance, but she was doing it for the titillation of the middle classes. Their guffawing could be heard from the leafy suburbs and, with every malapropism and faux pas, Jo was laughing all the way to her off-shore account. Jo took the girl out of Barking and served her up as prime-time amusement for the intelligentsia. The girls left behind became a punch line. Everyone else in the country viewed the WAG as a figure of fun; a piss-take; a council house court jester. Barking girls were supposed to see the WAG as an aspiration.

White working-class women were presented with a role model they didn't want. Jo celebrated an uneducated way of life and a pride in her shallowness that hurt the people she had left behind, because it was their truth; their reality. On her show, *At Home With Jo*, she once boasted that she had never read a book from cover to cover other than her and her husband's autobiographies. The country chuckled in disbelief. Teenage girls in Barking acknowledged the absence of bookshelves in their houses and sheepishly turned away.

They didn't want the national spotlight on their way of life. Their conscience told them what they really were. They didn't need Jo reminding them from her tacky gold-plated throne in her country mansion every Saturday night

They had all wanted Jo to simply go away.

And now that she had, the jealousy had gone. The insecurity had dissipated. Guilt had given way to a mawkish sentimentality. The white working class had been ashamed of their leading female voice. Now they had to make amends. They had to come out, not to pay their respects, but to say sorry.

JASON was stunned by the outpouring of grief. He looked down the long, straight stretch of Ripple Road and could only see tiled roofs and crying faces. They covered the pavements and spilled into the road, waved posters out of PVC windows and blew kisses from their cracked doorsteps.

Jason did not want to be here today. Apart from the fact he still remembered one of the last of the Krays' funerals (and what a macabre, nostalgic celebration for "Knees Up Mother Brown" lost London that had been), he felt a pang of guilt. He had sat in that office staring down at White City when he agreed, along with Jonathan and Tom, to set the ball rolling; to give the tabloids a little titillation and manufacture a TV audience. But no one saw this coming. No one could have expected this. Jason wasn't responsible for every adulterer and lunatic in London any more than he was responsible for young, brainwashed fundamentalists who sat in their bedsits in Beeston and entertained the notion of filling their backpacks with explosives. Jonathan had also figured that some of this funeral footage might be useful in drawing in the younger demographic of Jo's reality TV crowd.

But still, it didn't sit right.

Jason spotted a woman with dyed blond hair standing on the edge of the kerb. She was wearing a baggy Nike sweatshirt and had a couple of gold chains hanging over the top. One of them had a large, male sovereign ring dangling at the bottom. She clutched two children closely to her hips. All three of them were crying. Jason pointed her out to the cameraman. He grinned and zoomed in.

"Excuse me, madam," Jason said softly as they approached the woman. "I don't wish to intrude upon your grief, but I was just wondering if you would give us a couple of minutes of your time."

The woman's eyes narrowed as she examined the cameraman.

"Is this for TV?" she asked bluntly.

"Possibly, perhaps for a documentary."

The woman instructed her children to stand up straight.

"Yeah, all right, then."

"Thanks very much. What's your name?"

"It's Lisa."

"OK, great, thanks Lisa ... Are we ready to go? ... OK, Lisa, you seem to be very emotional today. In fact, it seems to be a very emotional day for the whole town. Most of East London seems to be here today to pay its respects. Why do you think that is?"

"She was just a real woman, you know what I mean?" Lisa said. "You felt like you knew her. You know, you watch TV most of the time and you don't know the people on there. But Jo was normal. She didn't put up a front. She talked like us. She talked just like how you or me would talk on the telly."

"As we watch the procession go past these streets in Barking, where both Jo and Jimmy grew up of course, do you think much of the sadness is due to how terribly things turned out for them both?"

"Oh, definitely. They always seemed like such a lovely couple, didn't they? They had so much in common. You know, they both came from round here and they were both great parents. Say what you like about her, but she did everything for their little girl. She was a great mother. She loved that girl. That girl will never have to work a day in her life, thanks to her mother."

"This is a tough question, Lisa, but she did have an affair. Well, we now know that she had several affairs, but the affair with her husband's best friend, do you think that changes your perception of her?"

"Not really. No one's perfect. That's why Jo was so popular. She was human. She made mistakes, you know. She made mistakes and the papers ripped her to shreds, but she always bounced back. Yeah, what she did was out of order, but there's no point talking about that now, is there? I mean the poor girl has paid for it, right? And anyway, it takes two, don't it? You notice he's not here today, is he? He's from around here too, but he won't be able to set foot in this place again. They'll have him swinging from a lamppost if he ever comes round here again."

"So you think Scott is to blame in all this?"

Lisa pointed at a weeping Jimmy, cradling his daughter, as the hearse trundled past the crowd.

"Look at him in there," Lisa said. "Just look at him. Ask him who's to blame in all this."

Jason nodded towards the cameraman, who swivelled round to zoom in on Jimmy. The cameraman pulled back to reveal the wreaths in the hearse behind Jimmy. One read: "BOUDICA OF BARKING."

It was red, white and blue.

The funeral procession stopped at the junction of Stuart Road. Jimmy slowly got out of the hearse. He crouched into the car and picked up his daughter. He lifted her out of the hearse and the crowd applauded respectfully. He reciprocated with a forced smile and a wave. The traffic on both sides of Ripple Road stopped and allowed Jimmy to carry his daughter across the street. The drivers waited. No one tooted their horns. No one revved their engines. An embarrassed hush fell over the crowd. Everyone watched Jimmy.

Jimmy took out an orchid and dropped it in the middle of Stuart Road. He peered down at Eastbury Manor House, a red-brick Tudor manor house which had always looked incongruous, surrounded by the repetitive 20th-century red-brick creations of the London County Council. He blew the old manor house a kiss and smiled.

Like most of the grand plans in their relationship, it had been her idea to get married in Eastbury Manor House. The location was so un-Jo-like that Jimmy had initially thought the scheme was a wind-up. He had expected a castle at least to justify the money *Hello* magazine were preparing to fork out. But as always, Jo was one step ahead of the game. Eastbury Manor House would be the last place anyone expected. She was going back to her roots, giving her wedding to her people, a morsel of celebrity thrown to the masses, a minor spoil of victory from Boudica of Barking herself. The tabloid possibilities were endless, and so were the zeroes.

Both Ross and Scott had insisted that the idea was ludicrous. Scott had been characteristically blunt. Why would we go back to that shit hole, he had said. It'll be a day of plebs pestering us for autographs and happy snaps. But Jimmy had won them over with the scheduling. They would only be at the house for an hour. Jo wasn't that daft. It was going to be straight out to Epping for a decent piss-up and then off to Barbados, where Jo had arranged with the paps for a spontaneous honeymoon beach shoot.

Jimmy stared at the old chimney stacks of Eastbury Manor House and thought about Ross and Scott at the wedding. Ross kept sloping off to call the bookies. Scott took pot shots at Jo's fake boobs. Jimmy had stomached the banter through dinner, but by the end of the night, he was ready to clump him. But Jo had talked him out of it. She had now saved that little fucker twice.

The paps had called out to Jimmy that day, screamed at him through the iron gates of Scott's house, told him about Jo, shouted that something had happened, that something wasn't right. They had stopped taking photographs. Their horrified reactions through those iron gates, their eyes, their silence, had told him to go back. Scott wasn't going to get his kicking. Jo had saved Scott again. Ross had destroyed himself, but Scott had been spared again.

Jimmy wiped his eyes and squeezed his daughter.

The funeral procession turned right at the Ripple Road mini-roundabout. Jimmy noticed the cemetery on the left and the Ford dealership on the right. He smiled. Change and progress had never really got on in Barking and Dagenham. The crowds waved as the hearse passed, and he tried to make eye contact with as many as possible. They were good people for the most part. They were Jimmy and Jo's people. Scott had slammed the door on his council house and never looked back. Ross had transferred his footy and betting and replanted his roots in Godalming, and Jimmy and Jo had chased the pound notes. The celebrity couple had bought the winning lottery ticket. What could possibly be more Barking than that?

A group of teenage girls held up a hand-made banner as Jimmy's hearse crawled towards them. It read: "She Was One of Us." Jimmy smiled at the irony. His dead wife had made a career of playing up on the stereotype: the Essex mouth and the fake tan in February, the media-savvy businesswoman celebrating her lack of intellect, the saintly working mother championing her desire to provide for her family. She had turned the Essex girl's dream into a media strategy because she would do anything—anything at all—to leave her Essex girl behind. The obvious route had worked initially. She had fulfilled the Essex girl dream earlier than expected. She married an English Premier League footballer. But the dream was over the moment a belligerent boot shattered Jimmy's knee ligaments.

Jimmy waved at the girls with the banner. He glanced down at his trousers and brushed some fluff off his knee. In many ways, he blamed his knee more than he blamed Scott. Jimmy earned more money as an agent, bought better clothes and lived in a bigger house than all of his footballers. It was a point of principle. But he was no longer a footballer. He was out of Jo's game.

Jason watched the funeral procession crawl between the stone pillars at the entrance of Rippleside Cemetery. He looked across at the Ford flags fluttering in the breeze at Dagenham Motors and smiled at the symbolism. Even Ford had unknowingly flown their flags at half mast for their local glamour girl. He noticed a couple in their early 20s standing on the kerb at the cemetery entrance. The girl wept openly. Her mascara ran down her cheeks as she blubbed. Her skin was startlingly orange. Her partner put his arm around her, but kept his distance. He was wearing a West Ham United jersey, presumably because he was a local boy and perhaps in protest. He scowled at the hearses as they made their way into the cemetery.

He's perfect, Jason thought.

"Excuse me, I don't wish to intrude," he said quickly, shoving his microphone under their chins and watching their eyes light up, as they always did, at the 21st century's greatest phallic symbol. "But can I ask you both why you're here today."

"Well, I'm 'ere because she wanted to be 'ere," the young man spat out.

"What's your name, sir?"

"Stuart."

"And do you live around here, Stuart?"

"I live just across the road, in Lodge Avenue."

"And you're obviously a West Ham supporter, so there's probably no love lost between the two clubs, but what is your view on what has happened in recent weeks?"

"It's just bang out of order, mate. You can't do that. You can't shag a mate's wife no matter how famous you are. And I'm not just saying that 'cos I'm a West Ham fan; I'd say it anyway, he's out of order."

"So if it was a West Ham footballer?"

"I'd say exactly the same, mate. I tell ya, right, do you know something? It costs me 50 quid to watch West Ham play. I don't even know how much a programme costs 'cos I ain't bought one in years. They take the piss. But I pay 'cos I've watched 'em all my life. Just like all Premier League fans. But then you got footballers like Scott and Ross just rubbing our noses in it. They're either pissing their money up the wall or shagging each other's missus. You can't do that to the kids. It's out of order. And then when the fuckers get caught, when they're caught red-handed with their dicks hanging out their best mates' wives, they get the hump with us. Start having a go at us, banging on about a lack of privacy and suing anyone who tells the story, and telling us all what a hard life they've all got. It's a different world, mate. They don't play by our rules no more. But they'll get it in the end. What goes around bloody comes around. I tell ya, you just wait till we get them down to Upton Park next season, see the stick they get then. They're finished, mate. Scott's career is finished. He's not a bad defender, he reads the game well and gets stuck in, but he's finished. You just can't do that. I mean, even in your job, if you sleep with your colleague's wife, you've gotta get the sack. I tell ya, you can quote me on that, mate. Scott is finished as a footballer in this country."

"That's a good point. What do you think about Scott's boss?"

The West Ham supporter smirked directly at the camera.

"Who do you mean? Charlie? Look, I like him, he's a bit of a character and he probably should've been England manager, but he's come from round here."

"What does that mean?"

The young man raised his tattooed forearm and pointed across the road to the Ford dealership.

"He should be working over there, mate."

Jason nodded to his cameraman, who zoomed in on the Ford logo. Jason wanted to kiss the bloke. The sound bite was priceless.

Jason moved his microphone towards the crying woman. She was rather pretty beneath the tan.

"Can I ask you why you're here today?" Jason asked tenderly.

"I don't know really, I just can't stop crying for the woman," she sobbed. "I 'spose it doesn't make much sense really. It's not like I knew her or anything. I don't even know why I'm crying for her. But I watched her show every week, and she made me laugh a bit. I don't know. I can't explain it really. I haven't felt like this since Princess Diana died and I didn't know her either."

Jason nodded his gratitude and stood away from the kerb to watch the hearses pass. As he struggled to take in the endless wreaths, the weeping women lined along Ripple Road and the camera crews shoving one another to find space, Jason smiled ruefully. The nation had stopped to witness her coronation. In returning home, the ex-footballer's wife had finally escaped.

She died the Boudica of Barking.

It was what she would have wanted.

twenty-five

CHARLIE pointed at a favoured reporter at the back of the press conference. The other journalists rolled their eyes. They had been in the game long enough to distinguish the wide-eyed innocents from Charlie's acolytes. This guy had been around for years.

"Yes, Billy," Charlie said cheerily. "Blimey, Billy, did your mother pick that tie?"

The other hacks guffawed loudly, not because the joke was funny, but because Billy was one of Charlie's boys and they were jealous. And the tie really was grotesque.

"How do you think you are going to work with the new owner?" Billy asked.

"Well, as you all know by now, I've known Al-Hakim for some time. I think the whole world has seen that bloody documentary by now."

Charlie stopped suddenly and surveyed the room.

"By the way, where are the boys at *The Sun*?" he asked, craning his head to take in everyone in the room. "Oh, there you are. Yeah, nice joke with the photograph, doing me up to look like Lawrence of bloody Arabia. Was that your idea? Yeah, very fucking funny."

Charlie studied the laughing faces. Of course it had been funny. That was the point. And of course it hadn't been their idea. It had been Charlie's. He needed to play them. He needed the story spun, turned on its head. The plebs had to reach the conclusion that Charlie was a slightly foolish, duped Falstaff, not a string-pulling Henry V, so Charlie had made sure that they arrived at that conclusion.

"But seriously, I've only really met Al-Hakim once or twice at the races and we've chatted a bit about horses, breeders and stables, but never really talked shop," Charlie continued. "I have no interest in big business and he had no real interest in discussing my hunt for a left-sided midfielder. But he has said publicly that the club will be given money to spend, and as a manager that's all you can hope for."

"And you've just signed a new contract, Charlie," Billy interjected.

"Yes, I have. To be honest, I nearly ripped their hands off. Look, I mean, let's be honest here. How many times have I sat here over the years and lamented the lack of funds? How I've managed to keep us in the top half of the Premier League most years on a shoestring budget, taking punts on players from the lower leagues and then selling them on to the big boys for four or five million. I've always said that as much as I admire the Fergusons, the Mancinis and the Ancelottis, I still believe that a lot of English managers could do the same if they had 100 million quid to spend every season. I might not have that, but I am lucky enough to have a new owner who's willing to put in some serious money. He is a serious football fan who wants to win some serious silverware."

"And he's not too concerned about the real controversy and tragedy surrounding you, your best players, your agent and the club."

It was Tom. Fucking Tom.

Charlie turned his head and faced his nemesis. Tom had stood up and glared at Charlie. There was an uncomfortable silence in the room. The contempt between these two men was explicit. Tom was aware that photographers in the room were taking his picture too.

Charlie took a deep breath and grinned at Tom.

"Ah, you all know Tom, here," he said, raising his arm to point Tom out to all the cameras in the room. "This is the TV reporter formerly known as a canteen cook. When he's not frying omelettes, he's hanging around in fancy dress shops looking for strange costumes."

"Can you just answer the question please, Charlie?"

Charlie sipped his milky sweet tea. The taste made him think of Tom. It always would now.

"I can't remember what it was."

"Well, let me put it another way," Tom said, making no effort to conceal his anger. "After the gambling scandal ruled out your best striker for the rest of last season, with speculation that he's on his way in the next transfer window, and your captain sleeping with your agent's wife ..."

"He was never really my agent, just an advisor. I think it was pointed out that ..."

"... And your captain sleeping with your agent's wife, and the tragedy that followed, and the documentary that showed your close relationship with that agent and the negative publicity that surrounded the club throughout the summer, and the allegations of illegal payments from other agents, why would a Saudi billionaire with no previous interest in the English Premier League or football generally, suddenly want to take over your club?"

CHARLIE heard Al-Hakim's lackey fumbling around with his intercom. Charlie was in no rush for the lackey to put him through. Facing the hacks was a doddle compared to this. He thought about putting the phone down, but he had come too far. He couldn't get out now even if he had wanted to. Those late-night phone calls from Al-Hakim's associates impressed upon him how important the deal was and what an integral part of that deal he had been. They couldn't have completed the takeover without him. They would be sure to inform the media that Charlie had made the takeover happen, even if it unexpectedly fell through. It was the very least they could do.

Charlie heard him take the phone off the receiver. He heard him clear his throat.

"Hello, Charlie," Al-Hakim said softly down the line. "Where are you calling from?"

"It's OK, it's fine. I'm outside."

"Good, as I'm sure you have been reading in your papers. Fleet Street has been getting carried away. Those little newspapers think they are the CIA with all that phone tapping."

"No, it's fine. I'm outside. Look, Hakim, something terrible has happened here. I don't know if you've heard about it yet."

"Of course, that poor girl and that poor man, Jimmy, is he OK?"

"He's gone away to be with his daughter and family. He's taking some time off, as long as he needs."

"That is a very good idea. Keep him away from the newspapers."

Charlie put his hand over the receiver and stared at that boy signing his first contract. He wanted to rip the fucking photograph off the wall.

"Look, Hakim, that documentary is going on TV tonight."

"Documentary?"

"The one about me and Jimmy and possibly our role with you."

"The thing at the hotel?"

"Maybe. I don't know what they will show. The sick bastards are rushing it out while everyone is still talking about Jo and Jimmy."

"Yes, that was terrible timing, terrible timing."

Charlie swallowed hard. His mouth had gone dry.

"So, er, what I'm saying is, I'll understand if you pull the plug. You don't need this publicity. I know you want to stay low-profile and I know you don't need this kind of aggravation."

Charlie heard Al-Hakim sigh down the line. He thought about his father. He thought about the second-hand car lot. He had always been so adept at polishing those old Fords.

"Er, Charlie, how is the other couple?"

Charlie frowned.

"The other couple?"

"Yes, er, Scott and ... er ... what is her name? ... Nicola. How are they? We need to keep a low profile now, so I need to know what they are going to do."

"Er, well, the thing is, they have separated. And from what I understand, there is no chance of a reconciliation. She's a determined, proud woman and you've got to admire her for it, I suppose."

"That's a shame," Al-Hakim muttered. "Business is always better around complete families. Do you think the divorce will be messy, in the newspapers?"

"Well, there's no knowing what the papers will do. I can try and control some of it. But I know the two of them won't say anything. Scott won't be allowed to, I can promise you that and Nicola won't say a word. It's not in her nature."

"We should wrap this deal up now then, within the next 48 hours," Al-Hakim said suddenly.

Charlie felt the phone shaking in his hand.

"Really? Are you sure?"

"It's the best way. It will give the media something else to focus on other than Scott and Nicola."

"What about the documentary?"

"Give the details to my London office. They will take care of it. You never took the suitcase. You left it in the hotel room. Everything else is easy. But you need some good news for Scott."

"What?"

"He needs some good news. We need to keep him at the club."

"Really? Are you sure? You don't want me to sell him? I reckon I could get around 20 million for him. That means a cut of around ..."

"I'm not concerned about that, but I understand you have a stake in this. By all means, sell the other one if you want."

"Ross?"

"We can talk about whatever percentage you usually feel is appropriate. But this Scott is different. He's our best player. I have to send the right signal as a new owner. We will be a buying club, not a selling club. We will be a buying family club."

"But I took him from nothing and turned him into a £20-million player. Ross is worth no more than 10 to 12 at the moment, and that was before the suspension. I don't wish to speak out of turn here, but that's a massive return for the club and it usually means that, as the manager, I could expect to get a commission of at least ..."

"Twenty million is not an issue right now. I need to win the fans over. Protests and boycotts are expensive. Look at Liverpool. They have two players worth almost 100 million and still, they sell the whole club for only 300. Investors do not like disruption. It makes them nervous. Uncertainty damages an investment, makes it look cheap. We need calm now. You always say that football is the results business. You told me Stalin and Hitler could be co-owners if you got them results every week. Well, get us some results. Use Jimmy. Make them play for Jimmy. They will try harder. Use Jimmy."

CHARLIE leaned forward and rested his elbows on the table. His eyes bored through Tom. He had been primed for this question. He was going to relish the answer.

"You see, Tom, what your documentary failed to show while it was doing all its grubby digging was the game itself," Charlie said slowly. "You didn't show a single piece of actual footage. Maybe you couldn't get the clearance. Maybe the documentary was too low-budget and you couldn't afford the rights. Maybe you spent all your money on the Lawrence of Arabia costume. I don't know. But you didn't show the game and when you strip away all the bullshit, that's the only thing that matters.

"After all those terrible things that happened to this club—and they were terrible—I gathered the lads in the dressing room before our next game. It was at home to Chelsea, do you remember? Just around the time of the documentary. No one gave us a chance. Everyone had written us off, saying Scott had played his last game for this club, saying I had managed my last game for this club. And I got the boys in the dressing room and I said four words. Do it for Jimmy. That's all I said. Do it for Jimmy. You can ask the other lads on the coaching staff, but that's all I said. We went out there and beat them 1-0, and Scott kept Drogba in his pocket all afternoon. He came off at the end of the game with tears in his eyes. He kissed the badge with tears in his eyes. That's all he had to do. No other words necessary. And people like you, people who have never played the game, people who look for the brutality rather than the beauty; you come out and pontificate about Scott not apologising publicly. Sometimes actions speak louder than words. That's how we do it in our game. When he kissed that badge, the crowd knew. They felt his pain and his pride. He didn't need to say anything.

"Next game, away to Blackburn, another potential banana skin, everyone was saying we'd get the backlash, that Scott would be crucified away from home. And they gave him abuse from the moment he stepped out to warm up, but he took it like a man and played the greatest game at centre half that I've seen since Bobby Moore took on Brazil in 1970. Even you boys had to acknowledge that they had seen something special that day. Suddenly, you're all calling for him to be called up for England. Two weeks earlier, you were calling for his head on a spike. Then you were calling him England's saviour. Suddenly, the recent past is forgotten. England's early exit at the World Cup is forgotten. Because at the end of the day, that's all that matters: the game. The players understood that. That's why they all played like men possessed. That's why all I said before the Blackburn game was do it for Jimmy. I said it for the rest of the season. Do it for Jimmy. And we took all 12 points from our last four games and sneaked into Europe by the back door. We did it for Jimmy. We made the Europa League without a penny from our new owners and our fans gave that team a standing ovation at the end of the last season. They carried Scott off on their shoulders. They chanted his name throughout the lap of honour. Because that's what the game is about, when you strip away all the bullshit. That's all that matters. It's only about the football."

Charlie watched Tom return to his seat. The other hacks scribbled away dutifully like mice on a wheel. It had been one of Charlie's better speeches. He had practised this one so it didn't sound rehearsed.

SCOTT sat tentatively beside Charlie. He surveyed the room carefully. Enough time had passed since Charlie's bombastic press conference to announce the towelhead's takeover and the press girl had been briefed carefully—no snipers. This was Scott's first press conference after all that stuff and he had every reason to be apprehensive, but she had done her job. He noticed the programme guy, the official club newspaper reporter, the local papers who took a few cheap shots in their regional rags but always lacked the balls to say anything provocative in Scott's presence, and a sprinkling of safe broadsheets and dependent fanzines. The press girl had warned each of them beforehand, individually and then again collectively: don't go there or you can kiss your press pass goodbye. There was European football and Al-Hakim's sexy shopping list for the journalists to think about. Their careers depended on the press pass. The club always had that leverage. Scott was back in his comfort zone.

"With the national team looking to rebuild with younger players, you must be delighted to be making your England debut," the programme guy piped up.

Scott couldn't remember his name.

"Yeah, I'm delighted, mate. This is every footballer's dream. Some of England's most famous players—Bobby Moore, Tony Adams and John Terry—played in my position and captained both club and country. I'm not saying I'm going to be an England captain. I'm not saying that at all. But I'm delighted to be following in my heroes' footsteps."

Of course, Scott was saying that. The England armband was worth at least an extra million a year and he needed it. That media whore of a judge had gotten a bit carried away on his moralising soapbox when settling the child maintenance.

"After what must have been a traumatic few months, you must be pleased with the way things have turned out," the fanzine guy said.

Scott examined the fanzine guy. He was new; older and fatter than the usual naïve idealists who worked on fanzines, but most definitely new. Scott turned towards Charlie who nodded briefly. The fanzine guy was enthusiastic, but he had made an indirect reference. This would be his last press conference.

"It's not been easy. But at the end of the day, I'm a footballer so I've just kept my head down and focused on the game."

"But are you not surprised with how quickly the mood has turned?" the fanzine guy interjected. "It's been quite extraordinary. Just a couple of months ago, *The Sun* was publishing cut-out-and-keep dartboards with your face superimposed over the bullseye. Now the papers are saying you should be the heart of the defence for the next World Cup. Are you surprised?"

Scott clenched his fists beneath the table.

"Er, I suppose that's not really a question I can answer," he said carefully. "Other people are there to judge my performances. Whether it's the media or the fans, they have a right to their opinion. I just go out every week and give 150 per cent. And if the fans are happy, then I'm happy. They just want their club and country to do well and I can understand that. We're all fans of the game ultimately. At the end of the day, it's all about the fans."

Scott signed the last of the programmes and smiled politely as the programme guy wished him all the best for his England debut. He watched the media girl, Alison, an attractive brunette in a designer suit, usher the programme guy out of the room and close the door behind him. Alison was alone with Scott and Charlie.

"Who the fuck was that prick from the fanzine?" Scott lambasted.

"Alison, I thought we agreed no outsiders for this press conference," Charlie added smoothly.

"I don't know who he was. He's obviously a new bloke. They change their staff all the time."

"Well, make sure the cunt doesn't get back in here again," Scott hissed.

Alison looked nervously at both Charlie and Scott.

"Er, it's only a fanzine," she stammered. "They've just got a few guys running it as a labour of love. They hardly get any advertising and they barely cover costs. Most months they run at a loss. They're one of the last fanzines left, but the fans like this one. It's very popular around the ground. They're usually very fair. That's why we let them in."

"They're not working for *The Big Issue*. Fuck 'em, I don't want them anywhere near me anymore," Scott declared.

Alison looked at Charlie for support. He walked across the press lounge, his slippers gliding effortlessly across the carpet, and gently put his arm around her.

"It's all right, Alison," he said chirpily. "He's got a lot on his mind. Come on, let's have a cup of milky sweet tea in my office and we'll update your media lists."

They headed for the door. Alison turned back. She wiped her eyes.

"I'm sorry, Scott, I didn't know. I'm sorry," she said.

"So am I," Scott replied.

He glared at her. Charlie smiled back at Scott and closed the door behind them.

Scott stood in front of the club logo on the press lounge wall. It hadn't been dusted properly. He thought about the recent phone calls from some of the boys at Chelsea and Manchester United, even cashed-up City, putting the feelers out, testing the ground for their gaffers. It was only a matter of time. His preference was United over Chelsea, but only just. The fans at both clubs had always sung about Nicola taking it up the arse when they were married, but the Chelsea mob had burned effigies of him outside Stamford Bridge. That took the piss. He wouldn't forget that. On the other hand, Chelsea had more money to spend than Manchester United. And as for City ...

"That was a quality little speech that, mate."

Scott realised he was falling towards the club logo. He threw out his arms, but it was too late. He heard his head crack against the top of the club's crest. He was falling backwards, drifting away from the club logo. The blood blurred his vision, dribbled down his nose and onto his Armani. The back of his head smashed against a chair and he found himself staring up at the heating vents on the ceiling and the club paintings on the back wall; sepia silverware celebrations on signed canvases.

Jimmy blocked his view of the club logo.

"For a monosyllabic prat like you, that was a great little speech. I almost believed you."

Scott blinked the blood out of his eyes and raised his arms towards Jimmy. He felt the blood dripping into his mouth.

"Jimmy, wait ... listen," he choked.

"Make sure you have a good game for England," Jimmy shouted. "I've got plenty of money still to make off your fucking back, especially if it's in an England shirt. It's in the contract and until you buy me out of it, you're gonna be paying for my little girl's private education until she does her PhD, you back-stabbing bastard."

Scott curled up into the foetal position. He spat some blood onto the carpet. He peered up at Jimmy and tried to speak, but there were no words. Scott could not apologise. Scott would never apologise.

Jimmy stared down at his oldest friend retching on the carpet.

"She had just missed a period," he muttered. "But she didn't know for sure. And I'll never know now, will I?"

Jimmy wiped the tears off his cheeks.

And then he kept on kicking.

twenty-six

JIMMY ran across the muddy field. He was excited. He was being summoned. He was going to perform one of his party tricks. He didn't mind. He was being noticed. He dashed across the penalty box and ducked as Ross tried to slap him across the back of the head.

"Piss off, you dickhead," Jimmy shouted breathlessly, flicking clumps of mud off his right boot towards Ross. Ross swayed effortlessly to his left as the mud sailed passed him.

"Don't do that, you'll mess up my hair," Ross yelled as he watched Jimmy sprint towards the men on the touchline.

Jimmy reached the touchline on the left side of the pitch, rested his arms on his upper thighs and inhaled sharply.

"You took your time running across the pitch there. What are you going to do if I suddenly change formation in the middle of a match and ask you to switch flanks?"

Jimmy looked up and wiped his perspiring forehead. His jersey sleeve left a streak of mud across his face.

"I'm sorry, Mr Charlie, it's just that Ross stopped me halfway and I ..."

Charlie put his arm around Jimmy's slender shoulder.

"It's all right, you daft sod, I'm only pulling your plonker," Charlie said reassuringly. "I wanted you to meet these two blokes here."

Charlie gestured towards two men dressed in scruffy suits and scuffed shoes. Their shirttails hung limply over the tops of their trousers. One held a notepad and a tape recorder, the other a camera.

"You're journalists then?" Jimmy asked them.

The journalists giggled and nodded towards a beaming Charlie.

"I told you about this boy, didn't I, Matty?" Charlie enthused. "The bugger signs on as an apprentice and then grills me about the clauses in the contract, didn't ya, you little bastard."

Jimmy shrugged his shoulders sheepishly.

"OK, Jimmy, listen," Charlie said slowly. "They find a man hanging in an old warehouse. He's killed himself with an old rope, hanged himself from the ceiling 20 feet in the air. There are no chairs, ladders, windows, ledges or steps anywhere in this warehouse, nothing except the man hanging from the rope, 20 feet in the air, above a puddle of water. How did he hang himself?"

Jimmy stared at Charlie quizzically.

"How did he hang himself, Mr Charlie?"

"Yeah, it's one of my mental puzzles. How did he hang himself? I've told these blokes you were a clever little sod. How did he hang himself?"

Jimmy kicked at the clumps of mud around the touchline.

"There's just a puddle of water under the dead bloke?" he asked.

"Yep, nothing else in the warehouse," Charlie replied, winking at the reporters.

Jimmy looked up suddenly.

"Ice," he said.

"What do you mean, ice?"

"He's stood on a block of ice, the ice has slowly melted into a puddle and he's hanged himself."

Charlie ruffled Jimmy's hair, bursting with pride.

"Good boy, I'll have another one for you next week. Now go and get your other two hoodies, we want all three of you over here for a photo."

Jimmy hared off towards Ross on the right side of the penalty box.

"You told him that beforehand," Matty, the young reporter, contended.

"Of course, I bloody didn't," Charlie said. "Why would I have to? If I wanted to bullshit you I would. No, I love these boys, bloody love them. Normally, you get one come through at any one time, or two if you are lucky, but never any more than that, ever. Well, it happened once, fair enough, with Fergie, and look what happened? He groomed them for the Treble. And I've got three of them right here, same town, same bloody council estate, same bloody school. They're best mates. They're almost telepathic. I've got my own Moore, Hurst and Peters, and even they didn't grow up together."

Matty rolled his eyes and laughed with his photographer.

"I'm telling ya. I'm not feeding you a line, not this time. I've never been so excited about three kids before. They are my Moore, Hurst and Peters. Quote me on that. Three boys, three different players, three different positions, three different temperaments, but they are magic together, bloody magic. Jimmy has a football brain like I've never seen. He's five stone soaking wet, but give him a ball and he takes off like a whippet. Ross is my Mark Viduka and Robbie Fowler rolled into one. He's big and makes a real mess in the box, but when he turns a defender, it makes me want to fucking cry. And he's a good-looking bastard. Look at him coming over now. He's Viduka and Fowler on the pitch and bloody Beckham off it. I'm gonna be able to retire on this kid. The only defender he doesn't turn is Scott. He's a bloody force of nature. He's got the least skill of the three of them, but you know who he is, don't ya? He's the Black Knight in *Monty Python*. If you chop his legs off in the penalty box, he'll come over and bite your ankles. Never seen anyone so determined. The boy is driven. I haven't seen anyone like him since me."

Matty laughed. He had only been covering Charlie's antics for a couple of years, but he already knew it was one of his oldest lines. Charlie hadn't used it for a while though. There hadn't been a prospect worthy enough.

Charlie watched his boys run over. Jimmy and Ross scampered over. Scott scowled and trotted across from the middle of the pitch half-heartedly.

"Can't we do this later," Scott shouted petulantly. "It's 1-1."

Charlie smiled at Matty.

"It's only a training exercise," he muttered, before glaring back at Scott. "No, we can't do it later, so get your arse over here now."

Scott trudged along the touchline and joined Jimmy and Ross. Ross tidied his shirt and adjusted his muddy socks. Jimmy craned his head to read the scribbling in Matty's notepad. Scott watched the game.

"Scott, look over here will ya," Charlie ordered. "Right, now, I've told these journalists all about you boys. So they are going to ask you just a few questions. Now, this is a national paper, not the local muppets. This is not your little clippings from the *Gazette* or the *Recorder*, the whole country is going to read this, so don't fuck it up. This guy here, Matty, is a good mate of mine and will ask all the questions. So answer honestly and make sure you tell them how great I am."

Matty nodded at Charlie and switched on his tape recorder. The three boys crowded around him.

"OK, boys, I'll ask you a question each, all right," Matty said. "Jimmy, where do you see yourself in five years' time?"

"On the right wing. My left foot is crap."

They all laughed.

"What about you, Ross?"

"Oh, I hope to be scoring the winner every week and owning the winner every week."

Matty looked at Charlie.

"He's talking about dogs," Charlie explained. "His old man half owns a couple of three-legged greyhounds over Romford, don't he?"

"Yeah, they're shit," Ross said honestly.

"He gives me great tips though, don't you, Ross? You popping in on the way home again?"

"Yeah, probably."

"Good tip?"

"About as good as last week and that one romped home for us. I'll probably go each way just to play safe."

"All right, I'll give you a few quid for me then as well. You better check with the other coaches before you leave as well. They'll probably want to put a few quid down."

Matty noticed that Scott had turned his back on him again to watch the football.

"What about you, Scott?" Matty asked.

Scott turned around.

"What?"

"Where do you see yourself in five years' time?"

"Er, well, playing for the first team, I hope, and if I keep my head down, maybe even knocking on the door for England."

"Really?"

"Well, Charlie says I've got the potential. The rest is up to me and no one will work any harder than me."

Matty examined Scott's face and scribbled in his notepad. The kid who looked like a ferret was the only one to drop the 'mister'.

"OK, fair enough," he said. "When you boys are not playing football, what else do you do?"

"Watch football," Ross shouted.

"Or play football on the PlayStation," Jimmy added.

The three boys all laughed together.

"Do you watch and play on the PlayStation together?" Matty asked.

"Yeah, most of the time," Ross said. "Scott likes to play me on the PlayStation because he knows he'll never get the ball off me out there." Ross pointed to the training pitch. Scott playfully pushed him in the chest.

"Piss off," he laughed.

"They're always like this, always up each other's arses," Charlie said. "I call them the Barking Boys, but really, they're the Barking bum bandits."

Charlie and the boys giggled. Matty glimpsed at his watch.

"But apart from the football," Matty interjected. It was starting to rain and he was getting bored. "Apart from the football, what else do you do?"

The three boys stared at the scruffy reporter in disbelief.

"What else is there?" Ross retorted.

"We grew up in Barking, mate," Jimmy added. "It's all we know."

"Football's everything," Scott muttered.

twenty-seven

AL-HAKIM laughed out loud. The Lawrence of Arabia costume was a great line. Charlie was certainly competent. Al-Hakim reached across and grabbed the remote control. Charlie was quite a speech maker. They had both agreed on the angle and approach, but the delivery was all Charlie. He was a skilled communicator, of that there could be no doubt, one of the most accomplished that Al-Hakim had seen, which was a trifle irritating. Charlie would be harder to remove when the time was right.

Charlie had to be sacked. That decision had been made the moment the English buffoon had accepted a case full of money from a confused Muslim in a circus costume. Everyone was driven by the dollars, but they blinded Charlie and impaired his judgment. The man was too greedy, too spontaneous and too populist. Those English Premier League cameras needed his cheeky persona. They sold him to the world as a "character." But Charlie the "character" would never boast the cool-headed credentials required to sell a new stadium project to immovable traditionalists.

Charlie had always been one of *them*. Al-Hakim had identified Charlie's failing from their lengthy discussions at the race track. It wasn't the money. The old man was born poor, so he would remain obsessed with being rich until the day he died. That was normal.

But he remained shackled to the ideals of the Beautiful Game. Charlie frequently denied it of course; claimed that he owed the game nothing and insisted a pro's limited shelf life in the game meant he should squeeze the ball for every last penny. But his guard occasionally slipped. He'd consider the fans' reactions. He'd factor in the supporters' opinions during takeover discussions.

He still thought the fans mattered.

Al-Hakim glanced up at the framed photograph on the wall of his London office. Charlie's ill-considered gift of an aerial shot of a packed stadium on match day had summed up the creaky manager. What purpose did the gift serve? The photograph was like a puerile cartoon. Thousands of grown men chanting simple songs like kids in a classroom; paying money they didn't really have to sit beside other grown men they didn't know and repeat nursery rhymes. *Twinkle, twinkle little star; how I wonder what you are.* They were children; singing and dancing children performing for fading stars like Charlie.

Children should be seen and not heard.

And yet, astonishingly, Charlie subconsciously pandered to these imbeciles. He took their feedback into account and understood their conservative traditionalism. He had never sided with the fans in business meetings with Al-Hakim, but he had acknowledged their existence.

Such naïvety would never do.

When the time was right, Charlie had to go.

Al-Hakim gazed over at the other framed photograph. Its frame was gold.

Nicola.

She flirted across the office at him, as she always did, smiling beguilingly. That was his major project now and one not without obstacles, but Al-Hakim was accustomed to subservience. It was the natural order of his world. Al-Hakim smiled back at Nicola's portrait. She was almost his. He had little time for football, but he would never grow tired of London.

Al-Hakim looked down at the blond head bobbing up and down between his knees.

"Deeper," he whispered.

TOM giggled as he watched Scott squirm for the Sky Sports News cameras. Using a mate with a grudge as a fanzine plant in the press conference had been a low blow; a childish, petulant display. Macca, his fanzine plant, had once written for the club's official weekly newspaper before he was sacked for questioning the decision to raise ticket prices during the economic downturn. They both had an incentive to upstage Charlie and sabotage Scott's England call-up. But they also accepted that Macca's antics were unprofessional and petty. Such immature behaviour was beneath Tom—or, at least, it used to be.

Tom moved some colouring books to one side and noticed marker pen scribbles across the sofa. He sighed and shoved his hand between two sofa cushions, pulling out a blue marker pen with no lid.

"Sarah, have you seen what she has done now," Tom shouted.

"I'm in the kitchen, Tom, what do you want?" Sarah replied.

"She's drawn all over this bloody sofa again. Why can't you stop her?"

"How do you expect me to stop her? And where do you expect her to go and draw? There's no bloody room in this place for an easel or a chalk board, is there? She just wants to play. It's not her fault if there's no room in this crappy flat."

"Yeah, all right, don't start," Tom grumbled.

Tom stared at the Sky Sports News broadcast, watching Macca interrogate Scott about his England debut. It was a silly, futile stunt that served no practical purpose, but it made Tom feel slightly better.

They were all still there. Despite everything, the fuckers were still there.

The documentary had gone out and rated through the roof. Jonathan and Jason had been delighted, chinking champagne glasses at a White City reception hosted by the grateful broadcaster. *Charlie's Army* had attracted the greatest TV audience for a football documentary since their three-part special on hooligans.

Jo's affair had sparked the unprecedented, nationwide interest in Charlie and Jimmy's fraudulent behaviour at the club.

Jo's death had killed it.

The English Premier League announced an ongoing probe that got lost in the funeral headlines. Jimmy the Sullied Agent became Jimmy the Saintly Widower and was removed from the equation. The muted calls for criminal action against Charlie were soon drowned out by the fickle roaring of the Three Lions demanding Scott's England call-up. The Saudi's legal team did the rest.

Tom had won his battle, but lost a war that he could never win. The game recovered immediately because Charlie was right; it was *their* game; *their* rules. The world's most popular sports league was also Britain's most private Masonic lodge.

Sarah stormed into the living room carrying their daughter. She dropped the little girl on Tom's lap.

"Your daughter has been trying to put her plastic plates into the oven," Sarah complained. "She thinks it's a dishwasher."

"Well, I told you she gets her brains from you."

Sarah noticed the TV channel in the corner of their cluttered living room. She shook her head.

"Let it go Tom, for God's sake," she said. "It's over. You've done the documentary, it went out, we caught up on the mortgage and now you've got the commission to do a new one on illegal immigrants. Build a bridge. Get over it."

Tom sat up suddenly and pointed at the TV screen. Beneath Scott's image, a breaking news story flashed across the bottom of the screen.

Tom and Sarah read the text together as their daughter picked up the blue marker pen and started scribbling on the sofa.

"Wow, that's amazing," Sarah admitted. "An England striker caught having an affair with his wife's sister. I wonder who it is."

"Who cares," Tom sighed.

"Quick, pass me the phone," Sarah said excitedly. "I must tell my mum."

Sky Sports News interrupted Scott's press conference to follow its new, breaking story.

Tom reached across the sofa and handed his wife the phone. Then he turned off the TV.

the author

In 1996, Neil Humphreys left Dagenham, England, to travel the world. He got as far as Toa Payoh, Singapore, and decided the rest of the world could wait. His 10-year sojourn in Singapore saw the publication of three best-selling works: *Notes from an Even Smaller Island* (2001), *Scribbles from the Same Island* (2003) and *Final Notes from a Great Island: A Farewell Tour of Singapore* (2006), and the omnibus *Complete Notes from Singapore* (2007). Neil then headed south for Geelong, Australia, where his fifth book, *Be My Baby*, was conceived and gestated in 2008. *Match Fixer*, his first novel, was released in 2010 to international critical acclaim, pleasing purists but irritating loan sharks and illegal bookies everywhere. He writes for several magazines and newspapers in Singapore, Australia and the UK. He still watches West Ham, writes for a Hammers fanzine and wishes Billy Bonds was still playing.

also by neil humphreys

Notes from an Even Smaller Island
Knowing nothing of Singapore, a young Englishman arrives in the land of 'air-conned' shopping centres and Lee Kuan Yew. He explores all aspects of Singaporean life, taking in the sights, dissecting the culture, and illuminating each place and person with his perceptive and witty observations.

Scribbles from the Same Island
Humphreys' back with yet more observations and ruminations about the oddball aspects of Singapore and its people. *Scribbles* also contains a selection of his work as a humour columnist.

Final Notes from a Great Island
All good things must come to an end, and before Humphreys makes his move down under, he re-visits all the people and places he loves in his final, comprehensive tour of Singapore.

Complete Notes from Singapore (The Omnibus Edition)
All three of Humphreys' best-selling works, *Notes from an Even Smaller Island*, *Scribbles from the Same Island* and *Final Notes from a Great Island*, in one classic book.

Be My Baby: On the Road to Fatherhood

Follow Humphreys on his most terrifying and hilarious journey yet—travelling the unfamiliar road to fatherhood.

Match Fixer

Once a promising graduate of the West Ham United Academy and tipped to play for England, Chris Osbourne, arrives on the Singapore football scene in a bid to right his faltering football career. But nothing has prepared him for the bent bookies, dubious teammates, underground party drugs scene and a seductively beautiful journalist that welcome him to life in paradise.